To: Jessica & Gene

[signature]

ABSOLUTE JUSTICE

By
Larry W. Pitts

Copyright © 2014 by Larry W. Pitts

Published by
Yawn's Publishing
198 North Street
Canton, Georgia 30114

All rights reserved. No part of this book may be reproduced or transmitted in any form or by any means, electronic or mechanical, including photocopying, recording, or by any information storage and retrieval system, without the written permission of the author except where permitted by law.

This is a work of fiction. Names, characters, places, and incidents either are the product of the author's imagination or are used fictitiously, and any resemblance to actual persons, living or dead, business establishments, events, or locales is entirely coincidental.

Library of Congress Control Number: 2014916315

ISBN:	978-1-940395-43-2	Hardcover
	978-1-940395-44-9	Paperback
	978-1-940395-45-6	eBook

Printed in the United States.

*For my daughter Jordan.
Everything is for you.*

> Two roads diverged in a wood, and I—
> I took the one less traveled by,
> And that has made all the difference.
>
> Robert Frost
> "The Road Not Taken"

CHAPTER ONE

My office is on the second floor above a Vietnamese restaurant on Broad Street. Next to the restaurant, a nondescript door directs your attention upstairs and advertises, *Nick Price, Private Investigations. Bonded, licensed, insured, and available twenty-four hours a day.* Upstairs on the pebbled-glass door of my office is a list of investigative services—*divorce, child custody, missing relatives, and surveillance. Ethical, reliable, and strictly confidential.* On my website is a more detailed advertisement of investigations: *domestic infidelity, GPS tracking, insurance fraud, workers' compensation, security consulting, accident investigations, and wrongful deaths.* Judging by the boastful list of services, it was easy to imagine teams of agents working diligently on your behalf—but in reality, there was only a lone-wolf investigator working from a hole-in-the-wall office in the low-rent section of downtown Atlanta.

It was four o'clock on a Wednesday afternoon, and since no one was beating down the door for my services, I was sitting at my desk thinking about calling it quits for the day. My girlfriend, Naija Patel, an OB-GYN who along with three other physicians shared a practice at The Atlanta Obstetrics Center, had one of her wine tasting soirees tonight with her highbrow friends; so I had the night to myself. As I sat at my desk, I was making my plans for the evening. My apartment was only blocks away. I had walked to work this morning, not expecting a wave of clients. I could leave the office, stop by the pizza place down the street, pick up a double pepperoni, and be home in thirty minutes. The Braves were playing the Giants on TV tonight and there was a six pack of Heineken in the fridge calling my name. A nearly perfect evening: pizza, beer, and baseball. After thinking about it another five seconds, I decided to call it quits. I got up, shrugged on my suit jacket and grabbed my fedora. I was ready to leave when the door swung open, and this woman walked in as if she owned the place. She stopped just inside the door and looked at me. She was a knockout, with shoulder-length auburn hair, huge, pale brown eyes, and heart-shaped voluptuous lips, painted red. She wore a white, low-cut blouse and a short light tan skirt that showed off her long legs. No stockings. Red high heels. She had the kind of looks that could make any man stand up and take notice. The day was looking up.

"Are you Nick Price?" she asked.

"Yes, I am."

"And you're a private investigator?"

I shot her a sly grin and motioned behind her. "That's what it says on the door."

She wheeled around and looked at the door as if she'd never seen it before. Then she turned back around, mimicked my grin, and said, "So you like to play."

"One has to amuse oneself when the situation arises."

A small smile played across her lips as if she had just thought of something funny. "I thought private eyes only existed in books and movies."

"I'm the real thing," I said.

She glanced around my small office, sizing me up to make sure I was the real thing. She looked at me a moment. Today I was wearing a dark gray suit, a white shirt with pale blue stripes, and a red and blue striped tie. I still had on my charcoal Borsalino fedora. I hoped she liked what she saw. I knew I liked what I saw.

"You look like you just stepped out of a 1940s movie," she said.

I love the nostalgic look from the late 1940s and 50s, and my fedora, with its wide brim that tilted down above the eyes, emanated the persona of a classic private detective. If it makes me look as if I just stepped from a 1940s movie, all the better. I like to stand out in a crowd.

"I dress for the part," I said. "Except I'm in color."

We stood there a second looking at each other. Then I asked, "Can I help you with something, or did you come in here to make disparaging remarks about my attire?"

"I didn't say anything disparaging about the way you dress," she said. That small, flirtatious smile spread across her lips again. "I like the way you dress. It makes you look mysterious."

She had a soft, sensual voice that no matter what she said hinted at sex.

"I'm all about mystery and intrigue," I said. Now it was my turn to flash a flirtatious smile. I can turn on the charm when necessary.

She looked around the office again and said, "When I came in a moment ago it looked like you were getting ready to leave."

"I have an appointment," I said. If you want to count my plans of watching baseball and drinking beer as an appointment. In reality, I had nowhere to go and nothing to do when I got there. But that wasn't any of her business.

"You can't be that busy," she said, glancing around my office again. "You don't even have a secretary."

"I don't need one," I said. "I keep all my appointments on my phone."

"Uh-huh," she said, and raised one eyebrow as if it were a question mark.

Apparently, she liked to banter. I decided to play along and see where it would lead. I took off my hat and sat it on the edge of my desk. Then I walked around the desk and sat down in my swivel chair. I motioned to one of the client chairs opposite the desk. She sat down and crossed her long legs. I looked at them. She had nice legs. When I looked back up at her, she was smiling at me. She had a nice smile to go with the nice legs. She was the total package.

I asked her, "How did you find me? Did someone I know recommend me?"

"Why does it matter?"

I flashed the sly grin again. "I need it for my Marketing department."

Again the eyebrow rose, "Marketing department, really? Where do you keep it? In your phone too?"

I grinned. "Here in my desk. Third drawer on the left."

She didn't say anything. Whatever role she was playing, she played it beautifully. I could tell she was a woman who knew how to play people to get what she wanted. And she was good at it. She would eventually get around to the reason she was here, but only on her own terms.

She stared at me a second, then said, "To be honest, I found you on the Internet. I saw your picture on your home page and was intrigued. You look like a private detective. You have a certain *je ne sais quoi*."

Right. That's me. Mr. Intrigue, master of the art of mystery. That is, when I'm not sitting at my desk with my feet propped up, bored out of my skull.

I motioned at the hat on the desk. "It's the hat," I said. "Men don't wear hats like they used to."

She said, "The picture on your website doesn't do you justice."

"I'm better in person," I said.

"Yes," she said, "I think a man that wears a hat looks sexy."

There was nothing to add to that so I remained quiet.

Then she asked, "Are you a good detective?"

"I'm good at everything I do," I said.

"I may want to hire you," she said, "if we get along. I don't do business with people I don't like."

"I don't work with people I don't like either."

"You'll like me," she said.

I liked her sitting in my client chair with her legs staring at me. The best legs I'd seen all week, and I do a lot of comparison shopping. Plus there was a nice body attached to the legs. But that didn't mean anything. With those looks and that sensual voice, she could make any man her prisoner. Then after she got what she wanted, she would chew them up, spit out the bones, and go looking for the next meal. But I wasn't on the menu.

I asked, "What's your name?"

"Julia Garrett."

"Pleased to meet you, Julia." To clear the air, I asked, "What do you do for a living?"

"I'm an actress," she said proudly. Then she continued, "I've been in television commercials and had a few non-speaking roles in movies filmed here in town. Plus, I've done modeling for magazines."

"I bet you're good at it," I said.

She gave me the flirtatious look again, but didn't say anything.

Time to get down to why she was here. "So, how can I help you?" I asked.

She remained silent a moment, as if she were thinking about something.

Finally, she said, "I need your help."

"Tell me about it."

"I'm not here about myself," she said. She paused a moment.

I remained silent. Waiting.

Then she continued, "It's my husband. His name is Jason Garrett." She said it as if I should recognize the name. I didn't.

"That name doesn't mean anything to you?" she asked.

"Should it?"

"I would think a man in your position would know the names of others in the law profession."

"I'm not in the law profession. I'm a private detective."

She flashed me an irritated glance, and then said, "My husband is a very prominent attorney."

"Never heard of him," I said. My dynamic personality came shining through again.

A wave of uncertainty washed over her face. "Maybe coming here wasn't a good idea," she said.

I looked at her a second. The flirtatious act she had been putting on had vanished. I wasn't sure why she'd done it in the first place. Maybe to size me up, or was it just to get attention? Nevertheless, I saw a worried woman in those huge brown eyes.

I said, "I can't help you, if you don't tell me what's wrong."

She stared at me a moment and then looked down at her hands in her lap. The earlier smile had disappeared. Then she said, "My husband is missing. He's been missing for over a week."

"Did you report it to the police?"

She flashed me the annoyed look again. "Of course, I did."

"And?"

"They took the necessary information and filed their report," she said. "But they haven't made any progress. I don't even think they're looking for him anymore."

"And you want my help?"

"Yes," she said. "It's been over a week and I haven't heard anything. Not from him or the police. I'm worried. I'm afraid something has happened to him."

Her eyebrows furrowed and her lips turned into a frown. She looked as if she were deciding what to do next. I bet she calculated every expression she made, analyzed every word before she said it, an actress that was practicing her lines. She had played the sultry *femme fatale* and was now choosing her next role. Maybe now it was the concerned and frantic housewife searching for her missing husband. She looked like she was about to cry. I bet she could cry, too, with real tears, any time the mood struck.

I asked, "Would there be any reason for him to up and leave without a word?"

"No," she said, without looking up at me.

"Has he ever gone missing in the past?"

"No."

"Taken off without telling anybody?"

"No," she said, and finally looked up at me. "He's never done any of those things. He's very structured. So much so that he is predictable."

"Does he have any enemies?"

"No" she said. "He's a corporate attorney. It's not like he works with hardened criminals."

"Does he have any bad habits? Gambling? Booze?"

"Of course not," she said. "He is a good man. He doesn't gamble. He hardly even drinks at cocktail parties."

"Any problems at home?"

This got her attention. She gave me the irritated look again. "What do you mean?"

"Do you and your husband get along?"

"Yes," she said. "We have a wonderful marriage."

"Any recent arguments?"

"No," she said flatly. "We're very happy."

"How long have you been married?"

"Nine years."

"Any children?"

"No," she said. "We both decided we don't want children, at least not in the immediate future."

There was no subtle way to ask the next question, so I simply dove in. "Is it possible there is another woman in your husband's life?"

She shot me a brazen look that said I shouldn't be asking such a personal question, especially to a renowned socialite of Atlanta. But I've always gone against the grain.

After a second of harsh looks, she said, "No. We have a good marriage." She motioned with her right hand at her body, and continued, "Look at me. I'm beautiful. I'm everything he needs in a woman. Jason would never cheat."

"How about you?" I asked. "Would you cheat?"

Her face flushed and her lips pursed together in a straight line. Her eyes clawed into me like talons. Then she exploded. "That's a terrible question. I will not sit here and answer such degrading questions."

I put my hands up, palms out, as if I were surrendering. I was certain the cops had asked her the same question, so it shouldn't have come as a surprise. Maybe she had anticipated the question and practiced her reaction in the mirror before coming to the office.

I said in reply, "I have to ask these type questions. I'm sure the police have asked the same things."

She stared at me a second before she responded. "I've gone over all this with the police already."

I didn't say anything. I looked at her a moment, waiting for an answer.

"No," she said finally. "I have never been unfaithful to my husband."

We were silent a moment to let the tension clear. Then I said, "So the police haven't come up with any clues to your husband's whereabouts?"

"No," she said. "I check with them every day, and they just blow me off. They tell me they'll contact me if there are 'further developments.' I'm convinced they're no longer looking for him."

"I'll need a list of acquaintances, business partners and such," I said.

"I anticipated you would," she said.

She reached into her purse and handed me a neatly typed sheet of paper with names and phone numbers. Listed beside each name was their association with Jason Garrett: family member, family friend, or business associate.

She looked me in the eyes for a moment and, as if on cue, a single tear appeared at the corner of her left eye. She dabbed it away with a tissue.

"Will you help me find my husband?"

When a person vanishes, the first step in the investigation is motive. Why would they suddenly disappear? Was their disappearance voluntary? Did the person suddenly decide he'd had enough and simply ran off? A lot of people do that. Just run. Either because they are fed up with their lives, or because of love. But if the disappearance was involuntary, that only meant one of two possibilities. Either they had been kidnapped, or something more sinister had happened to them. Since Jason Garrett's disappearance seemed involuntary—and the fact that no ransom had surfaced—I feared the latter, that Jason Garrett's disappearance had been because someone wanted him to vanish. But I didn't say anything about that to Mrs. Garrett.

Instead, I simply said, "Let me look into it."

CHAPTER TWO

I was having a drink with Detective Sergeant Mike Soratelli from the Atlanta Police in a small faux Irish pub on Courtland Street. There was not much about the pub that was Irish, but it was in a good neighborhood, with a mix of students from nearby Georgia State, cops from the precinct, and the downtown dwellers from the surrounding lofts and condominiums. You could eat if you wanted to, anything from steak to hot wings to potato skins. I wasn't eating today. I was having a beer. Soratelli was drinking scotch and soda. He was waiting for his food to arrive. He was a big, beefy Italian with a head like a concrete block. He had thinning black hair combed straight back. Soratelli had been with an out of state PD for twelve years before moving to the local department. I had known him since my days as a rookie cop, and he helped me when I needed a favor.

"Whaddya want now?" he said as soon as we got our drinks.

"What makes you think I want something?" I said.

"Every time you call me and want to have a drink, you want something."

"Maybe I just miss you," I said.

"Yeah, and I miss you too," he said. "Like a kidney stone. Now tell me what you want."

The bartender brought over Soratelli's order. It was an open-faced roast beef sandwich with enough brown gravy poured over it to render it unrecognizable. Just looking at it made my stomach hurt. But to Soratelli, it looked like heaven. He loved to eat and it showed. Call Soratelli anything you want, just don't call him late for dinner.

"Are you going to eat that?" I asked, pointing at the blob on his plate.

"Of course," he said. "I've had it before. It's great." He attacked the sandwich like a hungry bear.

"Does Doris know you're eating that junk?" I asked.

"No," Soratelli said through a mouthful of food. "And she better not find out, or I'll know who to come after."

"I wouldn't tell," I said. "But she'll probably notice you're ten pounds heavier when you get home tonight and wonder why."

"Doris loves me just the way I am," he said. "Big and lovable."

"I agree with the big part," I said. Soratelli and Doris had been married for twenty-six years and they were a perfect match. Despite the fact that Mike cheated on her with food.

While Soratelli ravaged the food, I took a sip of beer and glanced around the bar. It was seven o'clock and there weren't many patrons there. The evening happy hour crowd had cleared out. The only other people were a couple of guys in business suits at the other end of the bar, and a couple of college students in a booth against the wall, both with laptops.

Soratelli asked, "How's Naija?"

Naija Patel and I had been dating for nearly six months and, since meeting her, my life had changed for the better. Naija was everything I was not. She was beautiful, smart, and had a M.D. from Emory University and was a partner in an OB-GYN practice next to Piedmont Hospital. If opposites attract, we were the perfect couple. She was the only stability in my otherwise rough and chaotic life, and I was doing everything I could not to screw things up this time around.

I said, "Naija's good. Always busy with her patients."

Soratelli looked over at me. "How does a bum like you land a beautiful Indian girlfriend?"

"I'm handsome, debonair, and ..."

"...and full of crap," he said.

He smiled to himself with satisfaction at having finished my sentence for me. He took another mouthful of food, chewed a second, and then said, "You're lucky to have a woman like that. You guys talking marriage yet?"

"It's a little early for that," I said. "Besides, we like the way things are now."

"Maybe she can only put up with you part-time," Soratelli said. "Otherwise, you'd annoy her like you do the rest of the world."

"You may be right," I said.

The bartender brought me another beer and mixed Soratelli another drink. She was a tall blond with a little age behind her. She still looked good and was dressed in tight black pants and a white button-down shirt. She wore high heels that looked painful. I watched her as she walked down and served the two suits at the other end.

Soratelli finished his meal and wiped his mouth with his napkin. Then he took a sip of his drink, and let out a sigh of contentment, a bear that had just eaten his fill. "So," he said, "whaddya need?"

"What can you tell me about Jason Garrett?"

"He's missing," he said. "What's it to you?"

"I'm looking into it."

"Yeah," Soratelli said. "Who hired you?"

"His wife," I said.

Soratelli grinned, and said, "She's a looker, isn't she?"

"Yeah, she looks good. And she knows it."

"She's a classy broad," he said. "I like the way she carries herself. She exudes self-confidence."

"Exudes?" I gave him a questionable look. "You hear someone use that word or have you been studying the dictionary?"

"I know plenty of words," he said. "So why'd she hire you?"

"She wanted someone who has superior investigative skills, someone who's not afraid to take chances, bend the rules if necessary to get results. That's why I left the force. Too many rules."

"You left the force because they canned you because you're a smart aleck who can't follow orders."

I grinned at him. "I didn't fit in with the command structure."

"You don't fit in anywhere." Soratelli took another pull from his drink, and then asked, "Why'd she really hire you?"

"She isn't happy with the results from you guys."

"Missing Persons is looking for the guy."

"Sure they're looking for him."

"He's not the only guy missing in the city."

Right. No one cares if a lawyer goes missing. Everybody hates lawyers. They are like frogs. They're a necessary part of the ecosystem, but no one likes them.

"Well they haven't found her husband yet," I said. "That's why she hired me."

"You overestimate yourself," Soratelli said. "You think you can solve everyone's problems."

"I'm good at what I do," I said. Then I asked, "What have you got on Jason Garrett?"

"According to Missing Persons, his wife came in last week and reported him missing; he went to work but never made it back home. He usually worked late, so his wife wasn't worried until later that night. She reported him missing the next morning."

"What about bank activity? Credit cards?"

"Nothing. No ATM withdrawals. No money transfers. No activity on his credit cards."

"What about his cell phone usage?"

"Again, nada. The last cell call he made was at 6:20 p.m. the night he disappeared."

"Who'd he call?"

"Don't know," Soratelli said. "The call was to the switchboard at his office. It was probably transferred to an extension. No one remembers getting a call from Garrett at that time."

"His wife said his car is missing, too," I said.

"Yeah, it's a late model beige BMW. One of those $60,000 jobs. We've got the patrols on the lookout for it."

The bartender brought over a bowl of peanuts. I ate a few. Soratelli grabbed a handful and poured them in his mouth as if he hadn't eaten in days. I gave him a hard look as if he'd just eaten some of my lunch. I said, "Jason Garrett's a lawyer. Anything there?"

"No," Soratelli said. "He's a corporate lawyer at Schmitt & Lawson in Midtown. He does contracts and takeover requisitions. Real exciting stuff. I doubt he's ever been in a courtroom."

"What about the law firm where Garrett practices?"

"The only person that Missing Persons talked with was the senior partner at the firm. Guy named Charles Lawson."

"What did he have to say?"

"He didn't say anything," Soratelli said. "He's like any other lawyer I've ever met. The guy was tight-lipped."

"Why didn't anyone talk with the other lawyers at the firm?"

"Missing Persons said Charles Lawson wouldn't allow it," Soratelli said. He explained further, "In the report it says he wouldn't allow them to quote 'disrupt his law firm' unquote."

"Don't you think that's strange?"

"Yeah," Soratelli said. "But lawyers are strange people. They probably wouldn't have talked with us anyway, unless they had their lawyer in the room with them."

Then Soratelli laughed. I knew what was coming next. One of his jokes.

"Hey, this reminds me of a joke. There was a blind bunny and a blind snake that were best friends."

"That doesn't make any sense," I interrupted, just to get under his skin. "A rabbit and a snake can't be friends."

Soratelli gave me a disapproving look. "Are you gonna let me tell the joke, or not?"

I waved my hand. "Go ahead. Let's hear it."

"So, there's this blind bunny and a blind snake, and one day they decided to touch each other and describe what they felt. The snake felt the bunny's soft fur, long ears, and bushy tail, and after he described what he felt, the bunny cried, 'I'm a bunny! I'm a bunny!' Then the bunny felt the snake's scaly skin, his beady eyes, and his forked tongue, and after he described what he felt, the snake cried, 'Oh my God, I'm a lawyer.'"

Soratelli burst out laughing, as if it were the funniest joke he'd ever told.

So I gave him his due, and chuckled. "That's funny," I said.

"I thought it was, too," Soratelli said.

I finished my beer, and then asked, "You got anything else on the Garrett case?"

"That's all I have," he said. "Now you know as much as we do."

"So the guy just vanished without a trace."

"That's what it looks like," Soratelli said. "The guy just pulled a Jimmy Hoffa and disappeared."

CHAPTER THREE

The offices of Schmitt & Lawson took up an upper floor of One Atlantic Center in Midtown. The building was a fifty-story granite tower that highlighted Atlanta's skyline. I parked in a loading zone on 11th Street and walked the three blocks to West Peachtree.

The elevators at One Atlantic travel at approximately the speed of sound, and a few seconds after I selected Schmitt & Lawson's floor, the doors swooshed open and deposited me in front of the plush offices. Inside, the reception area was furnished with three leather sofas and several Chesterfield Queen Anne chairs. Pictures of the monuments in Washington, D.C. hung on the walls. The place looked as sterile and cheerful as a hospital operating room.

After talking my way past the receptionist, I made my way to Charles Lawson's ferocious-looking secretary, who scowled at me with a look that said she didn't approve of my existence, much less my presence in the office. She looked about fifty, with black hair streaked with gray that she wore pulled back in a bun so tight it made my scalp hurt. She reminded me of the nuns that used to beat the crap out of me in school. The brass name plate on her desk said she was Mable Williams.

"Hello, Ms. Williams," I said. "I'm Nick Price. I'm here to see Charles Lawson."

I gave her my prize winning smile. She didn't smile back. Probably frigid.

She shot me a scowl and checked her computer. "I don't have you on his appointment calendar," she said.

"I think he'll want to see me anyway," I said.

"What is this concerning?" she asked.

It sounded more like an accusation rather than a question.

I decided to take a more direct approach. I stopped smiling. No sense in wasting a perfectly good smile on a woman who probably hadn't been laid since the Reagan Administration.

I leaned over her desk a little and gave her the hard stare they teach in cop school. "I'm a detective," I said, "and I'm here to see Mr. Lawson. It concerns the disappearance of Jason Garrett. Now will you go tell Mr. Lawson that I'm here?"

She gave me a startled look, as if I'd threatened to punch her. She recovered quickly, however, and scowled at me.

"You should have told me you were with the police in the beginning," she said.

I didn't respond. No sense in correcting her.

She got up and went to the office behind her desk, tapped on the closed oak door, and went inside. A moment later, she came back out.

"Mr. Lawson will see you now," she said, but still gave me the disapproving look as if I were a bug who'd crawled in under the door. I'd seen the look a million times before. I gave her my surly, schoolboy I-showed-you look and moved around her desk.

Charles Lawson met me in the doorway of his office. He was a tall, thin man, and wore a navy blue pinstripe suit, a crisp white shirt, red tie, and gold cufflinks. The suit looked as if it cost more than my car. He had an oblong head that seemed as if it had been squeezed in a vise and a neck twice as long as normal. His Adam's apple protruded. He reminded me of a cartoon turtle stretching its head from its shell to look around.

"Detective," he said, tilting his head back and looking at me down his hooked nose. He didn't offer to shake hands. "I'm sorry, I didn't catch the name."

"Price," I said, "Nick Price." I was sure his pit bull secretary had told him my name. "I've got a few questions about Jason Garrett's disappearance."

"Do you have some identification?" Charles Lawson asked.

I gave him some. He looked at it closely, then handed it back.

"You're not with the police."

"Private," I said.

"I see."

He turned and walked back into his office. I followed him. He had a corner office that looked out toward downtown to the south. From this height, you could see the entire sprawl of the city. His office looked bigger than my apartment, and was better furnished. He had a leather sofa against the left wall where you could sit and look at the cityscape view below. Cherry wood bookcases lined one wall of the office, filled with volumes of law books. Next to another window, there was a huge glass-topped conference table with twelve leather and chrome chairs around it. Lawson went back behind his huge, cherry wood desk and sat down. He motioned to me to sit in one of the client chairs opposite the desk. I sat.

"How can I help you?" he said.

"What can you tell me about Jason Garrett?" I asked.

He tilted his head back and looked down his nose at me again. Apparently, it made him feel superior, the king regarding his loyal subjects.

"Unfortunately, I don't have anything to say that I haven't already told the real police."

He said it in that patronizing tone superiors use to inferior subordinates. But I wasn't one of them. I decided Charles Lawson was a snobby turtle. I wondered if I dangled a worm in front of him if he would snap at it. Probably not. This turtle had high standards.

Anyway, I let his crack slide. For the moment. At this early stage, showing my butt wasn't going to get me anywhere.

"I'd like to go over things again if you don't mind," I said.

He let out a disgruntled sigh, and said, "Certainly."

What he really wanted to say was 'get out of my office'. I waited.

Charles Lawson said, "He was…" then he corrected himself, "is one of our best attorneys. He would be one of my top picks for partner in a few years."

"Do you know any reason he would suddenly disappear?"

"No," he said. "As far as I know, there isn't a reason."

"Did you notice anything out of the ordinary before Garrett disappeared?"

"For instance?" he asked.

"Did he seem under any stress?"

"No," Charles Lawson said. "Garrett works hard and puts in long hours, as all the attorneys here do. It is a stressful job, but I wouldn't say he was stressed any more than the other associates."

"Did anything seem to be bothering Garrett before his disappearance?" I asked.

"No," Lawson said. "As far as I could tell, Jason was the same as always."

"And how was that?"

"Jason's a courteous and friendly person. He always makes a point to greet people in the morning. A genuinely nice guy."

"What about the other attorneys in the office?" I said. "Maybe they noticed something. I'll want to speak with them."

"No," Lawson said flatly. "That wouldn't be a good idea. Everyone in the office is terribly upset about Jason's disappearance. Having you asking a lot of questions would only disrupt the office."

Soratelli had been right. This guy played his cards close to his chest. In response, I said, "It may help me find him."

"I don't see how," he said. "His disappearance had nothing to do with this office. I can assure you of that." He added further, "Besides, I've asked the staff myself. They said Jason…Mr. Garrett…seemed perfectly normal before his disappearance."

This guy wasn't going to tell me anything. "Maybe I should talk with Schmitt," I said. "Maybe he noticed something."

"Robert Schmitt retired five years ago," Lawson said. "He lives in Florida." He seemed pleased to give me this news. Another person I couldn't talk to.

I'm not crazy about lawyers in general, and I was beginning to dislike this guy in particular. He was beginning to annoy me.

I tried a different approach. "What type of law did Garrett practice?"

"He's in our corporate litigation department," Lawson said. "Garrett handles some of our biggest clients."

"Did he handle any criminal cases?"

"Some of his pro bono cases may have been criminal. All our associates are required to handle at least one pro bono case a month. We work with Legal Aid to help the less fortunate." He added proudly, "We believe in giving back to the community."

I bet you do. I asked, "Did Garret mention any problems with any of his pro bono clients?"

"No," Lawson said. "Garrett is a very good attorney. I'm positive all his clients appreciated what he did for them."

"What about Garrett's regular clients?" I said. "Any problems with them?"

Lawson gave me an irritated look.

"Our clients are business professionals, Mr. Price," he said. "If there were a problem with one of our clients I would certainly have heard about it."

He hadn't answered the question. I waited.

"No," Lawson said finally. "He never mentioned issues with any clients."

"How many clients did Garrett handle?"

"I don't see why that's any of your business," he said.

I waited again. At this pace, I could be here all day and still not learn anything.

Lawson stared at me a second, sighed, then said, "Thirty."

"I'll need a list of those clients," I said.

"Absolutely not," Lawson said. "We have client confidentiality to respect here, Mr. Price. I'm sure you can understand that." He elaborated further, "In addition, involving them in a missing person's investigation could do irreparable harm to this firm."

He said it as if he were explaining it to a six-year-old. He was starting to get under my skin even more. Again, I took the high road, and said, "Talking with Garrett's clients could help in the investigation."

He took a deep breath and blew it out. He was getting tired of the questions—and of me. I was already tired of him.

Lawson leaned over his desk and pointed his finger at me, then thought better of it. He looked like a guy who pointed his finger a lot. He clasped his hands together on his desk.

"Let me make this clear," Lawson said. "As I said, as tragic as it is, Mr. Garrett's disappearance has nothing to do with this law firm, or its clients. Therefore, I won't allow you to hang around this office, disrupting the staff and asking a bunch of senseless questions. And I certainly won't allow you to harass our clients. Have I made myself perfectly clear?"

So much for the high road. Time to put this guy in his place. I stood up and leaned over his desk. "Let me be clear," I began. "I plan to investigate Jason Garrett's disappearance. So whether you like it or not, I'm going to keep asking questions, and keep annoying you so much you'll think you've got a giant tapeworm up your rear end that you can't pull out." I gave him the hard cop stare. "Now have I made myself clear?"

Lawson glared at me a moment and tried to look menacing. He failed miserably. He looked like he wanted to take a swing at me. I wished he would. It would give me a reason to punch him. He seemed more interested in protecting his precious law firm than finding Jason Garrett. Maybe this snobby turtle had something to hide.

Lawson said, "This conversation is over."

I replied, "For now."

I turned and walked out of his plush corner office with the cityscape view. I stopped at his secretary's desk, and said, "It was a pleasure meeting you, Ms. Williams." I flashed my favorite make-them-swoon smile. She didn't swoon, but she did give me a brief, slight smile and then it was gone.

I left. I felt good. I hadn't got any useful information, but I had accomplished two things: I had annoyed a pompous ass—plus, I had melted, if only for a second, the cold heart of Lawson's ferocious secretary Mable Williams.

CHAPTER FOUR

After making good friends with Charles Lawson, I decided to spread the love around by visiting another attorney. This one was on the list of acquaintances Julia Garrett had given me.

The law office of Vincent Carlyle was in Marietta, in a converted house just off the square. The office was modest, but tastefully decorated in early American furniture that went with the quaintness of the house. Carlyle's secretary was a good-looking woman of about thirty, with blonde hair that came down just past her shoulders. The name tag on her desk read: Carolyn Huff. She greeted me as if she had been expecting me.

"Hello, Detective Price," she said cheerfully. "Please have a seat and Mr. Carlyle will be with you in a moment. Do you want some coffee, or a soda?"

I had resolved to lower my caffeine intake. "Coffee will be fine," I said. "Black with two sugars."

I watched her as she stood up and went to a back room. Her skirt came down just above the knees. Nice shapely legs. It pays to be a seasoned investigator. After a moment, she came back with a huge cup with palm trees painted on the side. The coffee was fresh, as if it had been expecting me, too.

A moment later Vincent Carlyle came out of his office.

"Hello, detective," he said, shaking my hand. "I hope you haven't been waiting long."

"No," I said. "I was just getting acquainted with Ms. Huff."

Carlyle was about 5'9" with sandy brown hair, brown eyes, and a soft, southern-accented voice that immediately made you feel welcome. A big difference from my encounter at Schmitt & Lawson.

"Carolyn's great," Vincent said.

I bet she is. But I didn't say anything. Carolyn Huff sat behind her desk and I caught a glimpse of her legs again. I'm always looking for clues.

Carlyle led me into his office. It was a big contrast to that of Lawson's office. It was small and cramped with file cabinets. His desk was stacked with file folders of every color in the spectrum. A few law books teetered on the edge of the desk. An old, tattered trial bag, with more papers and folders sticking out, sat on one of the client chairs opposite Carlyle's desk. Carlyle maneuvered behind his desk and sat down. I sat in the other client chair.

"I've never met an actual private eye before," he said.

"Today's your lucky day," I said. I glanced around his cluttered office. "Nice office. How old is this house?"

"It was built in 1921," he said. "I bought it twelve years ago, did a lot of renovations and converted it to an office."

"Great location too," I said. "Close to the Cobb County Courthouse."

"I'm right up front where the action is," Carlyle said. "I can walk there in five minutes."

His office didn't have a cityscape view, but did have a good view of Glover Park where parents took their kids to play and on nice days office workers around the downtown square ate their lunch outside. Downtown Marietta had a small town quality to it though it was only minutes from downtown Atlanta.

Vincent Carlyle said, "Julia Garrett phoned me and said I might be hearing from you."

"Did she say anything else?"

"Only that she is unhappy with the way the police are handling her husband's disappearance," Carlyle said. He explained further, "Frankly speaking, I don't blame her. I would be upset myself if my wife were missing."

"It's understandable," I said. "What can you tell me about Jason Garrett?"

"We're casual friends," he said. "We're invited to the same dinner parties, same social functions. Occasionally, Jason, Julia, my wife Sherry, and I will have dinner together. They're nice folks."

"Any ideas about his disappearance?"

"I've asked myself that same question," Carlyle said. "I don't remember anything that would give an indication something was wrong. He's a dedicated husband, works hard at Schmitt & Lawson, always happy. A very likable guy."

"That's what I've heard," I said. "What about the other attorneys at Schmitt & Lawson? Know any of them?"

He thought a second, and then said, "No, I don't think so. Why?"

"Just curious," I said. "I ask a lot of questions until I uncover something interesting. Then I ask more questions and so on."

Carlyle asked, "Have you made any headway in Jason's disappearance?"

"Nothing yet," I said. I moved to another subject. "So you handle mostly criminal cases?"

"Yes, nearly all my cases are criminal."

"Do you know if Garrett handled many criminal cases?"

"If he did, it wasn't many," Carlyle said. "He specializes in corporate law. But he does pro bono work for Legal Aid occasionally, so he may have handled a few criminal cases."

"Do you handle pro bono work?"

He laughed and smiled. "Unfortunately, most of my work is pro bono." He laughed a little. "I'm on the public defender's roster. That's one of the downsides to being so close to the courthouse. Plus, I also work with Legal Aid."

Carlyle's secretary, Carolyn, knocked on the door and then came in carrying two cups of coffee in the same type cups with the palm trees on them. She placed Carlyle's cup in front of him, took my old cup, left the new one, and then sashayed out. We both watched her leave.

After she left, I asked, "What would Garrett do if he got a criminal case from Legal Aid he didn't feel comfortable handling?"

"We make referrals to each other," Carlyle said. He elaborated further, "That way our clients get the best representation. As far as the Legal Aid cases Garrett handled, they were the cases more suited to his expertise, like writing bad checks, DUI's, that sort of thing. In fact, I took a case off Jason's hands right before he disappeared."

"What type of case was it?"

He thought a moment, and then he said, "Assault, I believe."

He turned around, opened a file cabinet behind him and thumbed through several folders.

"Here it is," he said. He opened the folder, and glanced through the documents a moment. "It was an assault case."

"Anything special about the case?"

"Not really," Carlyle said. "The guy had priors, but nothing major. Petty larceny and one other assault charge. The guy's name is Roy Upshaw."

He handed me the case file. "You can make copies if you want."

"Thanks," I said. I glanced through the folder. The only thing that grabbed my attention was that Garrett gave the case to Carlyle the day before he disappeared. I asked, "Did you trade a case to Garrett for the one he gave you?"

"No," Carlyle said. "I didn't have anything that needed his type of legal help, so I just took the case off his hands."

"How did the case come out?"

"The charges were dropped at the last minute," he said.

"Anything strange about that?"

"I thought it a little strange that they waited until the last minute to drop it," Carlyle said. "The case was dropped a few minutes before the arraignment. That was a little weird. Usually, if charges are going to be dropped, they don't wait until we're standing in the courtroom to do it."

"Who did Upshaw assault?"

"A banker," Carlyle said. "Guy named Greg Little. He's a bank manager at First Georgia Savings."

"Why did Garrett ask you to take the case?" I asked.

"There were two reasons," Carlyle said. "One, it was an assault case, out of Garrett's expertise. The other reason is that Schmitt & Lawson does business at that bank. Garrett thought it would be a conflict of interest if he defended Upshaw."

"Why was Greg Little assaulted?" I asked.

"I'm not sure," Carlyle said. "Upshaw never said. He never said anything for that matter. The only information I got was that Upshaw accosted Little in the bank parking lot as Little was leaving."

"Was he trying to rob him?"

"Apparently not," Carlyle said. "Upshaw didn't ask for Little's wallet. He just walked up and started whaling on the guy."

"How did Upshaw get caught?"

"Another bank employee witnessed the attack and called police. They must have been in the area since they got there while Upshaw was still beating Little up. Says in the police report that Little was on the ground and Upshaw was kicking him."

"And this Upshaw guy never gave a reason why?"

"No," Carlyle said. "It's all there in the report. Upshaw refused to talk when he was arrested. He never made a statement, just asked for a lawyer right away."

"And Garrett got the case through Legal Aid?" I asked.

"Yes," Carlyle said. "The assault happened in Fulton County, so Upshaw was in the Fulton County Jail. Garrett went there and met with Upshaw, but when he discovered it was on the bank manager where Schmitt & Lawson does business, Garrett gave me a call and asked if I could take the case off his hands."

"So you went to the jail and met with Upshaw?"

"Yes," Carlyle said. "But Upshaw didn't say anything about the assault. The only thing he asked was when he could get out. I asked him a few questions about being able to post bail, and he just laughed it off as if it were funny. I took it to mean that he didn't have any money. At the arraignment I was going to ask for a lower bail but never got the chance."

I thought for a second, and then asked, "Why did Upshaw call Legal Aid? Why not just use the court appointed attorney?"

"I asked Upshaw the same question," Carlyle said. "He said that he didn't trust court appointed lawyers. He said they were all in with the cops."

"Did Upshaw know you're a court appointed attorney?"

Carlyle chuckled. "He didn't ask and I didn't say."

"What type of guy is Upshaw?" I asked.

"A true redneck," Carlyle said. "If you ever get a chance to see him, you'll know."

"So Upshaw beats up Little, then gets a get-out-of-jail free card."

"That's what it looked like to me," Carlyle said.

"And Upshaw was one of the last people to see Garrett before he went missing." I was mostly talking to myself now, formulating a time frame.

Carlyle nodded. "And then Jason Garrett goes missing the next day." He looked at me, and then asked, "You think the two are connected?"

"I don't know," I said. "Might be worth checking into."

CHAPTER FIVE

I didn't have a lot to go on, but since Roy Upshaw could have been the last person to see Jason Garrett before he vanished, I decided to pay him a visit. Upshaw lived in a trailer park in Bartow County not far from Lake Allatoona. When I turned off the highway, a rusty metal sign with faded lettering told me I had arrived at Southern Estates Mobile Home Park. A rutted dirt road snaked through the small trailer park.

I found Upshaw drinking beer outside his trailer. He sat in a plastic lawn chair that looked too small for his fat butt. A twelve-pack of light beer sat next to his chair. I took a glance around the place. A discarded washing machine sat in the front yard. Roy's trailer may have been new circa 1970, but now looked like it needed to be condemned. The trailer appeared to tilt slightly to the right, as if it were on the verge of tipping over on its side. Some of the windows were missing and had been replaced by planks of plywood. The rest of the windows were open. The front door was open; the top hinge broken. The door tottered as if it could fall at any second. I wondered if the trailer had running water. The rest of the mobile homes in the park didn't look any better. Some looked abandoned. Upshaw didn't have a yard to speak of, just bare ground. The place was so crappy, grass wouldn't even grow here. I didn't see a car parked in the bare patch of ground that may have served as a driveway. I parked in front of the trailer and got out of my car.

"Roy Upshaw?" I asked.

"Who wants to know?" he asked.

"I do," I said. "My name is Price."

"I don't care what your name is," Upshaw said.

He gulped more beer. He didn't stand up. He was a big guy, but fat around the middle. Too many of those cheap light beers. He was wearing an old gray t-shirt with the sleeves cut off. He had a barbed wire tattoo around his left bicep. On his right bicep, he had a skull and crossbones tattoo with blood running from the mouth of the skull.

"We need to talk," I said.

"Get out of my yard before I stomp you in the ground," Upshaw said.

"You can't," I said.

"What?" Upshaw shot me a really mean look. It probably scared other people he dealt with, but it didn't do anything for me. "What did you say?"

"I said you can't."

He jumped from his chair and stomped over to me. He gave me the menacing look again. Maybe he thought it worked better closer up. It didn't.

He said, "You're going to be talking with no teeth if you keep on." He was a couple of inches taller than I was. He liked bullying people, but it wasn't going to work with me. Carlyle had been right. This guy was the ultimate redneck.

"Clever comeback," I said, "but we still need to talk."

Upshaw glared at me through bloodshot eyes. He looked as if he were ready to fight. Maybe he was thinking about it. I could go a couple of rounds with him, but that wouldn't get me anywhere. I didn't come out here in the sticks to punch it out with the ultimate redneck in a trailer park. I needed information.

After a moment, he waved his hands at me and said, "Ah, what's the point." He clomped back to his chair and flopped down in it.

I walked over next to his chair. "I need to ask you a few questions."

He glared up at me. "You a cop?"

"Private."

"A private eye? Jesus Christ." He guzzled his beer, and tossed the empty can into an old rubber trashcan next to his chair. The trashcan was nearly full of beer cans, all the same crappy brand. "Well, get lost, Mr. Private Eye, before I kick the crap out of you."

I thought we just went down this road. I ignored his remark and said, "I'm looking for a missing person named Jason Garrett."

"Never heard of him," Upshaw said.

He opened another beer and gulped half of it.

"So you never heard of a guy named Jason Garrett?"

"That's what I just said."

I didn't want to stand here all day sparring with this backwoods yahoo. I decided to take a more friendly approach. I asked, "Mind if I have a beer?"

He glared at me again. "I ain't running a brewery," he said. "This twelve pack cost me eight bucks."

I pulled out a twenty and held it out. "This'll help cover the cost," I said.

Upshaw gawked at the bill and licked his lips. Then he glanced at me, snatched the twenty, and stuffed it into the pocket of his t-shirt.

"Help yourself," he said, and took another long pull from his beer.

I reached down and took one of the warm beers from the pack. There were only three cans left. Roy boy had been sitting here a while, seven beers and counting, excluding the eighth he held in his hand. He didn't appear drunk. He wasn't slurring his words.

I opened my beer and took a sip. The only thing worse than cheap beer is warm cheap beer. This stuff was terrible. Whoever said beer was made from horse pee must've been drinking this stuff.

"Good beer," I said.

"Damn straight," Upshaw said. "And cheap, too."

I said, "The guy I'm looking for is named Jason Garrett? He's a lawyer."

"Like I said, I never heard of him."

I took a picture of Garrett out of my jacket pocket and handed it to him. "Take a look at this," I said.

He took the picture, glanced at it and handed it back.

"Yeah, I recognize the guy," he said. "Didn't remember his name, though. He came to the jail after I was arrested."

He drank the rest of his beer, tossed the empty into the can next to him and opened another one. Just to be sociable, I took another sip of my beer. The taste hadn't improved.

"Did he help you with your case?" I asked.

"No," Upshaw said. "He didn't do anything. He came in and told me he would get me another lawyer to take my case."

"Did he say anything else?"

"No," Upshaw said. "That was it. Then he left." He paused a second, then asked, "So he's missing?"

"Yes," I replied. "Disappeared the day after he talked with you."

Upshaw glanced up at me, and said, "I don't know anything about that. I got my own problems."

"What did you tell the cops about the person you assaulted?"

"I didn't tell them anything," Upshaw said. "I wasn't going to admit to anything, know what I mean?"

I nodded. "And they dropped the charges against you."

"Yeah," he said. "I was glad. I was probably looking at some hard time because of my past arrests."

"Why did you beat up the bank manager?"

He shot a suspicious look at me a moment, sizing me up.

"You sure you're not a cop?" he said. "You look like a cop."

"I'm not a cop," I said. "I'm private." I took another small sip of my beer to show him I was his friend. I tried not to make a skunky-beer face. We were just two guys hanging out at the old trailer park, knocking back a few. He could trust me. I was his beer buddy.

He finished his beer and took another from the pack. He looked at the last beer in the box and seemed surprised that the beer was nearly gone. He checked the twenty in his shirt pocket and looked satisfied that more beer would be on the way.

I said in my friendliest voice, "So tell me, why did you beat up the banker?"

Upshaw looked at me again as if he were thinking about something. After a moment, he shrugged, and said, "What the hell? They dropped the charges anyway. I guess it doesn't matter now." He gulped some beer, then continued, "A guy came around a couple of weeks ago, said he had a job for me to do."

"Do you know the guy's name?"

"Daryl."

"He didn't give a last name?"

"No," he said. "He didn't have much to say at all, only that he knew I'd been in trouble before and had a job for me."

"How did he know you'd been in trouble before?" I asked.

Upshaw shrugged. "How should I know? At first I thought he was a cop, except he didn't act like a cop, know what I mean?"

Cops give off an aura that criminals can pick up on. I asked, "Why didn't Daryl do the job himself?"

"He said he'd been in trouble before, too," Upshaw said. "He said he would be recognized."

"Had you ever seen this Daryl before?"

"No," he said. "Like I said, the guy just knocked on my door and said he had a job for me."

"What was the job?"

Upshaw threw me an irritated glance. "To beat up the banker," he said. "That's what we been talking about."

I needed to wrap it up before he ran out of beer.

"Just to make sure I got this straight," I said. "A guy named Daryl shows up at your door, a person you don't know and have never seen before, and offers you a job to beat up a banker. Is that right?"

"That's what I just said," Upshaw said.

He drained his beer, tossed the can away, and took the last beer from the box. He popped the lid, and guzzled some as if he hadn't had anything to drink in days.

I asked, "How much did he pay you?"

"Five hundred," he said.

"How did you know who to beat up?" I asked.

"He took me to the bank and pointed the guy out," Upshaw said.

"Did Daryl tell you to say anything to the banker?" I asked. "Give him a message?"

"Yeah," Upshaw said, surprised that I knew this. "He told me to tell the guy to stick to banking."

"Did the banker know what you were talking about when you gave him the message?"

"I don't know," Upshaw said. "The guy was so scared I couldn't tell if he got it or not."

"What happened next?"

"So I was beating him up and he was on the ground, crying and trying to cover up, and then the cops showed up and busted me."

"Where was Daryl while this was happening?"

"As soon as the cops showed up, Daryl took off. He just left me there. I never saw or heard from him again."

"No honor among thieves," I said.

"Yeah," Upshaw said. "You got that right."

He had finished his last beer. He took the empty carton, crushed it, and tossed it in the rubber trash can on top of the empty cans.

I handed him the rest of my beer, which I didn't intend to finish, and said, "I better not finish this. I wouldn't want to get stopped by the cops." It was a way of getting rid of the stinking beer without coming across like a jerk.

"No sense it letting it go to waste," Upshaw said.

He took the can, turned it up. Then he patted his shirt pocket to confirm the twenty was still there. He seemed pleased. He had money in his pocket and more beer on the way. All was right with the world.

Since we were buddies now, Upshaw asked, "Can you give me a ride to the store so I can get some more beer? I can walk back."

"Sure," I said. I took out one of my cards and handed it to him. "Give me a call if you can remember anything else that may help me out." I didn't expect him to remember anything more, or perhaps anything at all after he gulped down more beer.

He looked at it a second and put it in his shirt pocket with the twenty. Then I drove him to the store to replenish his supply of skunky beer.

CHAPTER SIX

I didn't know whether Upshaw's assault on the banker had anything to do with Garrett's disappearance, but I decided it wouldn't hurt to check into it further. That's how some investigations go. You ask a person questions and they drop a name, and you go ask that person more questions and so on. Sometimes, it leads to a clue.

The next morning, back at my office, I gave Greg Little a call at First Georgia Savings. I was transferred around three different times—once to Customer Service, then to the Loan department, and finally to Little's secretary, a Mrs. Walker, who hesitated transferring me to Little. She inquired as to the nature of the call. I told her it was personal and that Mr. Little wouldn't want me discussing it with anyone except him.

Little picked up on the second ring. "Greg Little," he said in a voice so soft it sounded as if he were whispering.

I told him who I was and that I would like to come by the bank and talk about the assault.

There was a moment of silence on the line. For a second, I wondered if he'd hung up on me, but then in the same soft voice he said, "I dropped the charges."

"I know that," I said, "but I'd like to go over the details anyway. It may be connected to a case I'm working on."

"I don't think I'll be able to help you," he said. It sounded like more of a plea than a statement.

"It'll only take a moment," I said. "I can come by the bank and we can discuss it further."

"Oh, no," he said, a bit too quickly. His voice now took on a nervous tone. "Don't come to the bank." I heard him sigh. Then he said, "If we must talk, I'll meet you somewhere."

"I'll meet you at Mary Mac's Tea Room at one o'clock." I said. "I'll be out front. Lunch is on me."

Then I hung up before he had a chance to answer.

At one o'clock, I was standing outside Mary Mac's Tea Room on Ponce de Leon Avenue. Mary Mac's has been an Atlanta staple since the 1940s, featuring southern cooking that attracts locals and celebrities alike. Inside the restaurant, the walls are lined with pictures of celebrities and famous politicians that have dined here. There was a picture of Hillary Clinton, James Brown, Leonard Nimoy, Joe Namath, and even a picture of the Dalai Lama. When you come to Atlanta, you have to eat at Mary Mac's.

After a few moments, I saw a little man turn the corner from the back parking lot. He was a small bird who kept nervously looking around. He looked like he would jump out of his skin if someone tapped him on the shoulder. When he got closer, I saw a huge bruise on his left cheek, just below the eye. He walked slowly, as if it hurt to move.

"Mr. Little," I said.

He stopped and looked at me, startled, as if he hadn't seen me standing there. He was balding on top with just a half ring of short hair circling his head. He wore little horn-rimmed glasses that made him look like a bookworm.

"I'm Nick Price," I said and gave him a friendly smile.

He glanced around nervously again. No one jumped out at him.

"I guess we should go in," he said and headed for the safety of the restaurant.

The hostess seated us and we sat silently and looked at the menu. Each table had a supply of small pencils and order slips where you wrote down your own orders. Our waitress, Dorothy, a huge black woman, with a large bosom and a wonderful smile, picked up our order slips.

After she left, I motioned to the bruise on Little's cheek, and said, "Hurt much?"

Little lightly touched the left side of his face. "No," he said. "It looks worse than it actually is."

"What about the body punches you took?" I said. "Break any bones?"

"No," he said. "But my ribs are bruised and they hurt. I feel a little better every day."

"Good," I said. "Nothing hurt but your pride."

Little nodded, but didn't say anything. Getting beaten up is bad enough, but talking about it makes it even worse. Every time you talk about it, you relive it over again. It would bother anybody, especially if it's never happened to you before. And the last thing you want to do is talk about it. You just want to put it behind you and forget about it. I didn't blame Greg Little for not wanting to talk. But I needed to know why he had been assaulted. There could be a connection between his assault and Jason Garrett's disappearance.

"Tell me more about the assault," I said.

"I don't feel comfortable talking about it," Little said. He kept looking around the restaurant.

To reassure him, I said, "It'll be just between us. I know some of the details, but I'd rather get your side of it." I gave him my friendly smile again and waited. Little looked around the restaurant again, decided the place was safe, and leaned forward a little.

"Like I told the police," he said. His voice barely a whisper. "I came out of the bank around 5:15 and when I reached my car this huge guy came up and started hitting me."

"The guy who assaulted you. His name is Roy Upshaw. Ever see him before the assault?"

"No," he said. "If I'd seen him before I would have remembered him. The guy looks scary."

"Did he say anything to you during the assault?" I asked.

"I don't think so," he said, diverting his eyes. "If he did, I don't remember it. I was so scared."

"That's understandable," I said. "It must've been traumatizing."

Little nodded and said, "I've never had anything like that happen to me before." He paused and then continued, "You hear about stuff like that on the news, but never think it'll happen to you."

"So he just walked up and started beating you up?" I asked.

"Yes," He said. "He punched me and knocked me down and started kicking me. If the police hadn't come along, he may have killed me."

Our waitress, Dorothy, brought our food and refilled my glass of iced tea. Little had water that he hadn't touched. The food smelled great.

After she left, I asked, "Why did you drop the charges on Upshaw? You could've put him away for years."

He glanced around the restaurant again. No one lurked in the shadows.

"What about when he got out?" he asked. "He could come after me then. Next time I might not be so lucky."

"You may not have had to testify at the trial," I said. "A lot of these type cases are open and shut. The police caught him in the act."

"I just wanted to put the whole thing behind me. I didn't want it to drag out in court."

We ate our food in silence for a while. I love good southern cooking. In between bites, Little kept darting his eyes around.

"Did you have any contact with a guy named Daryl before your assault?" I asked.

"Daryl?" Little said. He looked confused. "Daryl who?"

"I don't know his last name," I said.

Little thought a second, and then said, "I don't recall anyone by that name. Why?"

"Just a name I heard," I said.

I didn't go into further detail. No sense in telling him that Daryl had been the guy that hired Upshaw. I didn't want to send the guy further over the edge. He was already a Nervous Nelly.

"What about the law firm of Schmitt & Lawson?" I asked. "What's your bank's association with them?"

He looked at me, startled. He suddenly seemed even more nervous. He hesitated, and then said, "They do business with our bank."

I asked, "Ever have contact with Jason Garrett from Schmitt & Lawson?"

Little thought a moment. "The name doesn't sound familiar."

"He's an associate at Schmitt & Lawson," I said. "He went missing the day after your assault. He picked up Roy Upshaw's case from Legal Aid, but then passed it along to another lawyer."

"I don't know anything about that," Little said.

We sat silently a moment. Little had barely touched his food.

"What about Charles Lawson?" I asked. "I know you have to be familiar with him."

He looked at me wide-eyed as if I'd pulled my gun on him. Then he quickly looked away and glanced around the restaurant again. The name had rattled him.

Little said, "Charles Lawson is the senior partner at Schmitt & Lawson. He comes in the bank occasionally."

"Why did you get more nervous when I mentioned Charles Lawson's name?" I asked.

"I don't know what you mean."

"Just then. When I mentioned Lawson's name, you nearly jumped out of your skin. Why?"

"I don't know what you're talking about," Little said. But I had touched a nerve.

"You know exactly what I'm talking about," I said. "When Upshaw was beating you up, he gave you a message. The message was to stick to banking. I just don't know what it means."

"I don't remember anything about that," Little said, looking down at his plate.

I leaned a little further over the table and glared at him. "Here's what I think," I said. "I think you know more than what you're saying, and for whatever reason someone sent you a message. So why don't you tell me what you know?"

I was going out on a limb here. I didn't know why Little had been assaulted, but I was convinced he knew more than what he was saying.

Beads of sweat appeared across his forehead. "I don't know what you're talking about," Little said. "And I don't know why I was beaten up."

"Did Charles Lawson have you beaten up?" I asked. I was reaching for the stars, but it didn't hurt to improvise.

"No, no," Little said. "Of course not."

"I think you're lying," I said. I gave him the hard stare.

He looked like he wanted to jump up and run for the door. It took him a moment to regain his composure. "I don't want to talk about it anymore," he said.

I leaned over the table and looked him in the eye.

"Why don't you tell me the truth," I said. "I can help you. But you have to be up front with me."

His face turned red with anger. "I don't need your help," he snapped. "I agreed to meet with you just because I didn't want you coming to the bank and causing a disturbance. This guy, Upshaw, assaulted me. I don't know why and I don't care. I just want to put the entire matter behind me. I consider the matter closed." He stood up and tossed his napkin on the table. "Please don't contact me again."

Then he walked away. I watched him go. This time he didn't glance nervously around to see if someone was going to jump out at him.

CHAPTER SEVEN

I was in my office sitting at my desk, thinking about lunch, and watching a baseball game on my laptop. Since I started watching baseball again, I subscribed to MLB TV so I could watch games whenever I wanted. They have live broadcast, or rebroadcast on-demand games. Today's game was live between the Cardinals and Cubs at Wrigley field. It was the last week of September and the game only meant something to the Cardinals. They were still in the wildcard hunt. But for Cub fans, another disappointing season was coming to a merciful end. The game was already five to zip in favor of the Cards, and it was only the third inning. I wasn't a staunch Cubs fan, but I thought all baseball fans would love to see the Cubs in the series one day. They hadn't been in the big show since 1945, and hadn't won the series since 1908. They were past due for a winning season, but it wasn't going to happen this year.

I was due as well to find some type of clue on the Garrett case. I had been on the case for four days, which meant Garrett had been missing for nearly two weeks, and I was no closer to finding him than when I started. The only thing I had discovered was that Charles Lawson didn't want me nosing around his illustrious law firm because I would "disrupt the office," and that Greg Little felt I would "cause a disturbance" at his bank.

But I was convinced that Garrett's disappearance and Upshaw's assault on Greg Little were connected, though I didn't have anything to substantiate my theory. There was a possibility that the two could be just a coincidence, totally unrelated to each other, but I wasn't buying it. I didn't believe in coincidences. So to get more answers, I would just have to keep digging until I uncovered a clue. If you turn over enough rocks, something eventually slithers out.

"I'm going to have to dig deeper," I said to my empty office. I had taken to talking out loud when I thought about a case. When I first began doing that I had wondered if I was off my rocker, but I'd always heard that you're not crazy unless you start answering yourself. So I was right as rain.

The phone rang. I reached over and answered it.

"How is my favorite detective today?" My girlfriend Naija Patel asked.

"Right as rain," I said, "now that I've heard from my Indian Princess."

"How is your new case going?" she asked.

"Not much to report," I said. "All I've managed to do so far is tick a few people off."

"You have a propensity to do that," she said playfully. "So what are you doing right now?"

"Just going over the details I have so far," I said. "Thinking about what my next move should be."

I heard her laugh a little.

"You're watching baseball, aren't you?" she asked. "Who is playing today?"

"How do you know what I'm doing?" I said playfully. "I might be sitting at my desk with my feet propped up."

"Because my favorite detective loves baseball and watches it every chance he gets." She giggled some more. "He missed it for all those years, and now can't get enough."

"What are you, psychic?"

"I don't have to be," she said. "We may have been dating for only six months, but I'm beginning to know you fairly well."

"I think you're just too smart," I said. "That's what I think."

We both laughed, but Naija was right. She did know me, despite the fact that we've only been dating for six months. She was very intelligent and intuitive. And she was radiantly beautiful. Since meeting her, my life had changed for the better. Up until six months ago, I hadn't watched baseball in years. In another life, or what seemed like another life now, I had played baseball. I had been a pitcher, a good one according to my trainers, with a chance at the big leagues. Right after high school, I went to the minor leagues, and for the next several years, I played with several minor league teams. Then I got my shot at the big leagues, but tragedy struck when I blew out my shoulder in my third start during spring training—and the injury ended my baseball career. Dejected, angry, and filled with bitterness, I turned my back on the game I had loved my entire life. Because of my anger, I couldn't see how lucky I had been, since most guys don't even get a shot at the big leagues. Instead, all I saw was that my dream had been shattered. I refused to go to any games, or watch games on TV, or check out the box scores in the newspaper. I slammed the door on that part of my life. But after meeting Naija, with her level-headed common sense and insightfulness, she convinced me that I could still love baseball, maybe not as a player but as a fan. She helped me heal my embittered heart. Now I watch baseball every chance I get. I'm an avid Braves fan, but I also like the Yankees, which is a form of sacrilege here in the South.

Naija said, "So you haven't told me who is playing."

"I haven't confessed to the crime yet," I said.

"Your silence is an admission of guilt."

"You're one smart cookie," I said. And I almost added, "That's why I love you so much," but I caught the words before they came out. We hadn't crossed that threshold yet, and I didn't want to scare her off by saying it too soon. But I wanted to say it. I felt I had found the person I had been searching for, the person known as "The One." Could you really fall in love in six months? I thought so. I know when I hear her voice I feel my heart race. I think that's a sign of love.

I heard her eating something, crunching in the background. Naija knew me well, but I was getting to know her pretty well, too. She was probably sitting at her desk, eating her lunch, or what she classified as lunch anyway, some carrots, a little celery, maybe an apple. I classified that as a snack, or bird food.

"Are you eating?" I asked.

"Yes," she said. "Even busy doctors have to eat."

"Let me guess," I said. "Carrots, celery, maybe an apple or some other fruit."

"You are a good detective," she said. "But today, I have some natural peanut butter to go with the celery."

"Sounds yummy," I said. "Not."

I imagined her sitting at her desk dressed in the scrubs she wears when seeing patients, the carrots and celery and peanut butter in front of her. Her long black hair up in a bun. Then I felt the familiar tug of longing when I talked with her on the phone.

"You should try more vegetables sometime," she said. "You may enjoy eating healthy."

"I eat my share of fruits and vegetables," I said.

"Yes," she said. "Along with the other things that aren't good for you."

"Man can't live off nuts and berries alone," I said. "He has to have a steak every now and then."

I always felt a mixture of gratitude, pride, and a degree of arrogance each time I spoke with Naija. The gratitude and pride was from the knowledge that she was with me. The arrogance came from the same fact that she was with me. I was lucky to have her, and knowing that I was lucky always took me back to gratitude.

"How is your day going?" I asked.

"I've been busy," she said. "I have a waiting room full of pregnant women right now. That brings me to the reason for the call. How would you like to take me to dinner tomorrow night?"

"What about tonight?" I said. "I could come by, pick you up, and take you to a great dinner and then back to your place for a night of hot romance."

"It sounds great," she said. "But I can't. I have my wine tasting group this evening."

"I can come to the wine tasting with you," I said.

"You came once before and hated it."

She was right again. I had gone with her a couple of months ago and hated it. I ended up sitting at the bar, drinking beer, and listening to them describe what a "wonderful bouquet" this or that wine had. The bar didn't even have a TV. I had been miserable. Why have wine tasting anyway?

To me, all wine tasted the same.

Naija said, "Besides, you'd be miserable. It is wine tasting, not wine guzzling."

"Maybe I just like to taste more wine than your highbrow friends," I said.

"Plus," she said. "I have to get up early tomorrow. I have a patient two weeks overdue, and I'm performing a cesarean in the morning at six."

"I hope everything comes out okay."

She caught the pun. "You're horrible," she said. Then she giggled. "But sexy, too. In a primitive way."

"I'm your Neanderthal man," I said. Again, I felt that wave of gratitude. Angels must have been looking down on me the day I met Naija. "And my heart belongs to thee." This time I couldn't stop the words before they escaped.

"And my heart is yours," Naija said.

We just crossed a threshold, I thought. Up until now, my previous relationships have been more of a rollercoaster ride, and they usually took a tailspin by the sixth week. In the past, the nature of my work took a toll on relationships. The women I dated didn't like the dangerous aspect of my profession. But so far, with Naija, that hadn't arisen yet in our relationship.

"Come by the office around five tomorrow," Naija said. "Then you can buy me dinner."

"I'll be there with bells on," I said and hung up.

CHAPTER EIGHT

The next day, I spent the morning going over the list of friends and acquaintances that Julia Garrett had provided me. I handled most of the people on the list over the phone. A few said they had only met the Garretts at parties and didn't know them personally. Others that knew them didn't have anything to help in my investigation. The last call I made was to a guy named Chad Livingston. Julia Garrett had listed him as a close friend to Jason. Sometimes guys tell close friends things they wouldn't mention to their wives. Livingston worked as a manager at a hotel on Marietta Street. He said he could meet me at two o'clock before his shift started.

I left my office on Broad Street and walked the two blocks to Marietta Street, and then turned right and headed toward the CNN Center. The hotel is adjacent to the CNN Center where the cable news giant broadcasts most of its programs. The center is also close to Philips Arena, the Georgia World Congress Center, and the Georgia Dome, where the Atlanta Falcons play. Inside CNN Center's atrium, a hodgepodge of fast food restaurants are splattered in all directions. The atrium looked like a mall food court on steroids. I felt my arteries hardening just walking through the place.

Around lunch time the place is like an anthill, especially if there is a convention at the GWCC. Today, however, at two o'clock, the crowd had thinned, leaving only the late lunch timers. When I had spoken with Chad Livingston earlier, we agreed to meet at the bar of an upscale restaurant in the South Tower of the hotel.

I took the escalator upstairs. The restaurant bar was next to the hotel registration desk. There was no one else at the bar. I ordered a beer and waited. Chad Livingston arrived a few minutes later.

"Mr. Price?" he asked as he approached me.

"Nick," I said and we shook hands. He was about thirty-five, tall, around six-three with a muscular build. He wasn't bulked up, like a bodybuilder, but was built solid like a tennis player or cyclist.

The bartender, a sharp-dressed black woman in black pants, a crisp white shirt and a black vest came over and Livingston ordered an iced tea.

"It's terrible," Livingston said after the bartender had left. "It's not like Jason to up and disappear like this."

"How well do you know Jason?" I asked.

"We've known each other for over twelve years," he said. "We went to college together at UGA. He went into law. I majored in business."

Livingston had a clear, concise voice. He enunciated each word. It was easy to imagine him calling the play-by-play of a baseball game.

I asked, "Exactly how close of a friendship do you and Jason have?"

"Pretty close," he said. "We play golf occasionally, and get together with our wives when we can."

"When was the last time you saw or spoke to Jason?"

"We played golf the Sunday before he disappeared."

"Anything seem out of the ordinary with him?" I asked. "Did he mention anything that may have been bothering him? Mention any problems?"

"No," Livingston said. "He was the same as always, and he didn't mention that anything was bothering him."

I took a pull from my beer. The bartender brought over a bowl of nuts and sat them on the bar beside my beer. I ate a few, then asked, "Would Jason confide in you if something were eating at him?"

"I think so," Livingston said. "We talk about everything, our jobs, wives, finances, just about everything."

"And he never indicated that anything was bothering him," I said.

"No," Livingston said. "But that's what's bugging me." He took a long drink of his iced tea, and continued, "Since Jason has been missing, I've gone back over everything we talked about that Sunday and he seemed perfectly normal."

"What about home life," I said. "Do you think he was happy with his marriage? Garrett ever mention another woman?"

Livingston grunted with a little laugh. "Not Jason," he said. "I've never seen him even look at another woman."

"Most guys at least take a gander at other women," I said.

"Not Jason," Livingston said, shaking his head. "Jason's not a typical guy. As far as he was concerned, Julia is the only woman on the planet."

The bartender refreshed Livingston's tea and brought me another beer. The bowl of peanuts was empty. Maybe it was a small bowl and only half-filled. She took the bowl, replenished the supply, and brought it back. It looked full this time. I ate a few more nuts.

"What about finances?" I asked. "He ever say anything about having financial difficulties?"

Again the head shake, then Livingston said, "I don't think he had money problems. He's raking in the chips with the lawyer gig. Nice car, nice condo in Buckhead, nice vacations every year."

"What about gambling?" I asked. "He do anything like that?"

"Not Jason," Livingston said in his announcer voice. "He's like a boy scout, straight and narrow. More like a choir boy. Jason doesn't even drink much. After we play golf, he nurses a beer while I have two or three."

I ate a few more of the peanuts, took a sip of beer, then asked, "Did Garrett ever mention anything about having enemies? Any of his clients ever give him a hard time?"

"He never said anything," Livingston said. "Most of his clients are corporate types."

"What about his pro bono cases? He must have run into clients a little rough around the edges in some of those cases."

"As far as I know," Livingston said, "he didn't handle hard criminal cases in his pro bono work. He passes those to colleagues who specialize in that type of litigation."

I looked at the half empty bowl of peanuts, then said, "Everyone I talk to says what a great guy Garrett is, and that he didn't have a reason to run off on his own."

"That's what bugs me," Livingston said. "Garrett would never do such a thing." He paused and took a sip of his iced tea, then said, "I'm worried something has happened to him."

"What do you think happened?" I asked.

"I don't know. I just know that Jason wouldn't leave without a word to anyone."

We sat silently a moment. I ate a couple of Brazil nuts I found in the bowl. I asked, "Know anything about Schmitt & Lawson?"

"Only what Jason has told me," Livingston said. "Jason seemed to like it there."

"What about the senior partner, Charles Lawson? Jason ever mention him?"

Livingston thought about that a second. "Not that I can think of," he said. "But Jason did say to me once that he thought Lawson was too controlling."

"How so?"

"He said Lawson had to see everything all the associates did. Nothing went to a client without Lawson's approval."

I ate the last few peanuts from the bowl. The bowl must have been smaller than I thought. I washed them down with the last of my beer.

I thought for a moment, then said, "If Garrett felt Lawson was too controlling, maybe Garrett grew suspicious about something at the firm."

"Could be," Livingston said.

"So maybe, I should look into Schmitt & Lawson a little further."

CHAPTER NINE

The Atlanta Obstetrics Center, where Naija shared the practice with three other physicians, was located a few blocks from Piedmont Hospital on Collier Road. I parked in the pay lot across the street and walked over to take her to dinner. I got there a little early, hoping that she had a short, late-day patient list. I hadn't seen her in six days and was excited.

When I stepped inside the waiting area, the angry stares of six pregnant women greeted me. They glared at me as if I had violated their inner sanctum. I felt like a flightless bird that had wandered into a cat convention. I didn't take the hostile stares personally. I think they would have greeted any male with the same cold, disapproving glare. Nevertheless, I was in hostile territory.

There were three leather sofas and four other leather chairs in the waiting room. There was a coffee table in front of each sofa, with an assortment of women's magazines on each table. Off to the left was a long check-in counter where the receptionist sat. The women in the waiting room glared at me as I walked across the waiting room and took a chair.

A nurse popped out of a door and said, "Mrs. Bradley to see Dr. Patel."

A very pregnant Mrs. Bradley, who looked as if she were ready to pop, struggled to get off one of the sofas. After she was upright, she shot me a quick, scowling glance as she followed the nurse into the back.

So much for Naija getting out early. My heart sank a little. I sat there like a big oaf, feeling out of place. There was nothing for me to do but sit, wait, and think.

I thought about how fortunate I was to have Naija in my life. Detective

Soratelli was right. I was one lucky stiff.

If opposites attract, then Naija Patel and I were meant for each other. Naija was everything I was not. She was beautiful, smart, spoke five languages, and had a Ph.D. from Emory University. She provided care for expectant mothers and nurtured unborn infants. She was empathetic and cared deeply about her patients. She meditated daily and associated with nice people who had dinner parties and wine tasting events. Naija hosted a book club in her apartment once a month where she and her highbrow friends met to discuss the latest bestseller. She was successful and led an organized life.

I, on the other hand, was a brazen private detective who led a disorganized life that sometimes involved violence. The only thing I've ever nurtured was a hangover. Some of my friends were cops who looked at the world through suspicious eyes, and my other friends were from the shadier side of society. I've never meditated in my life. And the only Ph.D. I have was one of hard knocks and street knowledge.

But fate brought Naija and I together, and I was fortunate to have her in my life.

I checked my watch. Only fifteen minutes had passed and another patient had been called for Naija. Nothing to do but wait some more.

When my baseball career came to a sudden end—although it didn't come to an official end until several month later but for all intents and purposes it ended that day—I was having the game of my life. It was my third start during spring training, and several major league scouts were in the stands watching me pitch that day. By the fifth inning, I had given up only one hit, and had struck out seven hitters. It was two outs in the fifth and I was ahead in the count. Then as I went into my windup about to deliver a fastball, I heard a loud snap in my right arm. It sounded like a gunshot going off. My right arm suddenly went limp, and the ball careened to the right behind home plate. The pain was excruciating. I fell to the ground, writhing in pain, holding my right shoulder. The x-rays showed I had broken my humerus bone in my pitching arm, snapped it completely in half. Then two operations and nearly a year of rehab later, it was apparent that I didn't have the right stuff any longer. And I found myself out of baseball forever.

A year later, I joined the police academy. And it was exactly what I needed. As a cop, I emerged myself in work, leaving both baseball and my resentment in the past. I liked being a cop and planned to make it my career. After a few years, I moved up to detective in the homicide division—but that's when problems developed. As a homicide detective, I discovered that taking orders and following procedures wasn't one of my strongest points. I did things my own way. Though I never broke the law, I sometimes bent the rules to get results. But it turned out that the higher-ups frowned upon such practices. And so like my baseball career, my police career came to an abrupt end three years after I made detective. That was five years ago. Then I got my P.I. license and hung my shingle as a private dick.

During those years as both a baseball player and a cop, I moved from one relationship to another. I would date a woman for a month or two, and then after the thrill of new-found romance dissipated, we would discover that we had nothing in common. During the cop years, some relationships ended because of the violent nature of my profession. A lot of women like the thought of dating a cop, but don't like the danger that goes with the job. Just ask any cop's wife. She would rather her husband be a baker, a banker, or a candlestick maker. Anything but a cop. At least in those professions no one shoots at you.

But all that changed when I met Naija.

We met at a dinner party, a dinner party that I almost didn't attend. A rich client I had worked for on an insurance fraud case had invited me to a dinner party. The client's name was Herald Bottom and he owned a local insurance company that had branches all over the Atlanta area. I almost didn't attend the dinner party, but changed my mind at the last minute. Good thing I did.

It was a small party, perhaps twelve people. I had arrived a few minutes early, but some of the party-goers were already there. Naija had been one of them. I noticed her as soon as I walked in. She was standing next to the fireplace talking with another woman, and her beauty and elegance captured my attention immediately. I'm not sure I believe in love at first sight, but I was certainly smitten the moment I saw her.

"So you're a private detective," she said after our host introduced us, and then wandered off, leaving us standing beside the open bar. "It sounds like an intriguing profession."

Her faint Indian accent was both calming and tantalizing at the same time. She was 5'4" with long black hair and dark, intelligent eyes. Her lips, painted red, accented her golden-brown complexion. She had on light makeup and not a lot of jewelry; gold hoop earrings, with four bangle bracelets on her right arm. No engagement or wedding ring. She wore a sleeveless red dress held up by two tiny spaghetti straps. She was the total package: intelligence, beauty, sensuality, and elegance.

"It's not as exciting as it sounds," I said. "The persona old movies give private eyes is one of tough-talking mysterious men who lurk around in dark alleyways. But in reality, I spend most of my time looking for clients."

"I must say you dress the part," Naija said, and smiled at me. "You looked intriguing and mysterious when I saw you come in wearing your overcoat and hat."

I was glad that she had noticed me. Ecstatic was more like it.

I said, "It's the hat. Men don't wear hats anymore like they did in the forties and fifties." I chuckled and said, "Not that I was around then."

She was drinking a glass of wine. I was drinking a Heineken.

"You're right," she said. "The only time I see men wearing hats are in old movies."

"You like watching old movies?"

"Yes," she said. "I think old movies are more realistic than the movies out now."

Great. She liked old movies. A woman after my own heart. I loved old classic movies. A couple of nights before, although alone, I had camped out in my living room with beer, pizza, and popcorn, watching a night of film noirs on TCM. Movies like *Murder, My Sweet* with Dick Powell, *The Big Sleep* with Humphrey Bogart, and *The Lady in the Lake* with Robert Montgomery. Not only was Naija beautiful and sexy, we actually had something in common. The night was definitely looking better.

Larry W. Pitts

We sat together during dinner and spent the rest of the evening talking to each other as though we were the only ones there. Looking into her eyes and listening to her soothing voice, I felt I could have stayed there talking with her forever.

Two days later, I called and asked her out. *Casablanca* was playing at the Fox Theater on Peachtree Street. To my surprise, she said yes.

We went to dinner and then went to see *Casablanca* at the fabulous Fox Theater. The Fox is one of the last old majestic movie theaters left in the country. When you sit in the theater and they dim the lights, you can look up and see the star-crusted ceiling flickering above. Sitting there in the dark with Naija on that first date, I had felt as if I were on top of the world.

On our second date, I gave Naija the CliffsNotes version of my stint in baseball, the shoulder injury, and the two subsequent operations. Afterwards, whenever the subject of my baseball career surfaced, I would quickly steer the conversation to other topics. I considered baseball a part of my distant past, and at the time, I wanted to keep it that way. Then one night at dinner, after we had been dating about a month, Naija asked me why I never talked about my baseball career. Even then, so early in our relationship, I felt so comfortable with Naija that I opened up to her, spilled my guts about my resentment, my anger, and my frustration at having been so close to my dream and then suddenly having it pulled out from under me. And in her practicality and levelheadedness, she helped me come to terms with my anger, and helped me see that I could still love baseball, perhaps not as a player, but as a fan. A few days later, Naija surprised me with tickets to a Braves/Yankees game, and we sat right behind home plate. Again, I felt as if I were on top of the world.

Though Naija and I both led busy lives, we tried to see each other at least a few times a week. Sometimes we manage to steal a weekend away together. We have a wonderful relationship. We were monogamous. We loved spending time together. Our lives complemented each other, though I felt she complemented my life more than I did hers.

As I sat there in her waiting room, remembering how empty my life had been before meeting her, I found it amazing how one person could enter your life and change you so completely in such a short time. In six short months, I felt I had become a completely different person.

Yes, I was a lucky man to have her in my life.

And then, there she was—my Indian Princess—standing beside my chair in the waiting room.

She had changed from the scrubs she wore when seeing patients, and she now wore a navy blue skirt that came down just above the knees. Her white blouse hugged her body perfectly. Her long black hair, which she normally wore in a tight bun when seeing patients, was brushed out and it cascaded down, framing her face. I looked into her huge dark eyes and felt like I was looking into my soul.

I stood up and gave her a brief hug and a peck on the lips. I beamed at the pregnant women in the waiting room and shot them a smirk. Their sneers now had cooled a little.

"Hi, handsome," Naija said, smiling at me, "been waiting for me long?"

"All my life," I said.

CHAPTER TEN

Naija and I went to dinner at a restaurant on Peachtree Street in Buckhead. The hostess seated us by the window and we ordered drinks. I was having a beer and she was sipping her wine.

After we ordered our salads, Naija asked, "When we were in the waiting room at my office, why did you look back at those women when you kissed me?"

I shrugged. "They looked at me funny when I came in."

Naija chuckled. "Looked at you funny? What do you mean?"

"They gave me dirty looks," I said defensively.

Naija laughed. "How old are you, twelve? They may have looked at you funny because they aren't used to seeing men in my office. It's sort of like their sanctuary."

"The way they looked at me, you'd think I slithered in under the door."

"They're pregnant," Naija said, as if that summed it all up.

"It's not my fault," I said. "I didn't make them that way."

Naija said in their defense. "They are uncomfortable, and their hormones are raging."

Right. If looks could kill, I would have been dead the moment I walked in the office.

"Their hormones aren't the only thing that's raging. They looked at me like they hated everybody with a Y chromosome."

Naija shook her head and laughed again. I loved it when she laughed. Her eyes glowed and her smile brightened the room. She said, "So did you feel vindicated when I came to your rescue?"

"Yes," I said and smiled at her. "That's why I gave them a gloating look."

"If you weren't so handsome and sexy," she said, "I would think you were twelve."

I gave her a flirtatious grin. "You want to come over to my house and play with me?"

"We'll have to see about that," Naija said, and took a sip of her wine.

The waiter brought our salads. I ordered another beer. We ate in silence for a moment.

Then I said, "You've been a busy girl lately."

"Such is the life of an obstetrician," she said. "Babies don't know how to tell time, so they decide when to be born."

"How did the delivery go this morning?" I asked.

I wasn't just making small talk. I was genuinely interested in her medical practice. I found her work fascinating, and I enjoyed hearing about the challenges she faced.

"Mother and baby boy are fine," she said.

"That's because she has such a wonderful doctor," I said.

"Your biased opinion is appreciated."

We were silent a moment, then Naija said, "Tell me about your new client."

"Her name is Julia Garrett," I said. "She hired me to find her husband."

"What is she like?"

"She's a knockout," I said, albeit too quickly, probably with a bit too much enthusiasm, too. I quickly added, "But not as much a knockout as you."

Naija giggled, and said, "Good save."

"I'm highly skilled at pulling my foot out of my mouth," I said.

The waiter brought my beer, smiled at Naija, and then left.

"So tell me about the case," she said.

"Not much to tell," I said. "The husband, Jason Garrett, is missing. He's a lawyer. He went to the office a little over a week ago and never returned home."

"Do you have any ideas as to what happened to him?"

"No," I said. "No one has seen him. No activity on any of his credit cards. No cell phone calls. Nothing." I took a sip of my beer, and added, "He doesn't have any bad habits either. No enemies. No mistresses. No gambling problems. No drug problems. It looks like the guy just vanished."

The waiter came and took our orders. He smiled at Naija again, and gave her all his attention while she ordered. He asked her all the right questions about how she wanted her food prepared. He didn't look at me when he took my order, and didn't ask any questions on how I wanted my meal cooked. I told him I wanted my steak medium-rare. He pretended to jot it down and then went away.

"I think our waiter is smitten with you," I said.

"He's just being nice," Naija said. "What about Jason Garrett's home life. Was he happy?"

"According to his wife he was. I also spoke with his best friend, and he confirmed that Garrett was happy."

"So you don't have any leads to go on?" Naija asked.

"Nothing substantial," I said. "The only thing that doesn't sit right with me is the attitude of the senior partner at the law firm where Garrett works."

"What's the name of the firm?"

"Schmitt & Lawson," I said. I then added, "I spoke with the senior partner Charles Lawson, and he wasn't helpful at all. In fact, he was more of a hindrance than help."

"Maybe he was just being cautious," she said. "After all, he has his clients' interests to look out for."

"At first I thought that too," I said, "but after a while I felt different. His reaction to my questions didn't fit."

"How so?"

"He seemed more worried about me snooping around his beloved law firm rather than helping me locate his missing lawyer."

"What are you going to do?"

I gave her an evil grin. "I'm going to snoop around his beloved law firm. See what turns up."

The waiter brought our order. Naija had the sashimi tuna salad. I had ordered the Hawaiian ribeye.

On the subject of Schmitt & Lawson, I said, "Another thing I'd love to see is Schmitt & Lawson's client list. See what kind of people the firm represents."

"Getting such a list could be difficult," she said.

"If not impossible," I said. "Lawson doesn't want me talking with his staff, much less his clients."

"Part of it has to do with client confidentiality."

"Confidentiality," I repeated. "I love it when you use big words. Turns me on."

Naija smiled at me with a gleam in her eyes. "Do you associate everything with sex?"

"With you, I can't control myself," I said. "Besides, it's been almost a week since I've seen you. I'm starting to turn blue."

Naija burst out laughing. A few heads turned our way. She put her left hand up to her mouth and blushed with embarrassment. Such an outburst was uncharacteristic of her. She was always reserved and under control. She quickly regained her composure.

"You've been counting the days?" she asked. She ate a small bit of her salad.

"Just a rough estimate," I said. "If I were shooting for accuracy…" I looked at my watch…"I'd have to say it's been six days, ten hours, thirty-seven minutes and seventeen seconds. But who's counting?"

"Apparently you are," she said, smiling at me flirtatiously.

We ate in silence for a moment. I was nearly finished with my steak. Naija still had half her salad left.

I said, "If I can't get a complete client list from Lawson, I'd settle for the clients that Garrett handled. There may be something there."

"There may be one way of getting the information," Naija said.

"Yeah? How?"

"Most business professionals take their work home with them," Naija said. "If Garrett kept client information on his personal computer, you may be able to access it."

"Smart thinking," I said. "No wonder your name means Daughter of Wisdom."

Naija smiled again and raised her eyebrows at me. "You would have thought of it in time."

"I doubt it," I said.

She said, "If you need help once you get his computer, my brother Satya may be able to help."

"He's the computer science geek at the college, right?"

"Yes," she said, rolling her eyes at me. "He has a Ph.D. in Computer Science from MIT. He should be able to help retrieve any information on the computer."

Our waiter brought the check and I paid. When we stood up to leave, Naija took my hand.

"By the way," she said, leaning over and whispering in my ear. "I'm turning blue, too."

CHAPTER ELEVEN

It wasn't quite dark as we left the restaurant. It was that strange time just after twilight and just before complete darkness. The temperature had dropped some as the day's light waned. Naija, forever cold natured, hugged my arm as we walked from the restaurant. In the parking lot as I held the passenger door for her—I'm old-fashioned enough to still open doors for ladies—I noticed a black Lincoln parked two rows behind my car with its motor running. Earlier, I had seen the same car pull into the parking lot behind us, but I hadn't seen anyone get out of the car. And no one had come into the restaurant directly behind us.

I closed the door and walked around to the back of my car. I had my keys in my left hand with my right hand up close to my chest so I could grab my snub-nosed .38 from my shoulder holster. I didn't pull the gun out. I didn't want to startle Naija. She abhorred violence and supported strong gun control legislation, but over the past couple of months, she had grown accustomed to me carrying a gun.

As I moved around the back of my car, I kept an eye on the Lincoln. It had darkened front windows, so it was impossible to see inside the car. I got in, started the engine, and flipped on the headlights. I glanced in the rearview mirror. The Lincoln's headlights blazed. I thought about it a moment. It could have been a coincidence. Maybe the occupants had gone to another restaurant in the area and were now just returning as we were. But I didn't believe it. Another possibility was that it might have been a different car altogether, just the same make and model. But I didn't believe that either. Tinted windshields weren't standard on most vehicles, so it had to be the same car that I saw before.

I backed my car from the parking space, and swung around to the next aisle of cars. In the rearview mirror, I saw the Lincoln back from its parking spot. I pulled from the parking lot and headed south on Peachtree. I checked the rearview mirror again, and saw the Lincoln pull in behind us three cars back.

It was close to seven-thirty and traffic crawled on Peachtree Street. I was quiet for a time. I kept checking the rearview mirror as we slowly made our way toward downtown. The Lincoln continued lurking behind us.

After ten minutes of silence, I said to Naija, "I've got an idea. Let's go to my place instead of yours."

"I thought we were going to my house for a night of hot romance," she said.

"We can still have the hot romance," I said, "only at my place."

Naija was looking at me intently. She had noticed the change in my demeanor. "Why the change of venue?"

My eyes darted at the rearview mirror again. Naija noticed.

"What's going on?" she asked. "Why do you keep checking the rearview mirror?"

"I think we're being followed," I said.

"Really," she said, with a hint of excitement in her voice. She turned around and glanced behind us.

"I think so. There's a black Lincoln three cars back. It pulled from the restaurant parking lot behind us."

We stopped at a red light and I glanced at her. Her eyes were lit up with excitement. Unlike other women I'd dated, Naija found my work intriguing, as if we were characters in a suspense novel, tracking down clues.

She glanced behind us again. "And you think they are following us?"

"I'm sure of it. The same car pulled into the restaurant parking lot behind us, but no one went into the restaurant behind us. Plus, no one came out behind us either. But the Lincoln was still in the parking lot when we came from the restaurant."

"Why do you think they're following us?"

"It has to be the Garrett case," I said. "Apparently I've asked enough questions to get someone's attention."

To make sure they were following us, I took a right on Spring Street, and a few blocks later took a left on 16th Street to West Peachtree. I hung a right onto West Peachtree, heading south, and then turned left at Biltmore Place. At the end of Biltmore, I ended up right back on Spring Street. All I had done was circle a few blocks. The black Lincoln stayed with me the entire time.

I had talked with several people on the Garrett case already, but hadn't come up with a single clue. Nevertheless, I had captured someone's attention. And that meant there was more to Garrett's disappearance than him simply running off to Tahiti. Suddenly, I began to get a bad feeling about this case, and about its outcome.

CHAPTER TWELVE

My condo was in a converted four-story building on Forsyth Street, a few blocks from my office. I pulled into the gated garage and drove to the second level. Evenly spaced sodium vapor lights glowed, giving the parking garage a pale yellow tinge. I swung around into a parking space that faced out onto Forsyth Street and cut the engine.

"Sit tight for a second. I want to check things out."

I got out and looked over the small concrete retaining wall overlooking Forsyth. The Lincoln had pulled into a parking space across the street. Its lights were out. I was slightly behind the Lincoln and high enough so that whoever was inside couldn't see me.

I waited.

No one got out of the Lincoln.

I waited some more. Several minutes went by. Naija got out of the car, walked over beside me, and glanced over the retaining wall.

"Which car is it?" she asked, hugging my left arm.

I motioned with a nod. "The black Lincoln across the street. They're still inside."

"What do you think they want?"

"They're probably just checking me out," I said.

I felt her grip on my left arm tighten slightly. "Are we in danger?"

I glanced over at her. The excitement was still in her eyes, but I saw a little apprehension, too. I hugged her. "No. They're just seeing what I'm up to." I looked at her, and she smiled at me. "You love this stuff, don't you?" I asked.

"I do find it exciting," she said. "I love the intrigue."

"Intrigue," I said. "I never thought of it that way."

"What do you think they'll do next?" she said. "Will they come up to your apartment?"

I chuckled. "I doubt it. But if they do, I have my two good friends Smith and Wesson to greet them at the door."

We watched a few moments more. There was no movement from inside the car.

"Let's go inside," I said. "They'll give up in a while."

"Do you think they'll come back?"

"Maybe," I said. "We'll find out in the morning."

The entrance to the apartment building was across the lot. To get into the building, you had to go through a small walkway to the elevator. The stairs were to the left of the elevator.

We took the stairs. Naija always takes the stairs. Another reason for her great shape. I followed her up. While she thought detective work was full of excitement and intrigue, I found excitement viewing her derriere moving up the stairs.

CHAPTER THIRTEEN

The next morning I awoke early, both relaxed and happy. It had been a wonderful night full of intimacy without any distractions. There had been no frantic, late-night calls from emergency rooms with unexpected births, and no middle-of-the-night calls from prospective clients for yours truly. Naija was nestled up against me, sleeping soundly, her left arm across my chest. Her hair lay splayed around her pillow. The sun was just rising and the early morning twilight lit the room just enough for me to see. She looked so beautiful lying there in my bed.

I moved her arm from around my chest. She made a humming noise and rolled over. I slipped from the bed and padded into the kitchen to make coffee. While it was brewing, I went into the living room and looked out the window. The window faced Forsyth Street. The Lincoln was gone, but I saw a black Chrysler parked on the corner. The motor was running. The overnight temperature had dropped into the low forties, and I could see the exhaust fumes coming from the tailpipe. I couldn't see who was in the car at this angle.

I went back into the kitchen and poured a cup of coffee. Then I went back to the window and watched the Chrysler some more. No one got out. If it were later in the day, I might have thought that whoever was in the car was simply waiting for someone. Maybe they parked and ran into one of the restaurants to pick up a to-go order or make a delivery. But not this early in the morning. At this time of morning the businesses along Forsyth were still closed. I couldn't make out the license number from this high up.

Since Naija was still asleep, I decided to check it out.

I strapped on my shoulder holster, put on a light pale blue jacket, grabbed my Yankees cap, and went out. I took the stairs down, but instead of heading to the garage, I went out the Luckie Street entrance and came around the building onto Walton Street. The car faced the other direction. I was behind it. There wasn't much foot traffic this early in the morning, so blending in with the crowd wasn't an option. I pulled my Yankees cap further down over my eyes and turned up my collar. Keeping my head down, I walked right past the Chrysler and got the license plate number. There were two men in the car. I could have taken them out if I had wanted to. They didn't seem to notice me. Nick Price, Master of Disguise.

I stopped at a newsstand on the corner, bought a copy of *The Atlanta Journal-Constitution*, circled the block and went back into the apartment building. The sun was up full now. Naija didn't have any appointments until ten-thirty, so I decided to cook breakfast. I went back into the kitchen, scrambled eggs, cooked bacon, made toast, and cut some fresh fruit. I cooked her some blueberry oatmeal, brewed her some green tea and added a little honey.

When I walked back into the bedroom, Naija was just waking. She was propped up against the headboard with the covers pulled up to her neck.

"Good morning, my Indian Princess," I said sitting on the edge of the bed and giving her a kiss.

"Did you go out?" she asked.

"I went out to get you the paper," I said.

She gave me a disbelieving look, but smiled.

"Something smells good," she said.

I responded in my best Shakespearean accent. "While thou have been sleeping," I said, "I've been working magic in the kitchen."

"Wow, you cooked breakfast and fetched the paper."

"Not only do I cook and fetch," I said. "I'm also good in the sack."

"And so modest, too." She pulled me close and gave me a kiss.

She hopped out of bed, slipped into her panties, put on one of my t-shirts from the dresser, and went into the kitchen. She sat at the kitchen counter and crossed her legs. I poured her some tea and served her the oatmeal. The cut fruit was on another plate on the counter. I spread some strawberry preserves on two slices of toast and poured myself another cup of coffee. I came around the counter, kissed her, and then sat beside her.

After a moment, she asked, "So Mr. Detective-slash-Cook, are you going to tell me the actual reason you went out?"

"To fetch thee the paper," I said.

She looked at me, one eyebrow raised, and gave me that disbelieving look again. I forked some of my eggs and ate a slice of bacon. She waited.

"I went out to take a look around," I said. "There's a different car parked outside now."

"So they switched cars?"

"Maybe they work in shifts," I said. "I don't know if it's the same guys from last night."

She thought a moment and ate a small piece of sliced cantaloupe, then asked, "What are you going to do next?"

"First I want to find out who's following me."

"How are you going to do that?"

"I'm a seasoned investigator, with superior investigative skills." I smiled at her and took a sip of coffee. "Plus, I got their tag number when I went to get the paper."

"Well, Mr. Seasoned Investigator, after you find out who is following you, then what?"

"Then I'll probably go and ask them why they're following me," I said.

"Then what?"

"If I don't learn anything useful from them, then I'll keep digging until I uncover a clue as to what happened to Jason Garrett." I took another sip of my coffee. "I just hope it's not too late."

Naija leaned over, kissed me on the lips, and then took my hand. She said, "You are very tenacious and have an unyielding determination, so I'm sure you'll get the answers."

I smiled at her. "You get all that from meditation?"

"No," she said. "I got that from looking up your profile in the Chinese calendar. You were born in the Chinese year of the dog."

"I thought you were Indian," I said, chuckling. "How do you know about all this Chinese stuff?"

Naija shook her head, and continued as if she were explaining something to a child. "Though I practice India's Dharma Buddhism, Chinese Zen Buddhism is closely related to that of India. In both Chinese and Indian Buddhism, you gain enlightenment through meditation."

"Well, what do you know," I said and grinned at her. "I think I gave you a little enlightenment last night."

Naija stared into my eyes, holding my hand, rubbing it slowly. With her sitting there in her underwear and my t-shirt, I realized one of us was overdressed.

She said, "Perhaps it was I who enlightened you."

I smiled and said, "Then I think I need some more enlightenment."

She stood up, peeled off the t-shirt, leaving only the sheer triangle of her panties. Then she took me by the hand and led me back into the bedroom.

CHAPTER FOURTEEN

I called Sergeant Mike Soratelli before we left my apartment and asked him to run the license plate number from the Chrysler.

"Has this got something to do with the Garrett case?" he asked.

"I don't know," I said.

"So why do you want me to run the plate?"

"Just checking something out," I said.

"Don't hold out on me."

"Never," I said.

"Made any progress yet?"

"None," I said.

"Then you're even with Missing Persons," Soratelli said. "They haven't made any either."

"Just run the plate and get back with me, okay?"

"Sure thing. That's why I'm here. To run down leads for you."

"To protect and serve," I said. "And I need some service."

"You need a lobotomy," Soratelli said. "Maybe it could help that crappy personality you have."

"Give me a call when you find out something on the tag number," I said and hung up.

A few minutes later, Naija and I left the apartment. I pulled from the parking lot and passed the Chrysler. In the rearview mirror, I saw it pull from the curb and fall in behind us a few cars back.

Naija glanced behind us, and said, "To get so much attention, you must've stumbled onto something."

I nodded, and said, "I wish I knew what it was. Then I would know what to do next."

"If they are so intent on following you, this must be serious."

I glanced over at her. Concern had replaced her cloak and dagger excitement from last night.

"Be careful," she said.

"Aren't I always?"

She looked at me and smiled. "No, I doubt you are."

"I'll be careful," I said.

I turned onto Collier Street, stopped in front of Naija's office, and switched on the emergency flashers. Horns blared as frustrated drivers swerved around us. I ignored them. The Chrysler pulled around and roared past.

"There goes your shadow," Naija said. "You better hurry and catch up."

"I'm sure they'll turn around and wait for me," I said.

I leaned over and kissed her. She got out of the car, and I watched her as she walked to the clinic door. She glanced back, waved, and then went inside. As I pulled from the curb, I felt that familiar longing I always felt every time we left each other. It felt as though a part of me had walked away.

CHAPTER FIFTEEN

I pulled into the lot I had parked in the day before and turned around. When I pulled back onto Collier, I saw the Chrysler speeding up the street. So much for me catching my shadow. It had caught up with me.

I called a friend of mine named Ray Norris. Ray owned a liquor store on Peters Street, and was well connected with the shadier sides of society. In fact, the liquor store was only a front for other less legal activities. If you knew the right people, you could get anything you wanted from the liquor store. I once went in for a bottle of Maker's Mark and left with a 37" flat-screen TV, and of course my bottle of bourbon. I've never asked Norris where he got his merchandise, and I didn't want to know. Ignorance is bliss.

"I need a favor," I said, when he answered the phone.

"You name it," he said.

Several years back, I had helped Ray's son Robert out of a jam. His son had been busted for possession of two joints at a concert a few days before he was set to go into the Navy. A stupid mistake that could have haunted him the rest of his life. The Navy had strict policies regarding any kind of drug possession charges, and even one as insignificant as pot possession could have ruined a promising naval career. I got the charges tossed. Now Robert had a distinguished career as a naval aviator. Ray Norris and I have since developed a good friendship based on respect and trust. I knew I could depend on Ray for help when I needed it.

"I've picked up a shadow," I said.

"How can I help?" Ray said.

"I need someone to follow them," I said. "I want to know what they're up to."

Ray laughed. "So you need someone to tail the tail."

"Exactly," I said.

"Tony's here," Ray said. "I'll let him know."

"I'll call you when I'm close," I said.

I went back downtown, turned onto Spring Street, and then took a right onto Peters Street. I called Ray back and Tony answered the phone.

"Ray told me you had a tail that needs tailing," Tony said.

Tony Veneto had worked with Ray at the liquor store for years, and I knew Tony helped Ray "acquire" the goods he sold from the store. Tony was a good-looking Italian with the physique of a body builder. He had dark piercing eyes, a strong jawline, jet black hair, and wore expensive suits. Whether it was his natural good looks or the excitement of sleeping with a mobster, women swarmed around him like bees on honey. Tony often boasted about the number of women he'd slept with. If Tony carved a notch on his bedpost for each woman he had slept with, it would look as if a beaver had gnawed on it. I had known Tony for several years through my association with Ray. Tony worked behind the counter at the liquor store and always carried a Glock in a shoulder holster. You know you're in a bad part of town when the clerks at the liquor store are armed to the teeth.

"I'll be passing there in a couple of minutes," I said. "I'm in a midnight blue Chevy Malibu."

I drove a dark, nondescript car in case I had to tail someone. But this time I was the tailee.

"Got it," Tony said.

"The Chrysler is two cars back," I said. "It's black."

"You want me to stay invisible?" Tony asked.

"If you can," I said. "Just follow them and see where they go."

"Got it," Tony said. "I'll call you back."

I drove past the liquor store and saw Tony, shoulder holster strapped under his massive biceps, climb into his bright red BMW. The Beemer wasn't the most inconspicuous car for a surveillance job. It stuck out like a sore thumb. But one makes do with what one has, doesn't one?

The Chrysler followed me. In the rearview mirror, I saw the BMW fall in line two cars behind the Chrysler.

I went around the block and back onto Spring Street, and then drove to my office on Broad Street. I swerved into the little alleyway between the Vietnamese restaurant and the adjacent building. In the rearview mirror, I saw the Chrysler pass. A few seconds later, Tony's Beemer flashed by. I got out of the car and walked to the corner of the alley. The Chrysler parked further down in a loading zone. I saw Tony turn right at the corner.

I stood and watched the Chrysler. After a moment, Tony pulled back onto Broad Street into a parking space a few spots behind the Chrysler.

Now I just had to wait and see where the Chrysler would lead.

CHAPTER SIXTEEN

I went up to my office, opened the blinds, and stood looking out the window. I could see the Chrysler parked further up the street.

I went to the small alcove that served as my kitchen area where I had a refrigerator, a toaster, small sink, and a coffee maker. I made a pot of coffee and poured a cup. I went back and checked on the Chrysler. It was still there. I went and sat at my desk, but I kept getting up to check on the Chrysler every fifteen minutes. It never moved. After an hour and thirty-five minutes, a police cruiser went by, gave a whoop of his siren, and motioned for the Chrysler to move. The Chrysler pulled off and a few seconds later Tony pulled out behind it.

I sat back at my desk with my feet up and thought about the case. There wasn't much to consider. I wasn't any closer to finding Jason Garrett than when I started. But maybe the Chrysler that had been following me would lead to a clue.

I went to my miniature kitchen and made a turkey sandwich. It's hard to think when you're hungry. Naija would be proud of me that I was eating healthy. I'm all about health food. Yeah, right.

The phone rang. It was Soratelli. We spoke a moment while I dodged his questions about why I wanted the license on the Chrysler run. Being a seasoned investigator, I skirted his questions without revealing any details. Finally, Soratelli gave up and gave me the information I wanted.

CHAPTER SEVENTEEN

While I waited for Tony to return from his surveillance job, I called Julia Garrett at her home. She picked up after the fourth ring.

"Have you made any progress in finding my husband?" she asked.

"I'm tracking down a few leads," I said. I didn't bother telling her that the only progress I had made was picking up a tail. Instead, I said, "I have a few questions for you."

"I'll do anything to help," she said.

Her voice still held a hint of sexuality. Maybe she always sounded that way.

"How much do you know about Schmitt & Lawson?" I asked.

"Not much," she said. "Jason never talked about the firm much."

"Did he ever mention to you about being unhappy at Schmitt & Lawson?"

I was standing next to my desk, looking out the window. The temperature outside had risen and the women from the nearby office buildings were out for lunch in full force. The view was spectacular. Atlanta has beautiful women.

"Jason is happy at the firm," she said. "He's working toward partnership."

"Did he ever mention anything that was bothering him at work?"

"No," she said. "He never mentioned anything like that. Why do you ask?"

"Just checking background info," I said. "Have you ever met any of the other attorneys at the firm?"

"Yes," Julia Garrett said. "We go to the company functions and holiday parties."

I asked, "Do you and Jason associate socially with any of the other attorneys?"

"No," she said. "Jason works all the time. So he doesn't have a lot of time to spend with friends."

"What about Charles Lawson?" I asked. "Ever met him?"

"I met him at the first holiday office party we attended several years ago," she said. "Of course, he was always at the subsequent parties, too. But I don't know him personally. Why?"

Now the sixty-four-thousand dollar question. I asked, "What's your opinion of Charles Lawson?"

"I really don't know him that well. I only spoke with him at office parties."

"Well, you've met him, so you must have an opinion?"

"Hmmm," she said.

There was silence on the line while she thought about that for a moment.

Out the window, I saw a particularly beautiful woman with long red hair come out of a Chinese restaurant across the street. She was tall and her dress was short. I wasn't the only person looking. Other men on the sidewalk twisted their necks around to take a gander.

Then Julia Garrett said, "My opinion of Charles Lawson is that he's a bit of a stuffed shirt."

I laughed.

"Are you laughing at me?" she asked.

The tone of her voice had changed a little, but she still sounded flirtatious.

"No," I said. "That's my opinion of Lawson, too. His shirt is certainly stuffed with something."

Julia Garrett chuckled. "That's a euphemistic way of saying it."

"Well, I am talking to a lady," I said. I paused a second, then asked, "Does Jason have a personal computer?"

I heard her laugh on the other end.

Now it was my turn to ask, "Are you laughing at me."

"Yes, I am," she said. "Are you sure you're not from the 1940s?" Then I heard her chuckle again. "Nearly everyone has a computer. But to answer your question, yes, he has a laptop."

"I'd like to come by and pick it up and have one of my technical associates take a look at it. It may lead us to a clue."

"Technical associates," she said, as if it were a question. "I thought you private eye types worked alone."

"I do," I said. "But I have people that help."

"You don't keep them in your desk drawer with your Marketing department do you?"

"No," I said. "These associates are real."

"That's good to hear." She chuckled, then said, "Yes, you can come by and pick up the laptop. When do you want to stop by?"

I looked at the clock on the wall behind my desk. It read 2: 22. I kept the clock behind my desk to keep me from staring at it when I'm not busy, which is a lot of the time. A watched clock never ticks. I thought for a second. I didn't know when Tony was going to come back from his surveillance job, and I didn't want to be out of the office when he came back. Plus, I had another lead I wanted to check out.

With that in mind, I asked, "How does tomorrow around noon sound?"

"That's fine," she said. "You have the address."

CHAPTER EIGHTEEN

An hour and twenty minutes later Tony walked into the office. He was carrying a six pack of Dos Equis. He was wearing a black shirt with white stripes and a gray suit that looked like it cost a couple of grand. I had to hand it to him; he knew how to dress. I sat behind my desk with my feet up. Tony sat in one of the client chairs and handed me one of the beers.

"You're not wearing your gun," I said. "Trying to turn over a new leaf?"

"No," Tony said. "I didn't want to scare the law-abiding citizens of the neighborhood."

He spoke with an articulate voice that had the resonance of a corporate CEO. I never understood how one second he would sound like a bank president and the next as if he were an uneducated thug. He changed the tone of his voice when it suited him.

"Where did our friends go after they left here?" I asked.

"They drove around for a while," Tony said. "Then they went east on I-20 and turned around and came back downtown."

"They wanted to make sure no one was following them," I said.

"No one except me," Tony said and smiled. "Finally they parked at Atlantic Station and switched cars. They got into a Chevy Suburban."

"They're being careful," I said.

"But not careful enough," Tony said. "Not when they're up against you and me."

"They didn't make you, did they?" I asked.

Tony looked at me as if I'd asked for his wallet.

"My car has one of those cloaking devices like on Star Trek," he said.

He finished his beer, opened another one. He handed me another beer, too.

"What did you find out about the Chrysler?" he asked.

"It was reported stolen two days ago," I said.

"So, they follow you in a stolen car, just in case you make them," Tony said. "Then switched cars when they're finished."

"Looks like they have something to hide," I said. "Where did they go after they switched cars?"

"They drove to a place on Monroe Drive, place called South Realty Group."

"Did they go inside?"

"Yeah," he said. "There were two of them. One was a muscular guy and the other one was fat."

"Would you recognize them if you saw them again?"

Again, he gave me the disapproving look. I knew Tony never forgot a face, name, or anything else he found important.

I said, "Did you get the tag number for the Suburban?"

He nodded, and then read it off to me from memory.

"South Realty Group," I said, more to myself than to Tony. "Never heard of it."

I opened my laptop, and began searching for South Realty Group on Google.

"I already did that," Tony said. He held up his iPhone.

"I'm more plugged in than you think," he said. "There's nothing on the web about them."

"Most businesses are on the web," I said. "Even I have a website."

"Yeah, I know," Tony said. He gave a small laugh. "You need another web designer. Looks like a high school kid did it."

"I paid a college student from Georgia State to design it for me," I said.

"Then maybe you would've done better using a high school kid," Tony said. Then he asked, "Why do you think they're tailing you?"

I thought for a moment. I didn't know why, but it had to be connected with Jason Garrett's disappearance.

"I don't know," I said.

"Maybe we should take a ride over there and ask them," he said. "If we ask real nice, they might tell us what we want to know. If they don't, then we can bust a few heads and ask again." Tony took a drink of his beer, and continued, "Chances are, they see a couple of thugs like us walk in, they'll start talking."

"We might just do that," I said.

I doubted gang busting in would give us any more information. In the end, it could complicate things more.

I said, "I thought you were a hoodlum."

"I graduated up to a thug," he said.

"I'm so proud of you. I always knew you would be successful."

CHAPTER NINETEEN

When Tony left, I closed up the office and headed toward midtown. There was one other person I wanted to talk to and see what information I could get out of them, if any. I drove north on West Peachtree Street and parked in the garage of One Atlantic Center. I checked my watch: 4:45. I was making two assumptions. One, the person I wanted to talk to didn't take MARTA and drove to work. Two, they parked in the garage at One Atlantic. If I were wrong on either assumption, then I would have to figure out another way to talk to them.

From the parking garage, I took one of the elevators to the concourse level and then took the escalator to the lobby. There were a number of people coming and going in the lobby, mostly going at this late hour of the day. After twenty-five minutes, I started to catch the eyes of the building security guys. It would only be a matter of time before one of them came over and asked what I was doing. But before they got the chance, I went back to the concourse level and hung around waiting and watching the office workers as they left the building.

Fifteen minutes later, the person I wanted to talk to came into the concourse. Suddenly the concourse was full of people. It was as if the ship was going down and everyone was scrambling for the lifeboats. The person of interest got in one of the elevators. I thought about taking the same elevator, but I knew I would be recognized. So I got in a different elevator and I went back to my car. I had backed into a parking space next to the garage exit. Now I just had to wait and watch when they came out of the garage. A few minutes later, I saw them go past me driving a late model Lexus SUV.

They turned left out of the parking lot and headed north on West Peachtree. I fell in behind them, two cars back. There was no reason for them to suspect they had a tail, so I followed closely. They turned left onto 17th Street, made a right on Atlantic Drive, and then pulled into a supermarket parking lot. We had driven less than a mile, and it had taken nearly fifteen minutes. Traffic was terrible this time of day; you could've walked it in five minutes.

I watched her get out of her car and go into the supermarket. I waited a few minutes and then went inside.

Inside, I cruised each aisle and spotted her in the pet food section. I pegged her as a cat person. I watched her as she moved further down the aisle. I walked up behind her.

"Hello, Ms. Williams," I said in a cheerful voice, as if I'd ran into an old friend at the supermarket.

Mable Williams turned around, startled that someone had called her by name. When she saw me, her eyes filled with recognition, and then a scolding contemptuous expression swept over her face.

"Mr. Price," Mable Williams said, "what are you doing here?"

I flashed my make-'em-swoon smile. She didn't swoon. She didn't even smile back.

"I followed you," I said.

"Why are you following me?"

She looked as conservative as she had when I first saw her. Her dark blue skirt went down past her knees. She wore a long-sleeved pale blue blouse. She wasn't wearing a wedding ring. Her hair, still severely pulled back, made her look like a ferocious librarian.

"We need to talk," I said.

"I don't have to talk to you," she said, and walked away.

I followed her.

At the dairy section, she stopped, turned around, and gave me a stern look, as if she'd caught me talking too loudly in the library. "What do you want?" she demanded.

"I'm investigating the disappearance of Jason Garrett and we need to talk," I said.

I glanced down at the basket she carried. It contained a couple of frozen dinners and a few cans of cat food. I was right. A cat person. Nick Price, Master of Characterization.

"If you continue following me," she said, "I'm going to call the police."

"Go ahead," I said. "Then you can answer their questions about the disappearance of Jason Garrett."

This was a lie. If she called the police, they would focus more on me harassing her rather than me investigating the disappearance of Garrett. But I was banking Ms. Williams didn't know this.

Her stern librarian countenance went to fear. "Why would the police question me?"

"Because you may have information concerning Garrett's disappearance," I said.

"But I don't know anything about it," she said.

"Did the police question you before?"

"No," she said.

"So you may have important information that you're not aware of," I said. "Did the police question others at Schmitt & Lawson?"

"No," Mable Williams said. "They didn't. They only spoke with Mr. Lawson."

"If there's a criminal investigation, they'll be questioning a lot of people, and they may start with you."

This wasn't exactly a lie. If there was an investigation, the police might question her, but it didn't mean they would start with her.

"My goodness," she said, drawing in a sharp breath. "Why would they question me? I don't know anything."

I ignored her question, and said, "And if they find that you've been holding key information on the case, you could be facing criminal charges."

This was a lie, too. But sometimes you have to improvise.

"You mean I could be arrested?" she asked.

She looked startled; as if I had just told her the police had an APB on her.

I said, "It would be better to talk with me now."

She walked toward the produce section. I walked beside her.

She stopped, glared at me, and then asked, "What do you want from me? I already told you. I don't know anything about Mr. Garrett's disappearance. I wish I could help you, but I can't."

I smiled at her. I gave her just the regular smile this time. No sense in wasting my make-'em-swoon smile. Now that I'd scared her, it was time to smooth things out, get her on my side. I said, "You'd be surprised how the smallest detail could lead to a clue."

"I'm under strict orders not to speak with you," Mable Williams said.

"Why?"

I don't know," she said. "I only follow instructions. I don't ask questions."

"Who gave you instructions not to talk with me?"

"Mr. Lawson," she said. "After you left he sent an e-mail to the entire staff instructing them not to speak with you under any circumstance."

"Doesn't it seem strange that I'm looking into the disappearance of one of the firms most valued attorneys and Mr. Lawson tells everyone not to help?"

"He said you would embarrass our clients, and cause irreparable harm to the firm," she said.

"And you believe that?"

"It doesn't matter whether I believe it or not," Mable Williams said. "I follow orders."

She looked nervously around, suddenly aware that she had been speaking with me all along. "If I'm seen talking with you, I could lose my job," she said, the tone of her voice suddenly lower.

"Don't worry," I said. "I'll never tell."

I smiled at her again. She shot me a stern look.

"I could use your help in finding Jason Garrett," I said.

I was going out on a limb. I didn't know which way this cat lady was going to jump. She could run back to Schmitt & Lawson and rat me out. Tell Lawson that the pesky private investigator followed her and started asking questions. But she didn't jump. She didn't run for the door. She just stood there looking at me. I knew she was deciding whether to talk to me or not.

"I don't see how I can help," she said finally.

"I think you can help plenty," I said. "You unknowingly may have information that could help me find Jason Garrett."

"What type of information would that be?" she said. "I'm not privy to confidential matters of the firm."

"But you're Charles Lawson's secretary, and you know the firm's internal operations. With that knowledge you could speculate."

"I could lose my job," Mable Williams said.

We were still standing in the produce section. We were nearly blocking the apple bin. People gave us disapproving glances as they maneuvered around us to get to the apples.

We were silent a moment. I waited, looking at her intently. She stood there and glanced around again. She was still considering what to do.

To help her make up her mind, I said, "For all I know, someone could be holding Garrett against his will. And we need to find him as quickly as possible. The more time that goes by, the greater the possibility of a bad outcome. Garrett's life could be at stake." I gave her my sad, pleading puppy dog look, and said, "Come on, Ms. Williams, I need your help. Jason Garrett needs your help."

She glanced nervously around again, checking to make sure no one had spotted her fraternizing with the enemy. Then she nodded her head.

"I'll do what I can to help," she said.

I smiled at her. She gave the briefest smile back, and then it was gone.

"Great," I said. I glanced down at the frozen dinners in her shopping basket. "Allow me to buy you dinner."

She glanced at the frozen dinners and twisted her lips as she thought.

I added, "I promise it will be better than a frozen dinner."

"Anything is better than frozen," she said.

CHAPTER TWENTY

So I followed her again, only this time she knew I was behind her. Again, it was a short drive that we could have walked. I'm not sure why she liked to drive short distances that were easier to walk. Maybe it gave her a sense of security being in her own car. Whatever the reason, she insisted on driving.

The restaurant we'd chosen was located a couple of blocks away on the ground floor of a nearby building. The restaurant was also on Atlantic Drive. Since a couple of buildings separated the south and north portion of Atlantic, you have to go around the block to get to the other side. Including traffic and the time for valet parking, it took nearly twenty minutes. We could have walked there in less than ten.

The restaurant had a modernistic décor with sleek cherry wood tables, with an open kitchen strategically placed in the middle. It was still early and there weren't a lot of people in the restaurant.

Mable Williams and I sat next to the window. Our waiter came to the table and told us they had an exceptional wine list and handed each of us a listing of their exceptional wine varieties. I imagined Naija and her frou-frou friends coming here for one of their wine-tasting soirees. I thought about giving her a call and telling her I was attending a wine tasting of my own, but then I decided against it.

Ms. Williams ordered a glass of Pinot Gris. I ordered the same. When in Rome.

Mable Williams said, "The part about a criminal investigation against me was just a ruse wasn't it?"

"Yes," I admitted. Then I explained, "But I had to get your attention. I needed to talk to you. I'm sorry if I alarmed you."

"You got my attention all right," she said.

"But the ruse got us here," I said.

Mable Williams smiled. She had a nice smile. It changed her entire face, making her look attractive and vibrant. She should smile more. It was better than the ferocious secretary/librarian look she normally wore. Maybe she didn't smile to keep people at bay.

I said, "Do you live close by?"

"I have a condo a couple of blocks from here," she said.

"Close to work," I said.

"Close to everything," Mable Williams said.

The waiter brought our drinks.

"Why don't you walk to work?" I asked.

Mable Williams shook her head. "In this city," she said. "Not a chance."

"I do a lot of walking. If I can walk where I need to get to, I walk." I took a sip of wine, and then asked, "What can you tell me about Schmitt & Lawson?"

"What do you want to know?"

"I don't know," I said. "I just keep asking questions until I find a clue. Then I go from there. How long have you been with the firm?"

"Twelve years."

"Are you married?" I asked.

"Widowed," she said. She took a sip of her wine, and then added, "My husband died thirteen years ago. Cancer. So I sold the house, bought the condo downtown, and got a job at Schmitt & Lawson."

"So you were there when Schmitt was still at the firm?" I asked.

"Yes," she said. "He retired five years ago."

"And now Lawson is the sole senior partner?"

"He holds fifty-one percent of the firm," she said.

"So he has the deciding vote on all matters," I said.

She thought about that a second, then replied, "Yes, I guess you can say that." She added, "But all the junior partners have complete faith in

Mr. Lawson."

"It's not like they have a choice," I said.

Our waiter came and took our orders. Mable Williams ordered the roasted salmon with seasonal vegetables. Seasonal vegetables usually mean steamed broccoli, a few green beans, and some carrots. Maybe those are the only ones always in season. I ordered the seared tuna with mashed potatoes. Mashed potatoes were always in season, too.

After he left, I asked, "What do you think happened to Jason Garrett?"

"I have no idea," she said.

"Do you think his disappearance has anything to do with Schmitt & Lawson?" I asked.

She countered with her own question. "What makes you think Schmitt & Lawson could be involved?"

"I don't know whether they're involved or not," I said. "But I find it strange that Lawson won't allow me to talk with the other associates at the firm."

Mable Williams said, "Mr. Lawson told everyone that Mr. Garrett's disappearance, tragic as it is, has nothing to do with the firm."

I took another sip of wine, and then asked, "Do you believe that?"

"Yes," she said. "I don't have a reason to disbelieve it."

The waiter brought our food orders. We ate in silence for a while. The tuna was delicious.

After a while, I asked, "What can you tell me about Charles Lawson?"

"He's been with the firm since he got out of law school twelve years ago," she said. "He works very hard, and so far he's made the right decisions for the firm."

"Does Lawson still handle clients?"

"Yes," she said. "He still handles some of the firm's more important clients."

"The high-dollar clients," I said.

She smiled again and chuckled. "They're all high-dollar clients," she said. "But some of our clients that have been with the firm a long time prefer Mr. Lawson handle their affairs personally."

"And you take care of his appointments and such?"

"Yes," she said. "The majority of my duty is handling his appointment calendar."

"Does Lawson ever have appointments that are not on his calendar?" I didn't know where I was going with this, but it didn't hurt to dig around.

"I'm not sure what you mean," she said. "All his appointments are on his calendar."

"I mean does he have people come to see him that don't have an appointment?"

"Occasionally," she said. "Some clients come in unexpectedly."

"Does Lawson have visitors that aren't clients?"

She thought about that for a moment, and then said, "There is one person who comes to see him who never has an appointment."

"Who is it?"

"I don't know him," she said. "The only thing he ever says when he comes in is to tell Mr. Lawson that Mr. Rueben is here."

"Rueben," I said. "Do you know his first name?"

"No," she said.

"What type of business is this Rueben character in?"

"I don't know that either," Mable Williams said. She added, "The only thing I do know is that Mr. Lawson always makes time to see him."

"How often does this Rueben come to see Lawson?" I asked.

She thought about it a second. "He comes around about once a month."

"And this Rueben never has an appointment?"

"No," Mable Williams said. "But Mr. Lawson always makes time to see him."

"And Lawson never tells you anything about what they discuss?"

"No," she said. "He never mentions anything about Mr. Rueben."

"Don't you find that strange," I said.

"I don't know," she said. "Mr. Rueben could be just an old friend of Mr. Lawson's."

Could be, but I doubted it. To change the subject, I asked, "Do you think Garrett could have simply run off?"

Mable Williams took a sip of wine and thought about that for a moment. "I don't think so. Mr. Garrett doesn't seem the type to up and run off." Then she explained, "He has a beautiful wife, and a wonderful future ahead of him at the firm. I can't think of a reason he would run away from that."

If Jason Garrett didn't disappear voluntarily, then something had happened to him. But I didn't say anything about that.

As if reading my mind, Mable Williams asked, "Do you think someone could have done harm to Mr. Garrett?"

Her voice had taken on an anxious tone.

"It's possible," I said.

She took a sip of her wine. "This is so terrible," she said. "Not only is Mr. Garrett one of our best attorneys, he is a very nice man. He always makes a point to stop and say hello. He's nice to everyone. I don't know who would want to harm him."

She looked as if she were going to cry. I reached over and patted her on the hand.

"There's no evidence that indicates that any harm as come to Garrett," I said. "But it is critical that we find him as soon as possible. That's why I need your help."

"I'm not sure how I can help you," she said.

We had finished eating. The waiter brought us another glass of wine.

I asked, "What can you tell me about the clients Jason Garrett handled?"

"I don't know any of the particulars about his clients," she said. "I'm just a secretary, not an attorney."

"But you have access to a list of Garrett's clients," I said.

"Of course," she said, "but how can that help?"

I said, "I'm not sure. It may not help at all. But if you can get me that list I'll see where it leads."

She looked worried again. Maybe she was thinking that coming here with me had been a mistake. I couldn't blame her for being cautious. She had only seen me once before and here I was asking her to break her loyalty to the firm.

"If Mr. Lawson finds out," she said, "I'll lose my job. I'd be breaking the firm's confidentiality with its clients."

"Don't worry," I said. "I'm not going to go gang busting in on any of the clients. I just want to see what type of clients Garrett handled."

"He handles all type of clients," Mable Williams said. "Individual and corporate clients."

She said it as if that simple statement would cover it. It didn't.

"It's not going to hurt to take a look," I said. "If there's nothing there to investigate, then no harm done." Then I added, "It could lead to a clue in his disappearance."

Now that it was getting later in the evening, more people came into the restaurant. Our waiter brought the check. I paid.

I gave her one of my business cards. "If you can send me the client list in the morning that would be helpful," I said. "I really appreciate your help."

She took it, looked at it a moment, and placed it in her purse.

"Don't use the firm's e-mail system," I said. "Use your personal e-mail account."

"I will," she said. Then she added, "Thank you for such a nice dinner, even if it was under a ruse."

"A ruse by any other name," I said.

"Is still a ruse," Mable Williams said and smiled again.

CHAPTER TWENTY-ONE

The next morning I awoke before dawn. I dressed in sweatpants and went for a run. The morning was crisp and cool with a temperature in the mid-forties. The perfect weather for a run. In the pre-dawn light, there wasn't much traffic on the streets. An occasional truck passed, making an early morning delivery to the many restaurants in the area. The only pedestrian traffic was the homeless people that always wandered the streets of downtown at all hours of the day and night.

I ran against the non-existent traffic on Luckie Street, turned up Forsyth Street, and then took a right on Marietta Street. I hooked a right at Spring Street and another right on Margaret Mitchell Square. The athletic club was on Peachtree Street. I worked out for an hour. On the way back to my apartment, I stopped at Dunkin' Donuts, ate two blueberry muffins and drank a cup of coffee. It was 8:10 when I got back to my apartment. I felt good. My muscles were tight and had that mild ache you get from a good workout. I took a long shower and got dressed. I put on a dark blue suit with gold pinstripes, a pale blue shirt, and a red tie with a matching breast pocket handkerchief. I strapped on my shoulder holster and tucked my 9mm inside. On the way out, I checked myself out in the living room mirror. Dressed to kill.

Since I needed my car later, I drove to the office instead of walking. I parked in the alley next to the Vietnamese restaurant. I had an agreement with the owner of the restaurant. He lets me park there, and if he needs any muscle, I'm just upstairs.

I went up to the office. The clock behind my desk read 9:15. I made a pot of coffee. While I waited for the coffee to finish, I went through yesterday's mail. Nothing exciting, a few bills and a circular that had a variety of advertisements from carpet cleaning to hair restoration. I didn't need either. I trashed everything, including the bills.

I checked my e-mail. The e-mail from Mrs. Williams had been sent this morning at 7:38. Jason Garrett's client list was attached. She was a very efficient secretary. Charles Lawson should give her a raise.

I poured a cup of coffee, opened the list on my laptop, and started studying the names. Along with Garrett's regular clients were the names of his pro bono clients. The only name that jumped out at me was that of Roy Upshaw. Beside his name in parenthesis was Vincent Carlyle's name.

After a while of staring at the screen, my eyes started to cross. I took a break, poured more coffee, and stood looking out the office window. What was eating at me was the way Charles Lawson had announced to the staff that Jason Garrett's disappearance had nothing to do with Schmitt & Lawson. If that were the case, then why would he instruct everyone not to speak with me? I wasn't buying that bit about disrupting his law firm. If one of the firm's biggest rainmakers were missing, Lawson should be telling the staff to help in any way necessary, not the other way around. It didn't make sense.

And what about this Mr. Rueben character? Who was he? Was he a part of this, too? I didn't know. Mr. Rueben could be just an eccentric client, someone who doesn't want anyone to know his business other than his attorney. But the more I thought about that, the less likely it seemed. Even if he were an eccentric client, he'd have an appointment on Lawson's calendar.

I hadn't made any progress on the case. I didn't have any concrete leads. Everything I had so far was speculation. I wasn't any closer to finding Garrett than when I started.

I drank more coffee and thought about the case some more. I didn't come to any conclusions. I looked out the window some more and watched the women go by down on Broad Street. An aptly named street, I thought.

The phone rang. It was Naija. "I had a break and decided to check to see how my detective is doing."

"I'm still chasing my tail," I said.

I told her about what I'd learned so far. Then I told her about the dinner with Mable Williams.

After I described the restaurant, I said, "You and your wine group should go there one night. I think your highbrow friends would approve."

I heard her giggle on the other end. "Our group has been there before," she said. "It's a nice place."

"I should have known," I said.

Then I told her about how Charles Lawson had instructed everyone at Schmitt & Lawson not to talk with me. I finished by saying, "I'm beginning to think Lawson doesn't like me."

"You just need to turn on the Nick Price charm," Naija said. "It worked on me."

"I don't think it would have the same effect," I said.

"It sounds like Lawson has something to hide," she said.

"Yes it does," I said.

"When are you going to pick up Jason Garrett's laptop?"

I glanced at the clock behind my desk. It was ten after eleven. "In about an hour," I said. "I'll drop it off with your brother Satya at the school. Maybe it will have some information on it."

"I hope so," she said. "Call me tonight."

She hung up.

Naija wasn't the only one hoping the laptop contained something that would lead to a clue.

When I left the office and pulled out of the alley, I noticed a black Ford Explorer parked across the street with two guys sitting in front.

CHAPTER TWENTY-TWO

The Garrett's lived on the twenty-eighth floor at Park Place in Buckhead. The ultra-luxurious forty-floor building, located on Peachtree Road, is one of Atlanta's who's who residences. It had once been home to Oprah Winfrey, Elton John, and Janet Jackson, and just like the Park Place in Monopoly, it was strictly high-dollar. Up and coming associates at Schmitt & Lawson must bring in some serious money. Maybe I should have gone to law school.

The valet took my keys and pulled the car into the parking garage. The security guys at the desk in the lobby didn't seem to notice me. Since I was dressed like a million, they probably thought I lived there.

I took the elevator to the twenty-eighth floor and pressed the buzzer at the Garrett residence. I waited. No one came to the door. I pressed the buzzer again and waited some more.

After a couple of minutes and three more buzzes, Julia Garrett opened the door.

Her eyes appeared slightly out of focus, as if I'd woken her. She looked surprised to see me.

"Mr. Price," she said. "What are you doing here?"

"We spoke on the phone yesterday, remember?" I said. "I said I would come by to pick up Mr. Garrett's laptop."

She wore red jogging shorts and a white tank top. The tank top hugged her upper body. Her toned shoulders and arms were tanned perfectly. Her auburn hair was pulled back in a loose ponytail. She was barefooted, her toenails painted a bright red. She didn't have on any makeup, but she didn't need it.

"Oh, yes," she said groggily. "Come in."

She turned and walked inside. The Garrett apartment was elegant and spacious with parquet floors in the foyer, living room, and dining area. Ten foot floor-to-ceiling windows gave you plenty of light and a spectacular view of the city. In the living room, two chenille upholstered Dunwoody sofas sat facing each other, and flanking one of the sofas were two cherry wood end tables. A marble figurine of Apollo sat on one of the end tables, standing guard. On the opposite table was a figurine of Aphrodite.

Julia Garrett sat on one of the sofas, crossed her legs, and motioned for me to sit down. I sat on the opposite sofa. She said, "To be honest, I had forgotten you were coming today." Her voice was thick, as if her tongue were still asleep. She seemed to be having difficulty focusing her eyes.

Then I saw the reason. On the end table next to her, Aphrodite stood watch over a nearly empty bottle of burgundy wine. A half empty glass sat next to the bottle. I glanced at my watch: twelve-ten. Now I knew why her speech was heavy. She was plastered. Maybe happy hour started early for the elite housewives of Atlanta.

I pointed to the figurine next to her, and said, "Aphrodite, the goddess of love and beauty."

She glanced at the figurine. "Aren't you full of surprises," she said. "I didn't think a man in your profession would know Greek mythology."

"Surprising as it sounds," I said, "I can read, too."

She looked at me a second, trying to decide if I was being facetious or just rude.

"I didn't mean it the way it sounded," she said.

"Don't worry about it," I said.

She waved a hand around the room, and said, "I'm the goddess of love and beauty around here."

She took her glass of wine and drank some, then asked, "Have you made any progress in finding my husband?"

"I'm chasing down a couple of leads," I said. "Do you know anything about the clients your husband handled at Schmitt & Lawson?"

"No," she said. "Jason never talked about his clients."

"He never mentioned anything about any of the clients?" I gave her a curious look. "Most husbands discuss their work with their wives."

"Not Jason," she said dismissively. "He never talked about his clients. He's a corporate attorney. Nothing exciting about that."

"Did he ever mention anything about Schmitt & Lawson? Whether there was anything going on at the firm that bothered him?"

Julia took a sip of her wine. "The only thing he ever mentioned about that place was how wonderful it was."

"So he never mentioned anything about the firm, or the clients he handled?"

"No," Julia Garrett said, waving her hand again. "Why all the questions about Schmitt & Lawson?"

I said, "Charles Lawson instructed the staff members at the firm not to talk with me. I find that strange."

She reached over, took the bottle from the table, and refilled her glass. "It's no surprise he's uncooperative. You've met Lawson yourself. He's arrogant. Thinks he's superior to everyone else."

She suddenly grew silent a moment. Then she looked at me seriously and asked, "Do you think Charles Lawson had something to do with Jason's disappearance?"

"Too early to tell," I said. "I'm just checking everything out."

"It wouldn't surprise me if he were involved," Julia Garrett said. "Or at least that law firm had some involvement with Jason's disappearance."

"What makes you think that?"

"Because that law firm was Jason's whole life," Julia Garrett said, as if she were spitting out the words. She took another drink of her wine. "Jason put in long hours at the office, and then came home and worked some more."

"Did that bother you?" I said. "Him working all the time?"

"It bothered me plenty," she said. "I felt jealous of that place. But…" she waved her hand around…"what could I do?"

"So Jason was happy at Schmitt & Lawson?"

"He loved the place," she said. "That's why I thought it funny when you asked if Jason had another woman. Not Jason. His other woman was named Schmitt & Lawson."

She paused a moment. Her eyes closed and I briefly wondered if she'd passed out. Then she came to again and continued, "He just worked all the time. He was never here. And when he was here, he really wasn't. Know what I mean?"

I nodded, but didn't say anything.

Julia gulped the rest of the wine in the glass. "It was like we weren't married any longer." Her voice was suddenly despondent. "I made sacrifices for Jason and his career. I put my acting career on hold to help him through law school. I was the perfect wife to him."

She wasn't looking at me any longer. She stared at her wine glass. It didn't matter. I don't think she was talking to me anymore.

She said, "Then when he got the job at Schmitt & Lawson, he completely changed. He became obsessed. That place took over his whole life." Then frustration and anger crept into her voice. "He stopped paying attention to everything else. Even to me." She waved her empty glass around. For a second I thought she was going to throw it against the wall. "Now look what's happened," she spat. "He's gone. Probably because of that place. I'll tell you one thing, Mr. Private Detective. There's something about that law firm that's not co…copahetic."

Her words were beginning to slur. She had managed to stick an h in the word copacetic. Time to get moving.

I said, "Maybe Jason's laptop will lead us to a clue."

"Maybe it will," she said.

Then she stared at me a second with a different look in her eyes. Funny thing about drunks, they can turn on a dime. She leaned back on the couch, uncrossed her legs, and put them up on the coffee table. The hand that wasn't holding the wine glass moved slowly up and down her thigh.

"I bet you don't work all the time. Do you?" she asked.

"Depends on how busy I am," I said.

"Are you married?" she asked.

"No," I said.

"Have a girlfriend?"

"Yes."

"Is it serious?"

"I think so," I said.

"I bet you give your girlfriend all the attention she needs," Julia Garrett said.

"I try," I said.

She poured the rest of the wine into her glass. The conversation wasn't going anywhere. I needed to wrap this up.

I said, "Do you have Jason's laptop ready to go. I'd like to get it to the tech guys as soon as possible."

"No. It's not ready to go." Her voice still held a tinge of anger. "It's in his office." Again, she motioned with the wine glass. Some of the wine sloshed out. "Down the hall. First door on the left."

I got up, leaving her sitting on the couch and went down the hall. In the hallway, pictures hung of Julia on various magazine covers. One of her sitting on a motorcycle in a bikini. On another cover was just a black and white head shot with her hair cascading down around her face. In stark contrast to the gray image, her lips were a vibrant red. Slightly parted. Sexy.

I went in Garrett's office. Cherry wood bookcases stocked with law books lined the walls. A matching desk sat to the right, facing the office door. The swivel chair behind the desk looked more comfortable than my bed. I sat in the chair. If I had a chair this comfy, I could prop my feet up when business was slow and take a nap.

Garrett's desk was neat. Everything strategically placed where it belonged. All the items on the desk aligned with the one next to it. Garrett had a little OCD. I checked the desk drawers. There wasn't much in any of them. There were several different colored folders in the file drawer. I glanced through the papers inside each folder. Nothing interesting. One contained bills. The other two had files that didn't mean anything to me. A red folder was labeled Schmitt & Lawson with several documents inside. I leafed through the pages, but nothing jumped out at me. I stuffed the folder inside Garrett's leather laptop bag. I would give the pages a better look later.

The laptop sat on top of the desk. I unplugged it and placed it in the bag. The power cord snaked down the side of the desk and disappeared beneath. I looked under the desk. The power cord was plugged into a surge protector deep in the foot well. I moved the swivel chair out of the way, crawled under the desk, and unplugged the power cord. When I was coming out from beneath the desk, I saw two bare feet standing there. Bright red toenails gleamed at me. I crawled from beneath the desk and stood up.

Julia stared at me the way a wolf looks at a rabbit.

"Do you think I'm beautiful?" she said. I noticed that she had replenished her supply of wine. This time with a chardonnay.

"You're very attractive," I said, hoping that would be the end of the conversation. I rolled up the power cord, placed it in the laptop bag, and zipped it up.

"You want to know something," Julia Garrett said.

Not really. I didn't like the sound in her voice, or the way she was staring at me. I'd gotten what I'd come for and was ready to leave.

She said, "When I first saw you, I thought you were handsome. And mysterious. Maybe even a little dangerous. A guy that knows what a woman wants and how to give it to her."

There was nothing to add to that, so I remained quiet.

"Do you know Jason hardly ever touched me," she said. "Look at me. I'm beautiful. Men would give anything to sleep with me. But not Jason. He never paid attention to this body. He was too busy working at that stupid law firm." She continued staring at me with that hungry look in her eyes. "I need attention. I need to be touched, caressed."

Then she came up to me, pressed her body against me, and wrapped her arms around my neck. "I want you to touch me," Julia Garrett said.

I didn't touch her.

Then she tried to kiss me. At the last second, I turned my head, and she kissed my cheek instead.

"I can tell you know how to satisfy a woman," she said. "I knew that the moment I first saw you. And I need to be satisfied. Take me into the bedroom."

I grabbed her wrist from behind my neck and pulled her arms away. "I don't think that would be a good idea."

"Why?" she snarled, changing her tone in an instant, "because I'm married?"

"That's part of it," I said.

She glared at me. "What's the other part?"

"I'm not unfaithful to my girlfriend," I said.

"She'll never have to know," she said, suddenly playing the seductress again. "No one will ever have to know."

"I would know," I said.

She tried to kiss me again. I performed the head turn maneuver again. She kissed the other cheek. I didn't think this is what the term "turn the other cheek" meant.

"Take me into the bedroom," she said.

"I can't do that." I took her by the shoulders and gently moved her out of my way. "I have to go," I said.

And again she performed the personality shift. I was beginning to think Julia Garrett had more personalities than Sybil. "What's the matter detective, boy?" she spat. "Afraid you can't satisfy me?"

I didn't say anything. This was a dead-end street.

She glared at me. Her eyes tore into me like daggers. Her lips twisted into a sneer. "All men are pigs! Pigs! Good for nothing pigs!"

I picked up the laptop bag and looked at her a second. What I saw was a worried, afraid, and frustrated woman whose husband was missing, and all she really wanted was for me to find him and bring him back home. Tears streamed down her cheeks.

"Get out!" she demanded.

"I'll let you know when I make progress," I said. Then I walked out of the office, down the hallway, and out the apartment door.

CHAPTER TWENTY-THREE

There had been a time in my past, especially in my baseball playing days when I tried to nail anything that moved, that I would have jumped Julia Garrett's bones like a duck on a June bug. But I wasn't the same person anymore, and I would never do anything to jeopardize my relationship with Naija.

When I reached the lobby, I stopped a moment and took a couple of deep breaths. That hadn't gone as I had expected. I felt like a piece of meat thrown into the lion's den. But I didn't blame Julia Garrett. She was scared and frustrated. You mix that with a little wine, and that can cloud your judgment. Her husband was missing and she wanted answers. Most people have done things they regret when alcohol was involved. I know I have. So I didn't read a lot into it.

When the valet brought my car around, I pulled from the exit at Park Place and drove down Peachtree Street. In the rearview mirror, I saw the black Ford Explorer several cars behind. I hadn't uncovered any information about Garrett's disappearance, but I had gotten attention. Maybe Garrett's laptop would lead to a clue.

I drove to the college to drop off the laptop with Naija's brother. I found Satya in the Computer Science Department sitting behind his desk reading student papers.

Naija had already spoken with him so he knew why I was there. I powered up the laptop.

"It is password protected," I said.

Satya didn't seem worried about it. "No problem," he said. "We can access the computer. I have a very competent group of grad students that love hacking into computers. They will love this."

"That's great," I said.

"What do you want to know?" he asked.

"Anything you can find that has to do with Garrett's law firm, Schmitt & Lawson," I said.

He nodded.

"Names, dates, files," I said. "How much time do you need?"

"We should have something for you in a couple of days," he said.

"Give me a call when you're finished," I said.

I left and drove back to the office. I had depleted the surge of energy I had earlier. I was exhausted, shocked, and hungry. Plus, I needed a drink.

I parked in the alley and went up to the office. I opened the windows to let in some fresh air. The clock behind the desk read three-ten. Close enough to happy hour. I sat in my chair, got the office bottle out from the desk drawer, and poured a shot in the glass I kept in the same drawer. I took a few sips and instantly felt better. It's not every day a beautiful woman throws herself at you. And it's not every day you turn her down. I felt proud of myself.

A few moments later Tony Veneto came into the office. He looked at the bottle on the desk and glanced at the clock behind my chair.

"Happy hour starting early today?" he asked.

"It started a few hours ago for some," I said.

He sat in one of the client chairs on the other side of the desk. Today, he was wearing khaki pants, a navy blue shirt, and an expensive looking sport coat. I noticed the bulge under his arm where he had his .357 hung.

"The early happy hour have anything to do with the case you're working?" he asked.

"Has everything to do with it," I said.

"Tell me about it," he said.

I told him about Julia Garrett. Not the entire story. I only said she was dressed provocatively and that she propositioned me. I told him about her getting mad and her practically throwing me out when I turned her down.

"She hot?" he asked.

"Smoking," I said.

Tony said, smiling, "Maybe I should go over and comfort her in her hour of need."

"Wait until I find her husband," I said.

I sat another glass on the desk and poured Tony a shot.

Tony got up and motioned out the window. "The Ford Explorer the one following you today?"

"Yeah," I said. "They're not very good at it. Unless they're trying not to be covert."

"Could be," Tony said. "Somebody's real interested in what you're finding out."

"So far, I haven't found out anything," I said.

"They don't know that," Tony said. "I still think we should ride over to South Realty and find out how much they know."

"Maybe later," I said. "There's something else I want to check out first."

I put my feet up on the desk. I felt better. A couple of stiff drinks will do the trick every time. I poured myself another drink.

Tony sat back down in the client chair. He poured himself a drink and propped his feet up on the other end of the desk. He said, "So if you don't want to go over to South Realty, why don't we go over to that law firm, see how much the guy running the place knows. We could go rough him up a little."

"Charles Lawson," I said. "Believe me. I've thought about it."

"Yeah, him," Tony said. "I bet he knows plenty."

"I bet he does, too," I said.

"Whatever you've stumbled into," Tony said, "it's big. Otherwise you wouldn't have captured all this attention."

Tony finished his drink and stood up to leave.

"Keep a sharp eye out," he said. "It's only a matter of time before the guys following you make a move on you."

CHAPTER TWENTY-FOUR

Later Naija came to my apartment for an evening drink. She had a last minute birth at the hospital so she didn't arrive at my apartment until nine-thirty. Even after a long day, she came in looking as chipper and fresh as if she had just awoken from a good night's sleep. Her beauty brightened the apartment the moment she entered.

"You're looking chipper," I said.

"I'm beat," she said. "I've been going nonstop since six this morning."

I handed her a glass of wine. I was drinking a beer. She took a sip.

"Wow," she said. "Are we learning how to pick out wines now?"

"You're starting to rub off on me."

She kissed me and gave me a devilish smile.

"Let me take a quick shower," she said.

"Can I come in and watch?"

"No," she said. "You have to wait here." She kissed me again. "Patience."

I sat on the couch and drank my beer. I thought about turning on the tube to see if a baseball game was on. The pennant race was in full stride. The Braves had a chance for a playoff berth if they won their final three games. But I decided to leave the TV off.

Fifteen minutes later Naija came and sat down beside me. She was fresh and clean smelling. She kissed me again. Her hair smelled like strawberries. I poured her a little more wine. She snuggled against me on the couch with her feet tucked under her.

"Hard day?" I asked.

Absolute Justice

"Hectic. I had a delivery this morning, then saw patients, and had another delivery late this afternoon."

"That's a lot," I said. "I know all your patients and babies are fine."

"Yes," she said. "The mother this afternoon was in labor for over sixteen hours. She was in so much pain. I gave her an epidural, but she was still uncomfortable."

"First child?"

"Yes," she said. "A lot of women have trouble with their first pregnancy. It's usually the most painful. Not to mention the emotional stress of having a first child."

She drank a small sip of her wine.

"What about you? Made any progress on your missing person case?"

"Not much," I said. "I found out a couple of things, but I don't know how they connect to the Garrett case."

"Did you pick up the laptop and drop it off with Satya?" she asked.

"Yes, he said he would have information about what's on the hard drive in a few days."

"If Garrett is like everyone else," Naija said. "He should have some type of information on his laptop pertaining to his clients and Schmitt & Lawson."

"I hope so, and I hope it leads to a clue."

"What else did you do today?" Naija asked.

"Picking up the laptop was the highlight of my day," I said.

"Did Mrs. Garrett give you any more information about what may have happened to her husband?"

"Not exactly," I said. "When I got to their apartment, happy hour had already started. I think it started around ten this morning."

"She was drinking?" Naija said, surprised.

I pointed to her glass of wine.

"She was having one of your wine tasting soirees," I said. "Except she was the only member of the group."

"How much had she been drinking?"

"She had downed most of a bottle by the time I got there," I said.

"Was she drunk?"

"Blitzed," I said.

Naija took another small sip of her wine. I finished my beer, went to the refrigerator, and got another one.

When I sat back down, Naija asked, "Did you offer to make her some coffee or something?"

"No," I said. "She's not paying me to be her butler."

"So what did you do?"

"I asked her where Garrett kept his laptop," I said. "And I went into Garrett's office to get it. A few minutes later, she followed me into his office."

I paused for effect and grinned at her. I took a sip of my beer. Naija looked at me with interest in her eyes. She knew I was teasing her.

"And?" she said. "What happened?"

"She came into Garrett's office and propositioned me," I said.

"She did what?"

"She propositioned me," I said. "In fact, she said that she could tell that I was the type of man that could give a woman what she needed."

"She made a pass at you?"

"It was more like an attack," I said.

I took another swallow of beer, and grinned some more.

"And what did you do, Mr. Studmuffin?"

"I turned her down, of course," I said.

"What did she do next?"

"She was persistent," I said. "She tried to kiss me a couple of times, but I pushed her away."

"So what happened next?"

Naija was looking at me intently, but I saw a hint of amusement in her eyes. She was enjoying this, me telling her how I fought off the lioness.

"Then I got the hell out of there."

Naija laughed. She took another sip of wine.

I smiled and said in my own defense, "I'm not some studmuffin that just gives it to anyone."

"You better not be," she said. "You're my studmuffin."

"Of course," I said. "My studness belongs only to thee."

She gave me an amusing, sensual look.

I looked at her. "What?" I asked.

She couldn't hold it in any longer. She burst out laughing at me.

"I wish I could have been there to see you in action," she said. "I know you have roving eyes, but when you receive an offer you run away like a scared little boy."

"I'm not so little," I said. "And I didn't run. I walked briskly away."

I paused a moment and took a sip of beer. Naija sipped her wine. She had stopped laughing but still had an amused look on her face.

After a moment, she asked, "Are you still being followed?"

"Yeah," I said. "They're easy to spot, but I don't think they care."

Then I gave her the details about Tony following the two guys who'd been tailing me to South Realty Group. I finished by saying, "I don't know how South Realty is tied to this, but it looks like they are somehow."

"Any more information on the law firm?" Naija asked.

"I got a client list from Lawson's secretary, but none of the names jumped out at me."

"It sounds like you've got your work cut out for you," she said.

"You've got that right. There are a lot of loose ends that don't connect."

She leaned over and gave me a kiss. "I'm sure you'll get to the bottom of it."

I kissed her back. She giggled.

"Now take me to bed," she said.

Later with Naija snuggled against me, I heard her steady breathing as she slept. She could always fall asleep at the drop of a hat. I closed my eyes and tried to sleep, too. I felt wonderful. For the moment, I wasn't a private eye. There were no clues to track down. I wasn't working on a missing person's case, and I didn't have people following me.

CHAPTER TWENTY-FIVE

It was time to talk with Charles Lawson. Again. I wasn't confident that he would tell me much, if anything, but I had been chasing my tail long enough. The only thing I had accomplished so far was picking up a tail, and I didn't know who was behind it or why. I was getting frustrated. I believed Lawson knew more than he was telling. Of course, he wasn't revealing anything. I also knew going to Schmitt & Lawson wouldn't do me any good. As soon as Lawson saw me, he would call security and have me escorted out of the building. I needed to surprise him, catch him away from his ivory tower.

At eleven in the morning, I was in the lobby at One Atlantic Center. I was dressed to the nines, wearing a dark blue pin-striped suit, crisp white shirt, and a red and white striped tie. The security detail at the front desk didn't give me a second look. I looked like a lawyer waiting for a deposition.

There were a lot of people going and coming from the building at that hour. At the coffee shop adjacent to the lobby, I bought a coffee, sat in the lobby, and waited.

At eleven-thirty I called Mable Williams. She answered on the first ring. Always the efficient secretary.

"I'm down in the lobby," I said. "I need your help."

"Mr. Price," she said. Her voice lowered to a whisper. "You could get me fired calling me here."

"Sorry," I said. "I won't keep you but a second. Can you tell me if Lawson has an appointment today for lunch?"

"One second," she said. I heard her typing on her keyboard. Then she came back on. "He doesn't have anything today. Why?"

I didn't answer her. Instead, I asked, "Where does he usually go for lunch?"

"If he isn't with a client, he sometimes just sends me to get him a sandwich. Other times, he goes to a little restaurant down the street."

"Thanks," I said. "Can you do me one more favor?"

I heard her nervously clear her throat.

"What?" she asked.

"Can you call me at this number when he leaves for lunch today?"

I gave her my cell number.

"Yes," she said. "I'll call you." She paused a moment. Then she said, "Mr. Price, I don't mind helping you, but I'm not good at this cloak and dagger stuff."

"You're handling it like a pro," I said.

We hung up. I finished the coffee and waited.

At twelve-twenty, Mable Williams called back.

"He's coming down the elevator now," she said. "He said he was going to lunch at the cafe. It's just down the street on the right."

"Thanks, Mable," I said. "You've been a great help."

"Guess what?" she said.

"What?"

"I've taken your advice," she said. "I've been walking to work. It's invigorating. I feel wonderful when I get to the office."

"I'm glad," I said. "I walk a lot myself. Thanks again, Mable. I really appreciate your help."

"I hope you find Mr. Garrett soon," she said.

"Me, too," I said. We hung up.

A moment later Lawson stepped from one of the elevators. Seeing him made me instantly think of a turtle again. A well-dressed turtle. He was talking with another guy in a charcoal three-piece suit when he exited the elevator. I turned my back and pretended to read the directory so he wouldn't recognize me. When he exited the building he went to the right, and I followed him down West Peachtree.

I watched as he went into a small restaurant a block down the street. The café was a small shop that featured wraps, pizza, burgers, and salads. I had thought a senior partner at a law firm would choose a more elegant restaurant, but instead he chose a place that looked like a bar and grill. I hung around outside until a waitress brought his food. Then I went in and sat at his table across from him.

"Charles," I said. "I'm disappointed. I thought the senior partner at a prominent law firm would eat at a more upscale restaurant."

Lawson looked up from the chicken wrap he'd been eating, startled that I had popped up at his table. "I'm not talking with you," he said.

"Charlie," I said. "Let's not start off on the wrong foot."

"Why don't you go away," Lawson said. "I'm not going to talk to you." He looked around the restaurant. I didn't know what he was looking for. Maybe a cop to make me leave him alone.

"Why don't you tell me what you know about Garrett's disappearance?" I asked.

"I'm not saying anything," he said.

"That's what bothers me," I said. "You're not saying anything. I find that a little suspicious."

"I've already told what I know to the real police," he said. "I've told you once that Jason Garrett's disappearance has nothing to do with me or my law firm."

He gave me his lawyerly courtroom stare. It was supposed to make him look mean. It didn't.

"What can you tell me about the banker, Greg Little?"

"Greg Little?" Lawson said. "I don't know anything about him."

"Your law firm has several accounts at his bank," I said.

"So what," Lawson said. "A lot of businesses in the area use First Georgia."

"But there's one difference between you and the other businesses," I said. "Greg Little was beaten up by a guy named Roy Upshaw, and Garrett got the case through Legal Aid to represent him. Then the next day, Garrett disappears."

"Two completely unrelated circumstances," Lawson said. "One has nothing to do with the other."

"Maybe," I said. "What can you tell me about a guy named Daryl?"

"Who?"

"Daryl," I said. "He's the one that hired Upshaw to beat up the banker."

"I don't know anybody by that name," Lawson said.

I said, "This Daryl guy gave Upshaw a message to give Little. While he was beating him up, Upshaw told him to stick to banking. Have any ideas what that was about?"

Lawson wasn't eating his wrap any longer. It remained on his plate. Maybe he had lost his appetite. The wrap didn't look very good anyway.

"I don't know what you're talking about," Lawson said.

"What can you tell me about South Realty Group?" I asked.

Lawson looked around the restaurant again. He suddenly seemed nervous like Greg Little had when I talked with him. Lawson glared at me a second, but this time there was a look of fright in his eyes. His little turtle eyes grew wide and his turtle neck seem to retract a little. If he had a shell, he would have pulled his head inside and hidden.

"Leave me alone," he said.

"Why don't you tell me about South Realty Group," I said.

"Leave me alone."

He stood up and marched toward the door. I don't think he paid for his half-eaten meal. I followed him out.

He bolted up the sidewalk, heading back to his towering shell at One Atlantic Center. For a guy who looked like a turtle, he could move fast.

I caught up with him halfway up the block.

I asked, "Why'd you bail when I mentioned South Realty? They got something on you?"

"I don't know what you're talking about," Lawson sneered.

"What about a guy named Rueben," I said. "What can you tell me about him?"

We reached the entrance of One Atlantic Center. Lawson stopped and nervously glanced up and down the sidewalk. Sheer terror had replaced the fear that had been in his eyes earlier. It occurred to me that he was afraid someone would see him talking with me. Maybe the guys following me around.

"Leave me alone," Lawson demanded. "I don't know anything."

"I think you know plenty," I said. Then I asked, "Why are you so nervous all of a sudden?"

Lawson took a deep breath, trying to muster up some courage. He shot me his most intimidating look. It didn't intimidate me in the least. "I know nothing of Garrett's disappearance," he said. "And I'm not answering any of your questions, so don't ever approach me again."

Then the turtle retreated into his high-rise shell.

CHAPTER TWENTY-SIX

I waited outside until Lawson was in the elevator. Then I went inside and took the stairs down to the concourse level, and then took another set of stairs to the garage. When I came out of the stairwell, there were two guys leaning against my car. They were the same two that had been following me in the Chrysler a few days before.

One was fat with a bad haircut. He looked like a boozer. His face was red and his bulbous nose was even redder. The other guy was tall and muscular with tattoos covering both arms. He probably thought the tats made him look menacing. He wasn't. At least not to me.

They didn't see me when I emerged from the stairwell, so I saw them before they saw me. I looked around. There was no one else in the garage. The perfect place to rough me up.

Then they saw me coming toward them.

I said, "Get off my car before your BO peels the paint."

"You saying we stink," Muscle Man said.

He gave me his meanest look. It wasn't mean enough. It didn't do anything for me.

"You catch on quick," I said. "You must be the smart one."

"Hey, hotshot," Bad Haircut said. "We're asking the questions here."

"You haven't asked anything," I said. "Why are you following me?"

"Shut-up," Muscles said. "We want to know what you're doing."

"What's it look like I'm doing," I said. "I'm talking to a couple of idiots."

Bad Haircut stepped up close to me. He smelled like cigarettes. His breath stank. "Why were you talking with Lawson?"

I leaned back a little. I didn't want his breath to knock me out. "I had some questions about my corporate investment strategies," I said.

They both glanced at each other. They probably didn't know what a corporate investment strategy was. Then they stared back at me. These guys were used to dealing with amateurs, scaring people just by acting menacing. They didn't know how to handle someone who talked back.

"Ok, smart aleck," Bad Haircut said. "How 'bout we beat the crap out of you and then you can tell us what we want to know."

"You can't," I said.

"We can't what?" Muscles asked.

"You can't beat the crap out of me," I said.

Muscles stepped forward and swung at me with a right cross. I moved my head at the right second and the punch brushed my shoulder.

I smirked at him. "Why don't you go pump some more iron and come back when you're man enough?"

Then I hit him in the nose. I might not be able to throw a wicked two-seam fastball as good as I used to, but I still had a mean right hook. Muscles staggered backwards. Blood gushed from his nose. Bad Haircut stepped up, took a swing at me and missed. I kicked him in the groin. He went down on one knee moaning loudly. I hit him in the temple with a right cross and he groaned and fell to the pavement. Muscles was more up to a fight. He came at me again and hit me with a right cross on the left cheek. He was wearing a diamond studded ring that tore the flesh below my left eye. I felt a warm trickle of blood stream down my face. Then he came at me again, aiming for my midsection, but I saw the punch coming and had time to tighten my stomach. The blow hit my ribcage on the left side. Pain ripped through my midsection. He had a good punch. He swung again, but this time I blocked it with my left arm. Then I hit him with a right uppercut to the larynx. He staggered back, clutching his throat, trying to breathe. I stepped forward and swung with a hard right hook that caught him in the solar plexus. The air swooshed out of him. Then I hit him in the face, left, right, left, and then another right. His face was a bloody blur. Blood poured from his nose and mouth. I hit him on the side of his chin with a left hook and he went down for the ten-count.

I turned around and saw Bad Haircut on his knees. He was fumbling for a gun from the inside of his suit jacket.

I kicked the gun out of his hand and it skidded under a car. Then I punched him in the left kidney. Bad Haircut howled and dropped back down to the pavement.

"Who wants to know what I'm up to?" I asked him.

He was still groaning, trying to reach around to his throbbing back. "I don't know," he croaked.

I reached down and hit him on the side of his face, hitting him just below the temple, next to the ear. He yelped, and tried to cover his head. Between the kick to the groin and the punches to the head and kidney, he was in a lot of pain.

"Maybe someone at South Realty Group sent you," I said.

"I don't know," he said again. It came out more of a groan than actual words.

"Perhaps I could beat the crap out of you until you tell me," I said. I raised my fist again to let him know I was serious.

"I don't know nothin'," he said. He held up a hand in surrender. "Honest. We were just supposed to find out what you were talking to Lawson about."

"Who hired you?"

"Guy named Barton," Bad Haircut said. "I don't know anything else. He just wanted us to find out what you were talking to Lawson about. Honest. Don't hit me anymore."

I stood over him a moment and thought about it. I didn't think he knew anymore.

I got in my car and I checked my face in the rearview mirror. There was a cut just below the left eye. A trickle of dried blood clung to my cheek, and a bruise was beginning to show around the eye. I started the car and pulled away. I glanced in the rearview mirror and saw both men moving slowly, trying to get back on their feet.

CHAPTER TWENTY-SEVEN

I went back to my office, washed my face in the bathroom sink, and checked it in the small mirror above the sink. I didn't look any better. The horizontal cut below my left eye was about a half inch in length, but it had stopped bleeding. The eye had swollen, and the bluish area under the eye had grown. It was going to look great by tomorrow morning. I got some ice from the fridge and fashioned an icepack from a sandwich bag. I went to my desk and poured myself a drink. I took a pull and felt the warmth of the bourbon in my throat. I sat down in my swivel chair, propped my feet up, and held the icepack to my face. The coldness of the ice stung for a moment, but then the soreness started to numb.

I hadn't gotten any concrete clues to Garrett's whereabouts, but now I knew two things: that somehow South Realty was involved in the case, and that somebody named Barton was very interested in what I was doing. Plus, I had a suspicion that Lawson was somehow involved in Garrett's disappearance.

When I finished icing my eye, I opened my laptop, brought up a browser, and typed in the Better Business Bureau site. In their search field, I looked for South Realty Group in Atlanta. The search came up blank. Next, I looked up the number for the BBB and punched it in.

A cheerful female voice answered on the second ring. "Hello, this is Bridgette, how can I help you?"

She didn't sound like she'd been in a fight earlier in the day.

"My name is Nick Price," I said. "Do you have any information on a company called South Realty Group?"

"One moment sir." I heard her tapping her keyboard. A second later, she was back on the line.

"I don't see any information on the company," she said. "Apparently they aren't a member of the BBB."

"Shouldn't a reputable company be a member?" I asked. I was a member. Even Ray Norris was a member, and I had doubts about his reputability.

"Most companies are," Bridgette said cheerfully. "It can help their business. A lot of potential customers come to us first before they use a company or service."

She sounded like a commercial. Maybe she was in their Marketing Department.

I asked, "Would you have any information if there had been any complaints about the company?"

"Yes," she said. "That information would have come up in my search for the company whether they are a member or not. We keep detailed records of complaints."

She sounded proud of the fact. I didn't want to wait for the next commercial, so I thanked her and hung up.

I twisted around to look at the clock on the wall behind my desk. It was ten after four. So South Realty wasn't a member of the BBB. Big deal. I was irritable, tired, and hungry. My face throbbed more intensely. I stood up, went into the small alcove kitchen area, and dumped the ice from the sandwich bag into the sink.

I went back to my desk and grabbed my suit jacket. I was putting it on when Tony walked in.

He said, "Looks like you hit someone in the fist with your face."

"You think this looks bad," I said, "You should see the other two guys."

"They the same two been following you?"

"Yeah," I said. "The guys in the Chrysler you followed to South Realty."

"What happened?"

I told him about going to see Lawson and about the two guys in the parking garage.

"The fat guy wasn't much of a fighter," I said. "But the muscle man packed a mean punch."

"You get any information out of them."

"Not much," I said. "I pressed the fat guy, and he said they were hired by a guy named Barton, but he didn't know anything else."

"You think they're associated with South Realty Group?"

"I think so," I said. "When I questioned the fat guy, he didn't seem to know what I was talking about, but he was in a lot of pain so it was hard to tell."

"I told you we should have gone over there and got some answers," Tony said. "If we had, maybe you wouldn't be so banged up."

"Maybe tomorrow," I said. "I've been in enough fights for one day."

"I think you're into something deep," Tony said. "I better keep an eye on you. Naija would kill me if I let something happen to you."

"You're all heart," I said. "But if you want to help, keep an eye on Charles Lawson. See where he goes. Who he meets."

"You got it," Tony said. "What you gonna do now?"

"I'm going home," I said. "I'm tired and hungry."

"Watch your back," Tony said. "These guys are playing for real."

We went out and I locked the door behind me. I drove to my apartment building and took the stairs up. Inside the apartment, I made a ham and cheese sandwich and washed it down with two beers. Then I took a long shower. Afterwards, I opened another beer and flopped down on the sofa. My face throbbed. There were a lot of loose ends to the case that didn't seem to lead anywhere. I needed some answers. Tony was right. It was time to pay South Realty a visit.

CHAPTER TWENTY-EIGHT

The next morning I checked my face in the bathroom mirror. My face looked like two miles of bad road. My left eye had turned black and a deep purple, and the cut had swollen a little. The cut still throbbed. I wondered how Naija would react. She hadn't seen me banged up yet.

I took a shower, dressed, and headed for the office. I was in my office with my feet up thinking about breakfast when Tony walked in. He was carrying two cups of coffee and a box of Krispy Kreme donuts.

"You must be psychic," I said. "I was just thinking about something to eat."

"How do you know any of these are for you?" he said.

"Because you're carrying two cups of coffee," I said. "A seasoned detective pays attention to details."

"Uh-huh," Tony said. "You weren't paying much attention to detail yesterday when muscle man punched you in the face."

"I had him right where I wanted him," I said.

"Right," Tony said.

He handed me a coffee. He sat in one of the client chairs and opened his cup of coffee. He opened the box of donuts and took out a glazed donut. I grabbed a chocolate.

"Still warm," I said. I took a bite.

"They make them for me when I go in," Tony said.

"It pays to have connections," I said.

We ate in silence. I got a strawberry-filled donut out and took a bite. Some of the filling drizzled on my chin. I wiped it with a napkin.

Tony grabbed another donut and said, "I didn't notice anyone outside when I came up."

"When I left my apartment, I didn't see anyone either."

"You think they've stopped following you?"

"Either that, or they've gotten better at it," I said.

"Maybe they'll try a different approach next time," Tony said. "Probably make a move on you for real."

I grabbed another donut and took a bite. "This case has turned out to be more than a simple missing person's case," I said.

"Yeah," Tony said. "And it looks like it's gonna get uglier."

We finished most of the donuts and sat with our feet up on the desk. The coffee was gone.

"I think we should go over to South Realty Group and get some answers," Tony said.

"Sounds good," I said. "I can't think of anything else to do."

"You're the detective, you're supposed to come up with ideas."

"I just did," I said.

"No you didn't," Tony said. "It was my idea."

CHAPTER TWENTY-NINE

An hour later, Tony and I pulled into the parking lot at South Realty Group on Monroe Drive. It was a small brick building in a commercialized area just off I-85. There were only three cars in the parking lot. The entrance was a glass door that had burglar bars on it. A black sign with gold lettering to the right of the door read SOUTH REALTY GROUP. In smaller text below was BY APPOINTMENT ONLY.

I motioned at the burglar bars on the door. "Not the best part of town for a business," I said.

"It is if your business isn't legit," Tony said.

We went inside. A platinum blonde woman with a bouffant hairdo that looked like it was leftover from the 60s sat behind a receptionist desk to the left. I guessed her to be around forty-five, but she looked older. There was a pack of Marlboro cigarettes on her desk.

Her makeup was too thick, as if she'd slathered it on with a paintbrush. The name plate on the desk read Paula Davidson.

"Hello, Mrs. Davidson," I said. "My name is Nick Price and this is my associate Tony. We'd like to speak with the person in charge please."

I was pleasant and courteous. I flashed a nice smile. She didn't smile back. She didn't seem happy to see us either. Maybe we were interrupting her smoke break.

"That's Mr. Barton," she said. "Do you have an appointment?"

She had a gravelly voice, as if her throat were lined with sandpaper.

Barton. Two clues just snapped together. "No," I said. "But I'm sure he'll want to see us."

"He only sees people that have appointments," she snapped.

She glared at us as if she were waiting for us to turn and leave. We didn't.

"He's not going to see you without an appointment," she growled. "He's very strict about that."

"Why don't you go tell him we're here," I said.

She looked at me with my banged-up face. Then looked at Tony, decided he looked more respectable, and beamed at him. When she smiled at him, her makeup cracked, giving her skin the texture of a dried up lakebed. I glanced over at him and shrugged.

"What's this pertaining to?" she asked. She wasn't talking to me. She was still gazing hungrily at Tony. Since she had fallen in lust with Tony, I let him do the talking.

"It's personal," Tony said. "He may not like a personal matter discussed in front of others."

I thought it sounded good. Apparently, she did too. She picked up the phone, whispered something into the receiver, and placed it back on its cradle.

"Someone will be with you in a moment," Paula said as she glared at me. Then she looked at Tony and smiled again. She produced a small compact from under the desk, flipped it open, and smeared on another coat of bright red lipstick. She drooled at Tony like a hungry she-wolf peering at a wayward lamb.

"You're a cute one," she said to him. "Tall, dark, and handsome."

"What about your husband?" Tony said, nodding toward the rock on her hand.

"What he doesn't know won't hurt him," Paula drawled.

A moment later, a muscular man in khaki pants, a blue chambray shirt, and a black sport coat walked into the receptionist area. I noticed the bulge under his left arm from a shoulder holster. Tony and I glanced at each other.

"I'm Dennis Black," he said. "I'm the office manager."

Why would an office manager pack a gun?

I said, "We're here to see Mr. Barton."

What's this about?" Black demanded.

I thought we had just covered this with the receptionist.

I said, "We didn't ask for you. We're here to see Barton."

"He doesn't see anyone without an appointment," Black said. "Didn't you read the sign out front?"

"Go tell him it's about Charles Lawson," I said.

Dennis Black shot me an irritated look. For an ex-pitcher who hardly ever got a hit, I was batting a thousand for annoying people.

"Wait here," Dennis Black said, through clinched teeth. He turned and walked down the corridor. Tony and I followed him. He stopped at a door with the name James Barton stenciled on the frosted glass, knocked, and opened the door. Then he noticed us behind him.

"Hey, I told you guys…"

Tony hit him with a right cross that knocked him further into the office. Then with precision and grace, as if he'd practiced the maneuver a million times, Tony reached into Black's jacket, took his gun away from him, and jammed his own .357 in Dennis Black's face. "Don't even think about moving a muscle," Tony said, "or it'll be your last thought."

"What's going on here?" a loud thunderous voice said. I turned around to see who was yelling at us.

"That's enough," the voice said again. "What's this all about?"

James Barton sat behind a huge cherry wood desk. At first glance, he looked like a little boy. He was a small man, thin shouldered, maybe 5'4", and 130 pounds soaking wet. He wore an expensive suit that fit his boyish frame perfectly. But what he lacked in stature, his voice made up for. It was deep and carried more weight than Barton had on his body.

Tony said to Black, "Don't try anything or I'll shoot you with your own gun. Tony put his gun away, but kept Dennis Black's Glock.

"I told them to wait up front," Dennis said, rubbing the side of his head where Tony had hit him. He straightened his jacket and tried to regain some of his dignity. When you have your gun taken away from you, you've already lost the fight.

"It's okay, Dennis," Barton said. "I'll talk with these gentlemen since they are so persistent."

Dennis nodded his head and stood beside the door.

James Barton remained seated. He didn't seem surprised to see us, and perhaps he wasn't since he had hired the two clowns that came after me.

"You're not going to pull anymore weapons are you?" Barton asked. He looked at Tony and then back at me.

"As long as no one starts trouble first," I said.

Tony handed me Black's gun, and then went and stood next to the wall so he could keep an eye on everyone. I pulled the clip from the Glock, ejected the round from the chamber, and sat everything on the corner of Barton's desk.

"What do you want?" Barton asked.

"What kind of business are you running here?" I asked.

Barton stared at me a second. He was hard to read. "Is that why you came busting in?" he asked. "To ask a stupid question about my business?"

"Humor me," I said. "I'm a nosy guy."

"Noses get broken from asking too many questions," Barton said. He continued to stare at me. I had to hand it to him. He didn't back down. For a little guy, he had guts.

I stared back at him and waited. He hadn't answered the question yet.

He said, "We're a real estate brokerage firm. We match buyers with sellers."

"Then why are you having me followed?" I asked.

"I don't even know who you are," he said.

"Cut the crap," I said. "You know who I am. You hired two guys to attack me to get info about a case I'm working."

James Barton looked at me without expression. His poker face gave away nothing. His eyes didn't blink. He was impossible to read.

"What are you talking about?" Barton said. His deep voice carried no inflection. "What case?"

I said, "A missing person's case concerning an attorney named Jason Garrett. He's missing. And right after I took the case, I picked up a tail."

"I don't know anyone named Jason Garrett," Barton said. "And I have no knowledge of anyone following you."

I ignored his remark. "At first I didn't do anything about the tail," I said. "I wanted to see where it would lead." I motioned toward Tony, and continued, "My associate here followed the tail to a parking lot, where they ditched the stolen car they'd been driving, got in another car, and then came here."

"That has nothing to do with me or my business," Barton said.

"I had the car they got into checked out," I said. "It's registered to this company."

Barton's deadpan expression never changed. "I don't know anything about it," he said. He looked over at Black. "Dennis, you know anything about this?"

"No sir," Dennis said.

"Sorry," Barton said. "I don't have any knowledge of you being followed."

He glanced at Tony, and then looked back at me. He was a good liar.

I asked, "Why do you want to know what I talked to Charles Lawson about?"

"I don't know a Charles Lawson," Barton said.

"Ever heard of a law firm named Schmitt & Lawson?"

"Never heard of them," Barton barked.

"That's strange," I said. "Yesterday, right after I talked with Lawson, your two goons accosted me. They wanted to know what I was talking to Lawson about."

Barton stared at me some more. "Again, I don't know what you're talking about."

I continued, "Their plan was to beat me to a pulp until I told them what they wanted to know. But it didn't work out that way. Instead, I beat them to a pulp and asked them questions. After some prodding, the fat one told me you hired them."

"I don't have any knowledge of the incident you've described," Barton said.

I knew he was lying. But I also knew I wasn't going to get anything out of him. But the dog in me couldn't let it go. Tenacious. Stubborn.

I asked, "What's your association with Schmitt & Lawson?"

Barton leaned over his desk and shot me his best stoic businessman stare. "Let me make this clear. I don't know a Charles Lawson, and I've never done business with Schmitt & Lawson." He glared at me a second, then added, "And I didn't have you followed. And I certainly didn't have you assaulted."

There was anger in his voice now. Maybe he wasn't such a cool cucumber after all. I felt like punching the little twerp in the face. Just a quick left jab to let him know I was serious. But I knew that wouldn't do me any good either.

Instead of punching him, I said, "You had me followed, and you had me assaulted. And I plan to find out why."

He took a deep breath. "I don't appreciate the way you and your associate here," he said, motioning to Tony, "have come in here, making unsubstantiated accusations. And if you try it again, I'll call the police."

"No you won't," I said. "You don't want the police nosing around your business."

"This conversation is over," he said. "I have a business to run. So if you gentlemen will excuse me."

"We'll talk again," I said. I stood up. Barton stood up.

"Don't bet on it," he said.

Tony and I walked out of his office. Paula Davidson was perched on the corner of her desk. She tried to look seductive, but it wasn't working for her. Instead, she looked like she was waiting for a bus. When Tony passed her, she beamed at him, handed him a small piece of paper, and said, "Why don't you give me a call sometime."

When we were outside, I said, "Yeah, Tony, why don't you give her a call? Maybe she knows something."

"Forget about it," Tony said. "Not happening."

CHAPTER THIRTY

The next day, Naija's brother Satya called and said he had retrieved the information I needed off Garrett's computer. I drove to the campus, and found Satya sitting behind his desk. He was thumbing through some papers when I walked in.

Satya peered at my face, noticed the black eye and the cut below it, and said, "Ah, Nick, you've been fighting."

"I got into a tussle with a couple of guys in a parking lot."

"There were two men against one?" Satya asked.

"Yes," I said. "And I was the one."

"You lost the fight?"

"I guess you could say I won, but one of the guys landed a lucky punch."

Satya shook his head, and said, "Fighting is not the solution for everything. Reasoning with one's adversaries is more effective." He smiled at me and then he added, "And less painful."

I chuckled. "You sound just like Naija." Then I said, "But I don't think reasoning with the guys that attacked me would have worked out in my favor."

"So some of the people you come in contact with are not reasonable?" he asked.

"You might say that." I motioned toward the laptop on his desk, and asked, "So, what have you got?"

"My guys retrieved everything off the computer associated with Schmitt & Lawson," he said.

He reached in his top desk drawer, took out a DVD case, and handed it to me.

"This has all the information on it," Satya said. "Jason Garrett kept detailed records. There was a lot of documentation on his computer."

"Maybe it will give me some insight into what happened to him," I said.

Satya nodded and said, "I took the liberty of having the Internet websites Garrett navigated to compiled as well."

"How can that help me?"

"It tells you all the sites Jason Garrett visited," he said.

I thought for a moment, and said, "So if Garrett was involved, say, in unsavory activities such as online gambling, or Internet dating, it would tell me the sites he visited. And if he researched travel destinations it would tell me that as well."

"Yes," Satya said. He then quickly added, "But I did not see any of those sites on the computer. Most of the sites were for legal reference material, such as the sites for the US Attorney General, the Federal Trade Commission, and Housing and Urban Development."

"I can understand the US Attorney's site," I said. "But why the FTC and HUD sites?"

"Perhaps he was researching for a client," Satya offered.

"Maybe," I said. But I didn't think so. Then I asked, "What other sites did he go to?"

"There was one site in particular that he visited a number of times," Satya said. "The FBI site. But, again, he may have been simply researching."

"Can you reconstruct the site to see what Garrett was reading?" I asked.

"Unfortunately, no," he said. "He navigated to the site's home page, and then conducted searches using the site's search engine, so we were not able to see exactly where he navigated."

"You find anything else interesting off Garrett's computer?"

"No," Satya said. "The documentation from his law firm, the website information, and the search details were the only items of interest found."

"Thank you for your help, Satya," I said. Then I added, "And thank your team of Internet sleuths for me as well."

He smiled and said, "I unlocked the laptop in case you wanted to look on the computer."

He placed the laptop back in its case, zipped it up, and handed it to me.

"I hope you find the information you're looking for, Nick," he said.

"I hope so, too. I haven't made much progress on the case so far."

"Naija told me a little about your difficulty in finding Mr. Garrett," Satya said.

I waved the DVD in the air. "Maybe the information on this will lead to a clue."

"Let me know if I can be of further assistance. My students enjoyed working on an actual case. I believe they are now infatuated with detective work."

"It's not as exciting as it sounds," I said. I pointed to my eye. "And it can be painful at times."

"Does Naija know you've been in a fight?"

"I spoke with her briefly, but I didn't go into any details."

Satya gave me a sly look, smiled, and said, "Meaning she doesn't know about the black eye."

"Exactly," I said. "I didn't purposely keep it from her, but I didn't bring it up either. I didn't want her to worry."

"Then I will not mention it either," Satya said.

CHAPTER THIRTY-ONE

I drove back to the office, opened the windows, and stood watching the foot traffic below. The clock behind my desk read 2:25. It was a nice autumn day with the temperature in the mid-sixties. I went into the small kitchen alcove and poured a glass of lemonade from the gallon jug I kept in the fridge. I sat at my desk, opened Garrett's laptop and booted it up. Then I opened my laptop to take notes on whatever I found. With two laptops on my desk I felt like a corporate bigwig who was so busy, just a single computer wasn't enough. I inserted the DVD Satya had given me into my laptop. I wanted Garrett's laptop open if I needed to verify any information. Then I began going through the documents Satya had retrieved.

The first thing I noticed was that Garrett was meticulous in keeping detailed records of every client he handled at Schmitt & Lawson. Good. But Satya was right. There were a lot of documents, and if they hadn't been in any kind of order, I could've been wading through them for months.

Garrett had been at the firm for five years, and each year had its own folder. In the yearly folders, he had additional folders for each month, and within them, there were folders for each client billed for that month. Compared to Garrett's neat folder structure, the documents on my hard drive looked like a trash heap.

I reasoned that if Garrett discovered something going on at Schmitt & Lawson that wasn't copacetic, then he would have made the discovery a short time before his disappearance. So instead of going through all the documents year-by-year, I went through the folders six months prior to his vanishing act. It was just a starting point. I could always go back further if necessary. I went through each folder, making notes of the clients and the type of documents filed on their behalf. There were documents for mergers, acquisitions, corporate restructures, tax litigations, a couple of corporate bankruptcies, and a few union contract negotiations. Plus, there were bills for each client. Garrett alone had raked in millions for the firm. No wonder he had been on the fast-track to partnership.

There was also a pro bono folder for each month, and inside those folders were at least one case per month. Most of the cases involved evictions, pleas for stop garnishments, and bankruptcies for the indigent. There were no criminal cases. Not even a DUI case. I wasn't expecting anything to jump out at me from the pro bono cases, but you could never tell if a client had been dissatisfied with his legal representation, even if it came from a pro bono lawyer.

After making a cursory glance through Garrett's documents for the past six months, I didn't see anything that gave an indication why Garrett had suddenly vanished. Another dead end. I checked my watch: 5:50. Three hours had gone by and I needed a break. My eyes were beginning to burn. Plus, I was hungry.

I left the office and walked down Broad Street to a sandwich shop called Anthony's. It was a New York-style deli run by a gruff Italian, and during lunchtime people lined up outside. But this late in the day, the place was nearly empty. I ordered the New Yorker, which comes with corned beef, pastrami, and Swiss cheese. The sandwich had enough meat on it for two meals. I ate it all anyway. Naija would have been disappointed with my dinner choice.

Afterwards, I walked back to the office and started back on the documents from Garrett's computer, going through more of the monthly folders. The only thing I noticed was that Garrett had logged more hours over the past three months. Normally, he put in twelve, fourteen, or more hours a day. Plus most weekends. But for the past three months, he logged sixteen, and some eighteen hour days. And all the weekends. Saturdays and Sundays. The guy lived and breathed Schmitt & Lawson.

The rest of the monthly folders contained the usual documents concerning mergers, acquisitions, tax litigation, and subsidiary filings, et cetera, et cetera. Real exciting stuff. As far as I could tell, all the documents looked legit.

Next, I checked through the websites Garrett had navigated to during the past six months. Nothing jumped out at me. Nothing indicated Garrett was doing anything suspicious. No indication he was in trouble. Just a corporate lawyer busting his rump. The only site that stood out was the FBI site. But I had no way of knowing why Garrett had visited the site. As Satya had speculated, Garrett could have been conducting research for a client, and I might have believed it—if Garrett wasn't missing. But he was missing, and I wasn't buying it for a second. I was convinced Garrett had visited the site for a reason. I just didn't know why.

I looked at my watch again: 9:40. How time flies when you're going through boring legal documents. I had been looking through folders and documents for over six hours and had come up with nothing. I was tired.

I was getting ready to call it a night when I noticed a folder outside of the yearly folders. I hadn't noticed it before. It was labeled: DISCOVERY. I opened it. Inside, were more monthly folders, with more documents inside each folder.

Great. More paperwork. I yawned but dove in anyway. Might as well wade through these now, I figured.

I opened the first document in the list. And then I had an ah-ha moment.

"Ah-ha," I said aloud.

At such a late hour, my voice boomed in the empty office.

I quickly scanned some of the other documents in the monthly folders. They were all the same type of documents. At the bottom of each document was the signature of Charles Lawson.

That didn't tell me anything. Since Lawson was the senior partner at Schmitt & Lawson, he simply could have been the attorney of record. There were also other signatures on the documents, but they didn't mean anything to me. I also noticed that on each document was a company named Tanner Investments. Alone or together, none of it meant anything.

But listed on some of the documents I opened, right along with Charles Lawson's signature, was the name South Realty Group.

Fantastic. A clue. I felt a sudden burst of energy. I was tired and my eyes burned from the strain of staring at the screen so long, but now I didn't want to stop.

Since taking the case, I hadn't discovered a single clue as to why Jason Garrett had vanished. But I had a hunch this was an actual clue. It wasn't much of one, but it did tell me one thing. That the little man with the big voice, James Barton, at South Realty Group had been lying when he said he never heard of Charles Lawson.

CHAPTER THIRTY-TWO

"**You got into a fight with** two men in a parking garage?" Naija asked.

We were having breakfast at a quirky little restaurant in Candler Park. Different colored paint covered each wall, one orange, one yellow, one a pale blue, and another one green. It was late Sunday morning and the little restaurant was like an anthill. We had had to wait outside for forty minutes before we got a table. When we finally got inside the restaurant, more people were still lined up outside. Naija wore a long-sleeved pink button down shirt and white Capri pants that showed off her derriere. I wore khaki pants, a blue chambray shirt, and a tan warm-up jacket to cover my gun. I had never been to the restaurant before, but Naija said it was a great place to eat. Judging by the looks of the mob lined around the building, she was right—but I still had my suspicions. With Naija's taste in food, I could end up eating tofu.

"Yeah," I said. "There were two of them and only one of me."

"And they just attacked you?"

"They would have," I said. "But I beat them to the punch."

She looked at me a second, and then said, "So you started the fight?"

"The fight was inevitable," I said. "I just gave myself an edge by starting it."

"What did they want?"

Our waitress brought the menus. She was young, pretty, and cheerful. She took our drink orders. I ordered coffee. Naija ordered tea. I looked around at the other tables. So far so good. No tofu in sight.

I answered by saying, "They were asking me questions I didn't like."

"So you got a black eye and a cut on your cheek because you didn't like the questions they were asking," Naija said.

"That's about it."

"You could've gotten seriously hurt, or worse."

"Not a chance," I said. "One of them was fat."

"And the other one?"

"He was muscular, that's how I got the black eye."

Naija shook her head in disbelief. I suddenly felt like a school kid hauled into the principal's office for fighting. She abhorred violence, but understood it was a part of my job. But she didn't have to like it either. I smiled at her. She shook her head again, but smiled back. She was wearing her hair down today and looked as beautiful as ever. I felt the familiar tug at my heart I always felt when I'm with her.

I looked at the menu. They had the standard breakfast fare: eggs, grits, but listed only turkey bacon on the menu. Not a good sign.

"I see only turkey bacon on the menu." Then I asked, "Do they have real bacon?"

Naija peered at me, and said, "If it's not on the menu I doubt they have it. But you can ask."

"And ask I shall."

The waitress came to take our orders. I asked about real bacon from a pig. Tough guys don't eat turkey bacon. Naija and our waitress passed a conspiratorial grin.

Then the waitress explained, "We only have turkey bacon. But it's very good and crispy."

I had my doubts about its goodness or crispiness.

"It's not going to kill you," Naija said.

Maybe it would. I could go into some type of shock because my body isn't used to me eating healthy. But I ordered the turkey bacon anyway, along with eggs, grits, and a biscuit. To my surprise, Naija ordered the same, with the exception of a wheat biscuit.

She took a sip of her tea, and asked, "After your fight, did you learn anything from the men who'd been following you?"

"The fat one told me who hired them," I said. I left out the part about me giving him some persuasion.

Then I told her about Tony and me going over to South Realty Group to get some answers. I didn't mention that we'd had to punch our way into James Barton's office. No sense in throwing fuel on the fire. I finished by saying, "But I still don't know why he had me followed."

"He must be involved with your case somehow," Naija said.

"He is. I just don't know how, or why."

The waitress brought our food. I eyed the turkey bacon suspiciously. I forked some eggs and then tried the grits. Both were great. I nibbled a little bacon. It was crispy. It tasted bland, but not too bad.

Naija watched me. "Well?" she asked.

"It's okay, but not like the real thing."

She smiled at me, leaned over, and kissed me on my cheek. Then we ate a moment in silence. Though I would never admit it in a million years, the turkey bacon wasn't that bad.

After a while, she said, "Did you learn anything from what Satya got from Jason Garrett's laptop?"

"That's how I know James Barton is involved with Charles Lawson."

Then I told her about the documents I found on Garrett's computer that linked James Barton to Charles Lawson. I concluded by saying, "I just don't know if the documents mean anything or not."

The waitress came and took our plates, refilled my coffee cup, and brought Naija another cup of tea.

After she left, Naija asked, "What kind of documents were they?"

"Real estate documents," I said. "Loan applications, deed transfers, that sort of thing."

"Those kind of documents are part of James Barton's business," Naija said.

"True, but why would Barton say he'd never heard of Schmitt & Lawson if he had dealt with them before?"

Naija thought for a second, then said, "If Barton is not being honest about his company's relationship with Schmitt & Lawson, then he could be conducting unsavory business practices."

"I was thinking the same thing," I said.

Naija smiled at me. "So Mr. Super Sleuth, what are you going to do next?"

"I'll keep nosing around until something jumps out at me," I said.

"And gives you another black eye," Naija said, smiling at me.

I leaned over and kissed her. "I'll try not to let that happen," I said.

CHAPTER THIRTY-THREE

I was in the middle of a dream when I heard bells ringing. In the dream, I was chasing someone and I pursued him down a dark alleyway. But when I reached the end of the alley, the dream suddenly changed and I found myself trapped by a violent lake of churning water. I couldn't go back or across the endless whirlpool. Trapped. The water rose inch-by-inch, coming toward me. Every nerve in my body screamed for me to wake up. That's when I heard a faint ringing. At first, I thought it was part of the dream, an unconscious alarm ringing in my head. I jerked awake. It was the phone. I picked up the receiver and groggily said hello.

"Hey, Sleeping Beauty," Detective Sergeant Soratelli's baritone voice boomed. "Wake-up."

I eyed the clock next to the bed: 5:15. "Do you know what time it is?" I croaked.

"Of course, I do," he said. "Now get out of bed. I've got something you'll want to see."

"What is it?"

"I'll tell you when I pick you up," he said. "Be in front of your building in thirty minutes." He hung up.

I eyed the clock again, swung my legs over the edge of the bed, and sat up. It wasn't daylight yet and the fog of unconsciousness still gripped me. I stood up and walked into the bathroom. I brushed my teeth, shaved, showered, and got dressed. At 5:45 I was standing on the curb in front of my building on Forsyth Street thinking about coffee.

Soratelli pulled up to the curb a couple of minutes later.

I opened the car door and got in the front seat.

Soratelli glanced at me, saw the black eye, and said, "You look like crap. What happened? You hit someone's fist with your face?"

Everyone's a comedian. "Something like that," I said. "What have you got?"

He handed me a cup of coffee. I pulled the lid off and took a tentative sip. Wonderful.

"We found your missing person, Jason Garrett."

He hit the pulsating lights that flashed across the dashboard and pulled away from the curb.

"Where's he at?" I asked.

"At the airport."

"At the airport?" I said. "You sure it's him?"

"Positive," he said. "His car was discovered in one of the long-term parking lots. One of the parking lot attendants was getting ready to have it towed because the parking fee had expired."

"So where is Garrett?"

"In the trunk," Soratelli said. "He's dead."

I shook my head. "I was afraid of that," I said.

Soratelli explained, "The attendant smelled something coming from the vehicle and called 911."

We were speeding down I-85 south, heading toward Hartsfield-Jackson airport. Soratelli drove like a bat out of hell and we pulled into one of the long-term lots less than fifteen minutes later.

Crime scene tape cordoned off an area around Garrett's BMW. Several police cars with their lights flashing crowded around the area. There were two crime scene vans and a coroner's van parked behind the police cars. We got out, ducked under the crime scene tape, and walked toward Garrett's car.

Lieutenant Matt Davis came over to us. He motioned toward me, and asked Soratelli, "What's he doing here?"

"He works for the vic's wife," Soratelli said. "He's been looking for the guy."

"Well, you can stop looking," Davis said.

Matt Davis was a solid built middle-aged man with graying hair at the temples. He had been a homicide detective for as long as I've known him, maybe since he was a baby. He had piercing brown eyes, no lips to speak of, and a chiseled chin. He was always impeccably dressed, and besides me, he was the only detective I knew that still wore a fedora. But that's where the similarities between us ended. Davis was a stickler for following police procedures and protocols. I, on the other hand—though I never broke the law as a cop—bent the rules when necessary to get results. And that had always rankled Davis.

We walked toward the BMW. The trunk was open. As we got closer, the smell hit me.

I started breathing through my mouth.

"Smells great, doesn't it," Matt Davis said. He motioned toward the trunk. "CSU is still going over the scene. We haven't moved the body yet."

Jason Garrett lay on his side in the trunk; his hands tied behind his back. Dried blood caked around his head.

Davis pointed at Garrett's head. "He took one shot in the back of the head," he said. "Execution style."

"Professional hit," I said.

"Looks like it," Davis said. "There isn't a lot of blood in the trunk, so he probably got popped somewhere else and driven out here." He glanced at me, then continued, "He's been here a while. We won't know exactly how long until the coroner's finished with him."

"He's been missing close to three weeks," I said.

Davis looked at me and asked, "How long you been working the case?"

"A couple of weeks," I said.

Soratelli added, "The vic's wife didn't like the way we were handling the case. So she hired him."

"What have you found out so far?" Davis asked me.

"Not much," I said. "A lot of loose ends that don't lead anywhere."

Soratelli went over and started taking the statement from the parking lot attendant who had found the body. He was a young black kid about twenty-years-old. He looked shook up. Understandable. I'm sure finding a dead body stuffed in the trunk of a car wasn't in his job description.

Matt Davis studied me a second, then asked, "How'd you get the black eye?"

"A couple of guys assaulted me," I said.

"Did it happen at One Atlantic Center?" he asked.

"No grass growing under your feet," I said. "How'd you find out?"

"I heard a call came in about three guys duking it out in the parking garage. I recognized it because it was in the same building where your vic worked. But by the time a patrol car arrived all three were gone. Know anything about that?"

"Timing is everything," I said.

"So why did they assault you?"

"They were asking me questions," I said.

"Yeah," Davis said, staring at me. "About what?"

"About this case," I said. "They assaulted me right after I talked with Charles Lawson."

"He's the senior partner where your vic worked," Davis said. "We talked with him when Garrett went missing. Tight lipped guy."

"You could say that," I said.

Davis stared at me another second. "So these guys that assaulted you, who were they?"

"I don't know," I said.

"But they were asking you questions about this case?"

"Yeah," I said. "They'd been following me since I picked up the case."

Davis said, "I'm sure you reported the assault to the proper authorities?"

"No," I said. "I know how over worked you guys are."

"Right," Davis said sardonically. "They still following you?"

"Not unless they've gotten better at it," I said.

"So these guys follow you around, and then they make a move on you, want to know what you're up to. Right?"

"That's about it," I said.

"And you being you," Davis said, "didn't tell them anything. Right?"

"Client confidentiality," I said and smirked. "Besides I didn't like them."

"So then they tried to beat it out of you."

"They didn't succeed," I said.

Davis turned and stared at me. "The way I see it, is that if you had followed proper procedure and reported the two assailants, we could have questioned them."

I stared back at him. "I questioned them myself. They didn't know anything."

Davis said, "And now the guy you've been looking for is found dead in the trunk of his car."

"That about sums it up," I said.

We were silent a moment to let the tension settle between us.

After a moment, Davis asked, "Why do you think Garrett was popped?"

"I don't know," I said. "There are a lot of loose ends to this case."

We watched as the CSU guys finished up their preliminary work with Garrett's body. Then two coroner's men moved in with a gurney. Both were wearing masks to stifle the stench. They put Garrett in a body bag, and then wheeled him to the coroner's van and loaded him inside. Davis and I were silent as we watched the van pull out of the parking lot.

"We're gonna have to talk with the wife," Davis said. "Think she's involved?"

"I don't think so," I said. "If she had him popped, why would she hire me to find him?"

"Maybe to throw us off."

"It doesn't fit," I said. "Complicates things. If she were involved, it would have been easier just to have Garrett popped without going through the trouble of hiring me."

"We'll have to talk to her anyway," Davis said. "You going to stay on this thing?"

"Yeah," I said. "I don't like leaving things unresolved."

CHAPTER THIRTY-FOUR

I was sitting at my desk thinking about lunch when Julia Garrett walked into the office. Today she wasn't dressed as a flirtatious *femme fatale*. Instead, she wore a conservative dress with a light gray skirt that came down just above the knees. Her blue button-down blouse didn't show any cleavage. The suit jacket matched the skirt. She came in and sat in one of the client chairs opposite my desk.

For a long moment, she didn't say anything, just sat there clutching her purse in her hands. I had spoken to her briefly over the phone after the discovery of her husband's body, but we hadn't met face-to-face, not since the incident at her apartment.

After a moment, she said, "I'm sorry about what happened at my apartment. I've never acted that way before."

"Don't worry about it," I said. "It never happened."

"Thank you," she said.

Julia Garrett looked at me a moment.

"What happened to your eye?" she asked.

The eye was healing, but there was still a slight purplish-black bruise beneath it. The black eye grabbed people's attention. It had become a conversation piece.

I said, "I got into a fight in the parking garage at Schmitt & Lawson."

"A fight," she said, intrigued. "What happened?"

I was getting tired of telling the story, but I recounted about the two clowns that tried to get information out of me.

When I finished, Julia Garrett asked, "Do you think they had anything to do with Jason's murder?"

"I don't think so," I said. I didn't mention I knew who hired the two clowns. I'd tell her when I learned more.

She was silent another moment, then she said, "The police questioned me."

"They have to talk with everyone involved," I said.

"It was a terrible experience," she said. "They were rude and invasive. They asked a lot of questions about our marriage. They asked whether we were happy. Was either of us having an affair? Did we have financial problems?"

"They have to ask all those questions to clear your name," I said.

"But they didn't have to be so rude about it," Julia said. "They questioned me as if they were accusing me of killing Jason."

"In a homicide, they always look at the spouse first," I said.

Her eyebrows knitted together. "So they consider me a suspect?"

I shook my head. "I'm sure they know you're not involved," I said.

"Instead of looking at me," she barked, "they need to focus on finding who really murdered my husband."

I nodded, but remained silent.

Julia was silent for a moment. Then she said, "The police wouldn't even tell me how he died."

"He was shot," I said.

She looked down at her hands in her lap, and then the grief and frustration she had been holding back boiled to the surface. Her shoulders shook as she quietly began to cry. She hardly made any sound, just the quiet sobs of a grieving woman.

After a while, Julia cleared her throat and dabbed at her eyes with a tissue. Then she looked back up at me, and said, "The whole time he was missing, I never lost hope that he would be found alive."

She dabbed at her eyes with the tissue again, and asked, "So what happens next?"

"The police will continue their investigation," I said.

"I don't have much faith in the police's ability to find Jason's killer," Julia Garrett said. "After all, they couldn't even find his…" She choked up again. She took a couple of deep breaths, and after a second, she added, "I want you to stay on the case. I want you to find out who killed my husband."

"I'd like to find that out, too," I said.

CHAPTER THIRTY-FIVE

Mable Williams called late on a Wednesday and asked if I could come to her condominium. She sounded nervous, even scared. Her normal ferocious, take-charge voice quivered when she spoke. She said she didn't want to discuss it over the phone. She gave me the address as I glanced at the clock behind my desk. It was 5:35. She would have just arrived home from the office. Something was up. I said I'd be right over.

I drove toward midtown and parked in a loading zone on 17th Street at her condominium complex. Mable buzzed me in. I took the stairs two at a time to the third floor and knocked on her door. She opened it immediately.

"Thank you for coming Mr. Price," she said.

"Nick," I said. "Call me Nick. What's up?"

"It's kind of silly," she said, "now that I've had time to think about it. I'm embarrassed that I called you, but I didn't know what else to do."

"You sounded nervous when you called," I said. "What happened?"

I followed her into the living room. It was an elegant, yet modest apartment with a spacious combination living room and dining room. There was a kitchen off to the left with a breakfast bar. Three wooden stools, painted black with white cushions, sat opposite the breakfast bar.

I sat on a leather sofa and Mable Williams sat opposite me on a matching leather chair. She was still dressed in her schoolmarms' attire she donned for work. She had her hair pulled back in the same familiar bun.

"What happened?" I asked again.

Mable Williams fidgeted with her hands in her lap. "Charles Lawson called me into his office today, and asked me if I had been speaking with you."

"What did you say?"

"I lied, of course," Mable said. "If I'd told him the truth he would have fired me on the spot. So I told him I haven't spoken with you since the day you first came to the office."

"What did he say to that?"

"He didn't believe me," she said. "He asked how you knew about the guy named Rueben. He said that I was the only person at the firm who knew his name, and then he accused me of giving you sensitive information about the firm."

"What did you say?" I asked.

"I told him I didn't know anything about it," Mable said. "I said you must've found out from someone else."

"What else did Lawson say to you?"

"He practically called me a liar," Mable Williams said. "He threatened to fire me. He said that if he found out I was giving you information, he would make sure I never worked in another law office again."

I studied her a second. She sat in her chair with her back perfectly erect, her knees together, and her sensible shoes touching each other. She kept nervously wringing her hands together. Lawson had really rattled her.

I leaned forward, my elbows resting on my knees. "I'm sorry I pulled you into this."

"I'm not," Mable said. "I wanted to help you find Mr. Garrett. But now that..." her voice cracked "...now that his body has been discovered Mr. Lawson has changed."

"How so?"

"He's a totally different person," Mable began. "He's jumpy all the time. Nervous. He yells at the associates and paralegals. The other day he called a paralegal into his office and I heard him yelling at her through the door. She was crying when she came out, and Mr. Lawson told me he'd fired her and to call security to escort her out of the building."

"Was Lawson yelling when he questioned you?" I asked.

"Nothing like the way he treated the paralegal," Mable said. "But he was so angry his face turned red. His whole body shook. It was scary. That's why I called you."

"Did he threaten you? Physically?"

"No," she said. "Nothing like that."

We were silent a moment, then I asked, "Do you know anything about a company called Tanner Investments?"

"The name isn't familiar," Mable Williams said. "Why?"

"I saw the name in some of the documents I found on Garrett's personal computer."

She thought a second. "They're definitely not one of our clients."

An awkward moment of silence passed between us.

Then she suddenly stood up. "I'm not a very good host," she said. "How rude of me. Would you like something to drink? A glass of wine? Beer?"

"Thank you," I said. "I'll have a beer if you have any."

Mable went into the kitchen to fetch our drinks. While I waited, I thought about what she'd said. There was still a lot I didn't know about the case. One, I didn't know Lawson's relationship with South Realty Group; two, I didn't know how the mystery man, Rueben, fit into the mix either. But I was certain of one thing—the discovery of Garrett's body had rattled Lawson, and now he was as jumpy as a cat. Maybe he thought his name was next on the hit parade. Good. I might be able to use his fear to my advantage.

A moment later, Mable came back into the living room with a stemmed glass of wine and a bottle of beer. I gave her a sidelong glance as she handed me the bottle.

She smiled at me as she sat back down in her chair. "You look a little surprised," she said. "Did you think someone that dresses like a librarian wouldn't have beer and wine in their home?"

I smiled guiltily. "Sorry. It was presumptuous of me."

"No offense taken," Mable said. "Just because I dress like a prude doesn't mean I am one."

"I never thought of you as a prude," I said.

"I just think a woman should dress appropriately for work," she said.

"Especially a woman of my position at the firm. Proper attire demands respect. There are a lot of younger women at the firm that dress as though they're going out to a night club instead of work."

She flipped off her shoes and tucked her feet underneath her on the chair. Then she reached behind her head, let her hair down, and fluffed it out. Her black hair, streaked with a touch of gray, was perfectly straight and radiant. The librarian look instantly disappeared. With her hair down, Mable Williams was a good looking woman.

"With the risk of sticking my foot in my mouth again," I said. "You're a good looking woman."

Mable Williams smiled, and said, "A woman always loves a compliment."

We were silent a moment as we both drank. Then Mable placed her wine glass on a coaster on the coffee table between us, then asked, "Do you think Mr. Lawson is involved with Jason Garrett's murder?"

"I don't know," I said. "But I think he's into something he can't control."

"Any idea what it is?" she asked.

"No," I said. "But the way you described his recent behavioral change, I think he's in over his head, whatever it is."

She picked up her wine glass, took a sip, and thought a moment. Then she asked, "Do you think I could be in danger?"

I caught the nervousness in her voice. This entire mess had rattled her, and now Lawson's barrage of questions had added to her anxiety. She looked scared, and had every right to be.

I took out one of my business cards, wrote my cell and home number on the back, and handed it to her. "If you ever feel scared, or threatened, give me a call, no matter what the time."

I sat my empty beer bottle on the coffee table and stood up. Mable followed me to the door.

"Thank you for coming over," she said. "I feel better now that I've talked to you about it."

To help calm her down, I changed the subject. I asked, "Are you still walking to work?"

"Yes," she said, her voice taking on a tinge of excitement. "It's a little over a mile and I love it. When I get to work, I feel invigorated."

"That's great," I said. "I feel the same way too when I walk." We were silent a second, then I added, "Call me if you need anything. And thanks for the beer."

I looked into her brown eyes. She really was a good looking woman. Then I opened the door and walked out.

CHAPTER THIRTY-SIX

Using my superior detective skills and Google, I found Tanner Investments on Piedmont Avenue close to Ansley Park. Their website listed Richard Murphy as the President and CEO. Since I didn't think I was in grave danger, I didn't take Tony along with me on this visit.

Tanner Investments was in a red brick building a few blocks from Ansley Mall. The building had tinted windows that were too high to see out from the inside and impossible to see into from the outside. A cheerful blonde receptionist that wore a tight red sweater with ample cleavage greeted me at the receptionist desk. The name plate on the desk identified her as Cheryl Swanson.

"Can I help you, sir?" she asked cheerfully. She seemed to vibrate beneath the tight sweater, as if she were bursting with excitement.

"Hi, Cheryl," I said, flashing a seductive smile. "Nick Price to see Richard Murphy."

"Do you have an appointment?" she asked. She smiled back with perfect white teeth. Her amble breast quivered beneath her sweater.

"No," I said. "But I think he'll want to see me anyway."

"What's this in reference to?"

"I'm investigating a murder," I said. I said it casually for effect, as if we were talking about the weather.

"A murder!" she gasped. Her blue eyes widened, and she seemed to vibrate more in her tight sweater. "Are you with the police?"

"I'm private," I said. I gave her one of my cards.

"A real private eye," she said, taking the card and staring at it, as if mesmerized. Then her eyebrows furrowed a moment as she thought. I could tell thinking wasn't one of her strong points.

I said, "Can I see Mr. Murphy now?"

"One moment," she said.

She picked up the phone, punched a few numbers and whispered something indiscernible in the receiver. She nodded and replaced the receiver.

"Come this way," she said.

I followed her through a door to the left into a huge office area filled with cubicles. As we walked between the cubicles, I could hear muffled office chatter and the clacking of keyboards. There were about ten cubicles with chest-high dividers. I couldn't see what the office workers were doing. At the back of the room, Cheryl stopped at the only office in the place. A plaque next to the door read: RICHARD MURPHY PRESIDENT & CEO.

Cheryl knocked lightly on the door, told me, "You can go right in," and left.

Richard Murphy stood up from behind his desk, reached over, and shook my hand. He looked about fifty with piercing green eyes with crow's feet at the corners. But he looked in good shape. I could tell he worked out regularly.

"Cheryl tells me you're a private detective," he said. "That sounds intriguing."

"It's not as exciting as it sounds," I said.

"Please sit down," Murphy said, motioning to one of the plush leather chairs that sat opposite his desk.

I sat. He sat in his big swivel chair behind his desk. The desk was mahogany and massive, with enough room to lie down on. Dual computer monitors sat on the left side of the desk. Before I had sat down, I had caught a glimpse of multiple stock screens displayed on the monitors.

I asked, "How's the investment business?"

"It's booming," Richard Murphy said, "if you make the right moves."

"Sounds interesting," I said. "And you always make the right moves?"

"I'm not perfect, but I give our clients a good return on their investments."

"What exactly does an investment broker do?' I asked. One of the best ways to get someone to talk was to ask them about their favorite subject. Themselves. Sometimes it works, sometimes not.

"Basically, we manage investment commodities," Murphy said. "We recommend commodities to clients, and we purchase those commodities for them." He paused and smiled at me. "For a fee, of course."

"Like stocks and bonds?"

Murphy nodded. "We offer a wide range of commodities to our clients."

"What about real estate?" I asked.

"Yes," Richard Murphy said. "We handle real estate commodities as well."

"That's risky nowadays, isn't it?" I asked. "With the real estate market the way it is?"

"It can be," he said. "You have to be more careful what you recommend."

I nodded but didn't respond.

Murphy said, "Cheryl tells me you're investigating a murder." He stared at me, and then his tone suddenly changed. "I thought that sort of thing was for the real police."

"I'm working with them on the case," I said.

Murphy nodded. "So how can I help you?"

"The victim was an attorney named Jason Garrett," I said. "The name mean anything to you?"

"Jason Garrett," Murphy said, continuing to look me in the eye. "The name doesn't sound familiar."

"He was an attorney for Schmitt & Lawson," I said.

"Schmitt & Lawson," Murphy said. Apparently he liked to repeat things. Maybe he learned that in CEO school.

"I'm sorry," Richard Murphy said. "I'm not familiar with them either."

It was almost the same thing that Barton had said when I questioned him. Maybe they took the same class on how to dodge questions.

I said, "I have information that you regularly do business with Schmitt

& Lawson."

He gave me an irritated look. His cordiality was gone.

"Perhaps you were misinformed," Murphy said.

"Do you know a guy named Charles Lawson?"

"No," he said. "I've never heard of him."

I asked, "What about South Realty Group? Ever do business with them?"

"No," he said. "I'm not familiar with that name either."

This was going as I had expected. Murphy was lying. And he knew that I knew he was lying. Whatever the documents I'd found on Garrett's laptop were, Murphy was involved. But he wasn't going to admit to anything.

But I hadn't expected him to. I was mostly on a fishing expedition.

I asked, "What would you say if I told you I have documents linking Tanner Investments to South Realty Group and Schmitt & Lawson?"

He shot me a hard stare, then said, "I would say the documents are fraudulent." Then he added, "Maybe someone is attempting to mislead you."

"That's possible," I said. "It's been tried before."

Murphy leaned over his desk, gave me the hard stare some more, and asked, "What exactly do you want?"

"I want to know what happened to Jason Garrett," I said. "Why was he killed, and who killed him."

His eyes stabbed into me like daggers. He didn't like me. And he didn't like me sitting in his plush leather chair asking him questions. Fine with me. I didn't like him either.

Murphy glared at me another second, and then leaned back in his chair. "I can't help you," he said. "So now if you'd excuse me. I have work to do."

He stood. I stood. We didn't bother shaking hands again.

He followed me to his office door.

At the door, Murphy looked me in the eye, and said, "I'd be careful if I were you. Investigating a murder could be dangerous. You don't want to end up like your murder victim."

"That's been tried before, too," I said. "Unsuccessfully."

CHAPTER THIRTY-SEVEN

When I got back to my office Tony was sitting in one of the client chairs with his feet propped up. An open pizza box from Rosa's Pizza down the street sat on the edge of my desk. Tony had already eaten two slices. Next to the box was a Dos Equis.

"I'm glad you brought food," I said. I grabbed a slice of pizza and took a bite. I hadn't had anything to eat other than a couple of muffins that morning.

"I brought beer too," Tony said, motioning toward the small office fridge. I went back, grabbed two bottles, brought them back to my desk, and handed Tony one.

"What are we celebrating?" I asked. "You shoot somebody?"

"No," he said. "I figured you wouldn't have anything here to eat or drink."

"You were right," I said. "There's nothing in the fridge but a light bulb."

"I thought I was gonna have the whole pie to myself," he said. "Where you been anyway?"

"Did papa bear miss me," I said. I grabbed another slice of pizza.

Tony grunted. "I just wanted to make sure nobody had shot you yet."

"Nothing like true friendship," I said.

We ate for a while in silence. I finished the first beer and went and got us two more bottles. The office windows were open and I could smell the mingling of aromas coming from the Vietnamese restaurant below. Tony stood up and took off his jacket. His .357 hung beneath his arm like a bazooka.

"So where'd you go?" he asked.

"I paid a visit to Tanner Investments and talked to the President, a guy named Richard Murphy."

"He give you anything useful?"

"No," I said. "He clammed up the same way James Barton did. Said he never heard of Schmitt & Lawson, or South Realty Group."

"You mention the documents you found?" Tony asked.

"I hinted at them," I said. "I just wanted to let him know that I was on to him."

"Smart," Tony said. "What do you think his next move will be?"

I replied, "I think they'll make a move on me sooner or later. Murphy even implied as much when I left."

"Yeah," Tony said. "What'd he say?"

"He said he'd be careful if he were me. Not to end up like my victim."

"I'd take that as a threat," Tony said.

"I did," I said.

"So you think Murphy's the ring leader?" Tony asked.

I nodded. "I think he's the one calling the shots." I paused for a second as I took a bite of pizza. Then continued, "I just wish I knew more about what he's up to."

"Whatever it is," Tony said. "He's not afraid to have someone popped."

"And he's not afraid to do it again," I said.

"All the more reason for you to watch out," Tony said. "He'll probably send someone after you."

Tony got us two more beers, and we both sat back and propped our feet up on the desk.

Then I told him about the frantic phone call from Mable Williams. How Charles Lawson threatened to fire her and how frightened she was of him.

"You think she's in danger?" Tony asked.

"I don't know," I said. "But she's scared."

"Lawson's worked up," Tony said. "He's running scared. He knows he's in over his head, and he has to be thinking he could be the next person whacked."

"He should be worried," I said.

We drank our beers in silence. Then Tony said, "You can talk to Lawson again."

I shook my head. "Don't think he'd listen." I thought for a second. "I could talk to his wife, though. If Lawson won't listen to me, maybe he'll listen to her."

"That might work," Tony said. "Might even save his life."

CHAPTER THIRTY-EIGHT

At five-thirty the next morning my alarm clock screamed to life. I slammed it off and sat on the edge of the bed in my boxer shorts. I still felt groggy, as if I hadn't had any sleep. When I have a difficult case, I immerse myself in it, totally, almost to the point of obsession. I live, breathe, eat, and although fitfully, sleep the case. Last night, I sat out on the small balcony of my apartment, took in the Atlanta skyline, and drank three bourbons while I thought about who killed Jason Garrett and why. But no conclusions had jumped out at me.

I got up and went into the kitchen, drank a glass of orange juice, and ate a blueberry muffin. Then I threw on some sweats and went down to the street in front of my apartment building. After performing a few stretching exercises to loosen up, I began with a slow run, gradually building speed. It was the first week in October and the temperature was in the mid-thirties. Great weather for a run. As I ran, I thought more about the case. I knew that the documents I had found on Garrett's computer linked Charles Lawson, James Barton, and Richard Murphy together. And I was convinced they were pulling some sort of scam, though I didn't know what it was. Why else would they lie about not knowing each other? I was also certain Richard Murphy was the ringleader of the group. He had remained cool and confident when I talked to him, which told me this wasn't his first rodeo. For all I knew, Richard Murphy could be the person behind Jason Garrett's murder. He may not have been the actual triggerman, but he could be responsible for putting the hit on Garrett. Of course, this was all speculation without any real evidence, but

I had learned through my years as a cop to trust my instincts.

Then there was Charles Lawson. Something about him kept nagging at me. I didn't understand how Lawson got involved with a career criminal like Murphy in the first place. It didn't add up. You don't go from being a successful, prominent attorney to an accessory to murder—not without something happening in the middle. I didn't believe Murphy could have recruited Lawson into the scheme with just the enticement of making a lot of money, especially through illegal means. There had to be something more, a link between the two. The only explanation I had was that Lawson must have been doing something illegal before getting involved with Murphy. Then Murphy had discovered Lawson's secret, used it against him, forcing him into cooperating in the scam Murphy was running. No honor among thieves. But what had Lawson been up to beforehand? I had no idea—but I had a hunch. So I resolved to look into Lawson's recent past to get some answers.

I knew Lawson was in way over his head and was feeling the pressure. He had to be thinking he could be the next to die, shot in the head and stuffed in the trunk of his car. He was getting desperate. So desperate, I thought, that he wouldn't hesitate to sic the dogs on someone else to get the monkey off his own back.

Then I thought of Mable Williams. She had been terrified the night I went over to her apartment. Though she tried to hide it, I had seen it in her eyes. But she had every right to be afraid. One of her colleagues had been murdered. I didn't know whether she was in danger or not, but I had recruited her into this mess so I couldn't allow anything to happen to her.

I ran for four miles and worked up a good sweat. Nothing like a good run in the morning to get the heart pumping.

When I got back to my apartment, I felt invigorated. I took a hot shower, got dressed, and was about to leave for the office when my cell phone rang.

"Rueben is here," Mable Williams said in a low voice. "He arrived a few minutes ago."

My heart skipped a beat. "Where's he at right now?"

"He just went into Mr. Lawson's office," Mable Williams said, her voice nearly a whisper. "When Mr. Lawson saw Mr. Rueben, he looked terrified, like he'd seen a ghost. Rueben looks dangerous." Then to my surprise, she added, "I took a picture of him just before he went in."

My heart jumped in my throat. "You did what?"

"I took a picture of Mr. Rueben," Mable Williams said. She sounded proud of the fact, despite the danger it entailed. She continued, "It's not very good because I didn't use the flash. I'm sending it to you now."

I didn't know what to think about her taking a risk like that, but there was nothing I could do about it now. "Let me take a look," I said. "I'll call you right back."

I brought up the attachment on my cell phone. The picture was of a man's profile, not too clear, but good enough to tell what Rueben looked like. I smiled. Super-sleuth-in-training Mable Williams had come through for me again.

I forwarded the picture to Tony, and then called him.

"I just forwarded you a picture of Rueben," I said. "He's in Lawson's office now."

"I can be there in fifteen minutes," Tony said.

"The picture's a profile shot," I said, "but good enough for you to recognize him."

"What do you want me to do?" Tony asked.

"Just stay with him and see where he goes," I said, and hung up.

Then I called Mable Williams at her office number. She answered immediately.

I thanked her again, but then implored her, "Promise me you won't take another risk like that again."

"I promise," Mable Williams said. But then she added in her take-no-prisoners voice, "But if they think they can scare me off, they've got another thing coming."

"Just don't take any unnecessary risk," I said. Then I added, "I've got someone coming over to follow Rueben when he leaves."

"I hope your man is careful," Mable Williams said.

"Don't worry," I said. "The guy I have coming over can take on the Russian army."

"Do you need me to do anything?" she asked.

"Not with Rueben," I said. Then acting on my speculation about Lawson, I said, "But I could use your help with something else."

"What do you need?" She was always ready to help. God bless you Mable Williams.

I thought for a second. The oldest date on the documents from Garrett's laptop was about six months ago, so following my hunch, I would only need to go back a few months before Lawson got involved with Murphy. I said, "Can you get me a list of clients that Lawson met with between six to nine months ago?"

"The list could be long," Mable Williams said. "What do you need specifically?"

"I'm only looking for new clients that Lawson signed or tried to recruit," I said. "Particularly wealthy clients. And I only need people Lawson recruited. I don't need anything from the other associates."

"No problem," she said. "Plus, I'll send you a list of the clients Mr. Lawson handles personally. It may help you find Mr. Garrett's killer." There was a brief pause, then Mable Williams continued, "I hope Mr. Lawson isn't involved with the murder, but judging by the way he's been acting lately, I'm afraid he's involved in something."

"We'll just see how it plays out," I said.

"I'll email you the list by the end of the day."

"That's fantastic," I said. "Thanks so much for helping me. I couldn't do it without you. You're a sweetheart."

"You know how to swoon a gal," Mable Williams said.

CHAPTER THIRTY-NINE

Later that afternoon I was in my office waiting for Mable Williams to email me the list of Lawson's prospective clients when Tony walked in. He was carrying a bag from Stan's Sandwich Shop down the street. I hadn't had anything to eat since the muffin that morning and I was starving. I stared at the bag like a hungry dog stares at a bone. If I had a tail, I would have wagged it.

"Perfect timing," I said. "I was thinking of getting something to eat."

Tony put the bag on my desk, opened it, took out two Styrofoam containers, and handed me one. Then he pulled out two bags of chips, both barbecue.

"I figured Dick Tracy needed some nourishment," he said, sitting in one of the client chairs.

"Your deductive skills are improving," I said. "What would I do without you?"

"You'd probably have to eat that bird food Naija tries to get you to eat," he said.

"In other words, I'd starve to death," I said. I got up and went into the small kitchen alcove, brought back two beers, and handed Tony one.

"You can't eat that vegetable crap all the time," Tony said.

"I agree," I said. "Man cannot live on tofu and turkey bacon alone; he must have a club sandwich every now and then." I flipped the lid on my container. It was a club sandwich with ham, turkey, and bacon, with mayo on toasted wheat. A lot of places now offer turkey clubs without the ham, but not Stan-the-man down the street. He has the real thing. I dug in.

We chowed down in silence. After a while, I asked, "Were you able to track Rueben from Lawson's building?"

"Yeah," he said swallowing a mouthful of sandwich. He took a sip of beer before continuing. "I waited around in the parking garage and he walked right past me. He's one bad looking dude."

"A tough guy, huh?"

"No," Tony said. "The dude's ugly. You should see this guy's face. No wonder he scares the hell out of people."

"What's the matter with his face?"

"He's got a lot of scars," Tony said. "Deep scars, pockmarks."

"Maybe an ex-fighter," I said.

"Could be," Tony said, "but some of the scars are long and deep, like he's been cut a few times."

"Some fighters get cut a lot," I said, "especially the ones that aren't any good."

"This guy doesn't fit into that category," Tony said. "This guy's face looks like it's been chewed up in a meat grinder. Those scars aren't from boxing. More likely knife fights."

"So he would look scary to regular guys like Lawson?"

"Yes," he said. "He probably scares people just by staring at them."

I got up and retrieved two more beers from the fridge, and walked back to my desk.

Tony took one of the beers, and said, "The guy looked out of place in Lawson's building. He tried to blend in by carrying a briefcase, but people still stayed clear of him."

"I wonder what was in the briefcase," I said.

"It could have been empty," Tony said.

But I doubted it. If Rueben came to see Lawson unannounced, he may have been carrying more papers related to whatever scam they were running. I still wasn't sure what role Lawson played in the scheme, but having a lawyer involved could make the scam seem legitimate.

I took a sip of beer, and thought a moment, then said, "Rueben's probably the muscle. He could be the one that killed Garrett."

"He looks like he could get the job done," Tony said. "When he walked past me in the garage, I noticed the bulge in his suit jacket. He was packing heat."

"Which confirms my muscle theory," I said. "Where did he go?"

We both had finished our sandwiches. We stacked the empty Styrofoam containers on the corner of my desk.

"I followed him over to our friends at South Realty Group," Tony said. "He went in and stayed there around a half an hour. Then he went over to Tanner Investments and stayed in there about an hour. When he left South Realty, he was still carrying the briefcase, but when he left Tanner Investments, he no longer had it."

"So not only is he the muscle," I said, "he's also the carrier."

"Looks like," Tony said. "Whatever he had in the briefcase, he left at Tanner."

"You get his tag number?"

"Of course," Tony said, smiling. Then he read it to me from memory. I've never known Tony to forget anything. I wrote the tag number down.

I thought for a second, then said, "Here's what I think. The documents on Garrett's computer had Lawson's signature on them. So suppose Rueben has more documents for Lawson to sign. He takes the documents to Lawson, has him sign them, and then he takes them over to South. Then James Barton does what he needs to do, and then Rueben delivers everything to Richard Murphy. Nice and neat."

"It's a way of making sure Lawson does what he's supposed to," Tony said.

I leaned back in my chair, propped my feet up, and thought for a moment. Tony propped his feet up on the other corner of the desk. We were both silent a moment as we drank our beers. After a moment, I asked, "You learn anything from following Lawson around?"

"No," Tony said. "Following that guy is as exciting as watching grass grow. All he does is leave home, goes to the office, and then goes back home."

"What kind of house does he live in?"

"Place looks like a mansion," Tony said. "His house must have cost a few mil. It's on Habersham Road. I don't know how much a lawyer makes, but Lawson must be pulling in a lot of jack to pay for a house like that."

He pulled his phone out, punched the screen a couple of times, and showed me a picture of a huge house that looked like a hotel. Four families could probably live in it and never interfere with each other.

"That's a lot of house," I said.

"Maybe we're in the wrong racket," Tony said. "You're smart, why don't you take the lawyer exam."

"It's called a bar exam," I said. "And you have to go to law school first."

"It's worth it if you pull down enough money for a place like that," Tony said.

I thought for a moment, then asked, "You find out anything about Lawson's wife? She have a job?"

"The only job she's got is spending money," Tony said. "She goes shopping every day and then has lunch with her rich friends at expensive restaurants. She wears a lot of expensive looking jewelry too." He paused and laughed a second, then said, "If I wasn't working with you, I might rob her for her jewelry."

I shook my head and grinned at him. "It's good to have a career."

Tony shrugged. "A guy has to make a living."

I finished my beer and thought for a second. "So Lawson's living in an expensive house with an expensive wife. Maybe he is doing something other than practicing law."

"He's gotta be doing something," Tony said. "Just keeping his extravagant wife happy probably cost a couple of mil a year."

"Maybe I'll drop in on Lawson's wife," I said.

CHAPTER FORTY

After Tony left, I grabbed the phone and called Detective Sergeant Mike Soratelli. He answered on the fifth ring.

"You guys making any progress on the Garrett case?" I asked.

"Nada," Soratelli said. "We've got nothing. No suspects. No motive. No reason why anyone would want to kill Garrett. You got anything?"

"A few loose ends, but nothing substantial."

"We don't even have the loose ends," Soratelli said.

"I need you to run another tag number for me," I said.

"You keep asking for numbers run, but I don't hear anything back," Soratelli said. "Are you holding out on me?"

"I wouldn't treat a friend like that," I lied. "I'm in the same boat as you. I don't have anything to report. The other numbers didn't lead anywhere."

"What makes you think this is any different?"

"I've got a feeling about this one. I'm due for a hit."

"And I'm due to die one day," Soratelli said. "Let's hope you hit before I die. What you got?"

I read him the tag number from Rueben's car.

"I'll call you back," he said, and hung up.

Twenty minutes later Soratelli called back.

"The tag number you gave me belongs to Jack Rueben," he said. "Why are you interested in him?"

I wanted to throw him a bone, but I knew if I did, he would run with it. If Rueben were the triggerman, Soratelli would get his murderer. But what about James Barton and Richard Murphy? They'd scatter like flies—probably set up another scam in another city. I didn't want partial justice. I wanted absolute justice. I wanted them all. So, Soratelli would have to wait.

"I'm just following a hunch," I said.

Soratelli grunted. "I know you're holding out on me. But let me give you some advice on Rueben. Watch yourself around this guy. He has a long rap sheet."

"Tell me about it," I said.

"Seven arrests for assault and only one conviction. That was on one of the assault charges. Did two months in county lockup. Two arrests for extortion, but the charges were dropped." He paused a second, then added, "He has three other arrests on lesser charges. Carrying a concealed weapon and the other two arrests were for just being a troublemaker."

"Sounds like a real nice guy," I said.

"Have you seen the mug on this guy?"

"No," I lied.

"He's got a face not even a mother would love," Soratelli said. "He looks like someone hit him in the face with a pizza. And it stuck. He's one bad hombre, so watch out."

"I will, Mom, I promise," I said. "When was the last time he got pinched?"

"A couple of years ago," he said. "The assault charge."

"And he's only been convicted once?"

"That's what it says," Soratelli said.

Our crack justice system at work. Rueben's rap sheet was long as my arm, with violent offenses, and he's only done sixty days. Let the hooligans run loose on the streets, while some poor schmuck gets busted for a little pot and does five years.

Soratelli asked, "Why are you so interested in Jack Rueben? You think he's involved with the Garrett case?"

"I don't know," I lied again.

Soratelli cleared his throat. "You don't know or you're not saying."

I had piqued Soratelli's curiosity. I had to give him something. Otherwise, he would keep pestering me.

"I've got a suspicion," I said. "But I don't have anything concrete."

"But you think Rueben's involved? Right?"

"Could be," I said. "But I don't know for sure."

Soratelli paused a second, then asked, "You think he's the one that popped Garrett?"

"He fits the profile, doesn't he?"

"He sure does," Soratelli said. "Got any evidence to back it up?"

"No," I said, and hung up before he could ask any more questions.

CHAPTER FORTY-ONE

The email from Mable Williams contained thirty-seven names of prospective clients Lawson had solicited. Fourteen were businesses. I crossed them out. If my hunch was right, I didn't think businesses would be a part of Lawson's scam. He would only be interested in personal clients. Out of the remaining twenty-three names, ten were clients, meaning Lawson had convinced them to trust him. People tend to trust lawyers, taking what they say as the truth. The remaining thirteen names Mable had listed as non-clients. I sat back in my chair, propped my feet up, and read over the entire list again. No names jumped out at me. But I hadn't expected them to.

First, I started calling the names listed as clients. The first four calls, I got voice-mails. I left my name and number, asking for a call back. The next five clients refused to talk to me, one telling me their financial affairs were none of my business. Others simply hung up on me.

On the next call, a woman answered.

"This is Nick Price," I said. "I'm a private investigator working on a case. Is Martin Stevens available?"

"My husband's not home," the woman said. She paused a second, making me wonder if she'd hung up. Then she added, "He's a doctor."

She had a soft, seductive voice that sounded like a whisper.

"Yes, that's what I have listed," I lied. I wrote down physician next to his name on my list. Maybe Naija knew him. I asked, "Mrs. Stevens, what type of medicine does your husband practice?"

"Cindy," she said. "You can call me Cindy."

"Ok, Cindy," I said. "The type of practice?"

She paused again. "Oh, I don't know exactly. He's a doctor at Northside Hospital."

"You don't know what type of medical practice he's in?" I said. I tried not to sound surprised.

"No, I don't know," she said honestly. "He's a surgeon."

Apparently, Cindy Stevens wasn't the sharpest pencil in the box. I hoped she wasn't performing surgery any time soon. I pushed ahead.

"Perhaps you can answer a few questions," I said.

Another pause. "I'll try," she said. She didn't sound certain of her answer. Maybe she had trouble answering anything other than her name.

"Are you and your husband a client of the law firm Schmitt & Lawson?" I asked. I found myself speaking slowly, as if I were speaking to her in a language she didn't understand. I gave her a hint. "It would involve financial matters."

"Oh," Cindy Stevens said. "I really don't know anything about our finances. Martin takes care of that."

I imagined Martin took care of everything. I wondered what Mrs. Stevens looked like. With that soft, sensual voice, I bet she was a knockout—but with an IQ only in double digits. Beautiful but dumb as a rock.

I asked, "Do you remember meeting with a man name Charles Lawson?" I threw her another hint. "Perhaps you and your husband would have gone to his office. This would have been a little over a year ago."

The pause surfaced again. "I don't think so."

"Do you accompany your husband on meetings concerning financial matters?"

"Oh, no" she said again. "Martin takes care of all that stuff."

This wasn't going anywhere. I was talking to a light post with the light out. "Perhaps I need to call back when your husband gets home."

"That's a good idea," she said. "I'll tell him you called." She paused again. I assumed she was thinking. Then she said, "I've got an even better idea."

"What's that?" I couldn't wait to hear her brainstorm.

"Why don't you come over at eight o'clock," she said. "Then you and Martin can have a martini and talk in Martin's study."

Maybe she was a genius. "Good idea. Tell Mr. Stevens I'll come over at eight."

"I certainly will," she said, suddenly excited. Then she added, "I make a great martini."

"I bet you do," I said, and hung up.

Just talking with her had made me feel dizzy. I leaned back in my swivel chair, propped my feet back up on the desk, and closed my eyes until the dizziness passed.

CHAPTER FORTY-TWO

The next call I made was to a guy named Frank Owens. Mable Williams had him listed as a non-client, which meant that he didn't bite when Charles Lawson made his spiel. I dialed the number and tapped my pin on the desk as I listened to the phone shrill at the other end. No answering device picked up. On the twenty-fifth ring, someone answered.

"Hello," a man's voice boomed.

"Is this Frank Owens?"

"Yeah. What do you want?" he demanded. He had a strong heavy southern accent.

"My name is Nick Price. I'm a private investigator, and have a few questions about the law firm of Schmitt & Lawson."

"What about them?" He sounded angry, as if I'd interrupted him from something.

I consulted my notes quickly. "I understand Charles Lawson contacted you about six months ago."

"Yeah," he said. "What about it?"

"I'm working on a case," I said. "And it involves Schmitt & Lawson, specifically Charles Lawson."

"Lawson," Frank Owens said, as if he were spitting out the name.

I asked, "Did Schmitt & Lawson represent you at any time in the past?"

"Yeah," he said. "Robert Schmitt was my lawyer back when I still ran my construction business. He's a stand-up guy. But Lawson, I didn't like him. He seemed like a crook to me."

Right you are, Mr. Owens. "You said you were in construction?"

"Yeah. For forty-two years," Frank Owen said. "I ran one of the most profitable home construction businesses in the South, Owens Construction. My son runs it now."

"When did Schmitt & Lawson stop representing your company?" I asked.

"Five years ago. I retired. When my son took over he switched to another firm."

"And you didn't hear from the firm until Charles Lawson contacted you six months ago?"

"That's right," he said. "Lawson called me out of the blue, said he had a business proposition for me." Owens chuckled. "He said it was an investment opportunity of a lifetime."

I thought for a second. Six months ago. The timeline seemed right. If my hunch was right, whatever scam Lawson had been running began to dry up about six months ago. Then out of desperation, Lawson began calling former clients he hadn't spoken to in years to lure them into his scam.

I asked, "What happened after Lawson called you?"

"Lawson came to the house and showed me this proposal that guaranteed thirty-three percent on an initial investment."

"Thirty-three percent," I said. "That's a big return."

"That was my reaction, too," Frank Owens said. "Sounded too good to be true."

"Do you remember exactly what kind of investment Lawson offered you?"

Frank Owens paused another second and then said in his strong southern voice, "Yeah. Lawson told me he represented a woman in a wrongful death suit. Her husband had died on the job. The payout was for a million dollars, paid out over a three-year period. Lawson told me the lady needed the money right away. Lawson said he had negotiated a payout for her of seven-hundred and fifty-thousand payable immediately."

"And Lawson wanted you to invest the seven hundred and fifty thousand," I said.

"Right," Frank Owens said. "Lawson told me that he could pay me the full million in installments over a three-year period."

"Making you the thirty-three percent return on your investment."

"That's what he claimed," he said.

"Did he show you documentation to back up his claim?" I asked.

"Yeah," Frank Owens said. "But the documents looked suspicious to me."

"What was suspicious about them?"

"All the names were blacked out," he said.

"Did Lawson say why he had the names blacked out?"

"Lawson said it was because of client confidentiality."

"But you didn't buy that story, did you?"

Frank Owens chuckled again. I think he was enjoying talking about Lawson's big investment spiel. "Absolutely not," he said. "He probably thought I was some dumb southern hick that couldn't add two and two. But I know a scam when I see one."

This was great. Not only did Frank Owens turn Lawson down on his investment scheme, he also knew what kind of documentation Lawson was offering to back up his scam. I felt as if I were in Vegas and had hit the jackpot.

"Then what happened?"

"Then I told him I wasn't interested in his 'business proposition' as he put it," Frank Owens said. "You should have seen the look on Lawson's face when I turned him down. Looked like he'd lost his best friend." Then Owens added, "I had to work hard for my money. I put in long hours, neglected my family, and I wasn't about to hand some of it over to someone that talked like a crooked used car salesman."

After we hung up, I had to laugh. It was easy to imagine Lawson on a used car lot, peering down his long nose, and trying to swindle some poor schmuck out of his money.

CHAPTER FORTY-THREE

After hitting the jackpot with Frank Owens, I felt I was on a roll. Later that evening, I headed to the home of Dr. Martin Stevens and his wife Cindy, who by her own account made great martinis. The Stevens lived in a remodeled two-story Victorian on Euclid Avenue in Inman Park. I love Inman Park, with its old homes built in the early 1900s, and its laidback community atmosphere that many other areas of town lack. The house of Dr. Martin Stevens was painted battleship gray with white trim and had a wraparound front porch. A white picket fence fronted the property. I climbed the brick steps and rang the bell, and the front door swung open immediately and a young blonde who looked to be in her mid-twenties greeted me.

"Hi," she said in that voice I'd heard over the phone that sounded like a seductive whisper. "I'm Cindy Stevens. You must be the private detective." She seemed excited as a puppy to see me. Cindy Stevens was pretty and had an innocence about her that made her even prettier.

"Nick," I said. "Nick Price." I shook her delicate hand.

"Martin's waiting for you in his study," she said, swinging the door open and ushering me inside the foyer. There were bamboo hardwood floors throughout the house. To the right of the foyer was an elegant living room furnished with antique European-style furniture. To the left, a spiral staircase led upstairs.

"Follow me," Cindy Stevens said.

I followed her down the hallway until she opened a door on the left and led me inside.

Dr. Martin Stevens stood next to a massive antique mahogany desk. He looked to be in his mid-forties with a touch of gray at his temples. He was wearing khaki pants and a green sweater vest. He had an unlit pipe in his right hand.

"Hello," Dr. Stevens said as I came into the room. He moved the pipe from his right hand to his left and we shook hands. I introduced myself again and gave him one of my cards. He took it, read it over, and placed it on the desk.

"Would you two men like a martini?" Cindy chirped. Then she looked at me and added, "I make a great martini."

"That would be very nice," I said.

Cindy left and Martin sat in one of the Queen Anne chairs opposite the desk. I sat in the other chair.

I said, "This is a very nice home."

"It was built in 1915," Martin said. "Of course, it's been completely renovated. Some by the previous owner, but there was still a lot to do when I bought it five years ago."

Cindy sailed back into the room carrying a silver tray with a pitcher and two martini glasses on it. The martini glasses were in transparent colors of blue and red. She sat the tray on Martin's desk and poured each of us a drink.

"You boys drink up," she said. "I made plenty."

After Cindy left, Martin motioned with his unlit pipe toward the door. "I met Cindy in a restaurant bar one night," he said, as if an explanation were needed. It wasn't, but it seemed like something he said to all his guests. He continued, "I was waiting to be seated, and Cindy was the bartender." He took a sip of his martini. "It was love at first sight. She's twenty-six and I'm forty-five. We've been married a little over three years now."

"Age is just a number," I said.

He took another sip of his drink, then said, "Cindy tells me you're a private investigator."

"Yes," I said. "I'm investigating a murder." I said it to get his attention. It did.

"A murder," he said, his eyes suddenly growing wide. "Who was murdered?"

"An associate at Schmitt & Lawson. His name was Jason Garrett."

"Jason Garrett," Dr. Stevens said. His eyebrows furrowed together as he thought a moment. "I'm sorry. I don't know him." He looked at me, and then asked, "What has that got to do with me?"

I ignored the question. "I'm just gathering information at this point." I took a sip of my martini, then asked, "But you are familiar with Schmitt & Lawson?"

Martin Stevens nodded. "The firm has handled my personal affairs for years."

"And which associate handles your affairs?"

"Charles Lawson," he said. "He's the senior partner, but he still handles my legal affairs because of my longtime relationship with the firm." He took another drink, then added, "He handled the closing on this house, and revised my will when Cindy and I got married."

"So Lawson would be privy to your finances?" I prompted.

"Yes, of course," Martin Stevens said.

Time to get to the point. "Mr. Stevens, the reason I'm here is to ask you about an investment you may have made recently with Lawson."

Stevens suddenly grew concerned. "Yes, I made an investment with him a little over a year ago. In fact, Mr. Lawson came here to the house to discuss it with me."

It was easy to imagine Lawson sitting here, drinking one of Cindy's fabulous martinis, and swindling her husband out of his money. I asked, "Was the investment opportunity a lawsuit settlement case he had negotiated?"

Martin refilled his empty martini glass. "It was a wrongful death lawsuit. Lawson told me that a client's husband was killed on his job and the widow had won a million dollar lawsuit against her husband's employer. But the money was held in a trust to be paid over a three-year period."

I spoke up and finished for him. "Then Lawson told you the widow needed the money right away, and that he had negotiated a settlement for her."

Dr. Stevens looked surprised that I knew this. He took another belt of his martini. "That's exactly what he said."

I said, "And that's when Lawson mentioned the investment opportunity?"

"Exactly," he said. He picked up his pipe and looked at it. He was suddenly nervous. I didn't blame him. I was here investigating a murder and asking him personal questions about his finances. He put his unlit pipe in his mouth and clamped down on it. Then he took it back out. "Old habit," he said. "I don't smoke it anymore. I quit when Cindy and I got married. Now I just carry it around with me."

I nodded. "How much did Lawson negotiate the settlement for?"

"Seven-hundred and fifty thousand."

I took another sip of my martini. Cindy Stevens was right. She did make a killer martini. I asked, "Did Lawson ask you to invest the entire seven-hundred and fifty thousand?"

I watched as Martin gulped more of his drink. "Lawson said I could invest the entire amount, or invest a partial amount with other investors he had lined up."

"But he convinced you it would be more profitable to invest the entire sum?"

Stevens nodded, staring at the floor. He didn't say anything.

"How did Lawson tell you you'd receive payment for the investment?"

Martin Stevens looked me in the eye. "He said it would be paid back in quarterly installments over a three-year period."

"Giving you the full amount of the settlement," I said. "A cool million."

Dr. Stevens nodded. "A thirty-three percent return." He paused, then said, "Now that I've said it out loud it does seem too good to be true. Doesn't it?"

He drained his glass and refilled it. His third drink. I had only drunk half of my first.

I asked, "Did Lawson show you documentation to back up his claim?"

"Yes," he said, nodding his head.

"And the documents he showed you had the names blacked out, didn't they?"

Again, he shot me a surprised look. He had to wonder how I knew so much, but he didn't say anything. Instead, he simply nodded.

"And Lawson told you the names were blacked out because client confidentiality?"

Dr. Stevens nodded his head again. The worried expression on his face grew darker.

I asked, "So you've gotten a few of the payments already?"

"Yes," he said. "The first couple of payments were on time."

"And the recent payments?"

"After the first two, the next payment was late," Stevens said. "And short."

"Did you call Lawson about it?"

"Of course," he said. He glanced at me, then quickly went back staring at his pipe. "Lawson told me that there must have been an accounting mistake and that he'd look into it and make sure the remainder of the payment was added to the next one."

"Did he make good on his promise?"

"Yes," Dr. Stevens said. "The last two payments I received were on time and for the full amount."

Of course, they would be, I thought. That's probably about the time Lawson got involved with Richard Murphy.

I took a sip of my martini, then asked, "Were the payment checks drawn from First Georgia Savings?"

Again, the look as if I'd been getting my information from a crystal ball. "Yes," he said. "Why do you ask?"

"Just following a hunch," I said, and let it go at that.

He finished his drink and poured himself another one. His fourth.

We were silent a moment. Dr. Stevens finally put the pieces of the puzzle together. He asked, "Do you think my investment is at risk?"

"I don't know," I said.

"But you're here investigating a murder of an associate at Schmitt & Lawson, and asking questions about Charles Lawson. Is he involved in the murder investigation?"

"I'm not sure," I said. "Like I said before. I'm just gathering information."

"But you suspect enough to investigate him, and the investments he's offered."

I looked at him and nodded.

Then the gravity of it hit him. He downed his drink and poured himself another. His fifth. He wasn't slurring his words yet, but the effects of drinking so many that quick would hit him all at once. "He made it sound like a very solid investment," he said discouragingly. "It was nearly all of our retirement savings." He sounded like he wanted to cry. He took a drink of his martini and looked at me. "Does making such an investment make me gullible?"

"No," I said. "It makes you human."

"But I'm a doctor," he said. "People depend on me to make the right decisions. If word gets out I've made such a blunder of my own finances, it could ruin my career. Who wants to go to a doctor that can't even manage his own affairs?"

There was nothing to say to that, so I remained silent.

I had had a good day. I had learned that Lawson had been running some type of investment scam—really nothing more than a Ponzi scheme, peddling phony paperwork, and no doubt pocketing a huge portion of the money. But a Ponzi scheme only works as long as you have an endless supply of investors. But Lawson's investor pool had begun to run dry. Then desperate for money, he tried to peddle his bogus documents to loyal clients like Martin Stevens, swindling them out of their life savings.

I had also learned that the payments for the scam had been drawn on First Georgia Savings. So maybe the scared little bird Greg Little wasn't such an innocent victim after all. Greg Little could have been a part of Lawson's scheme from the beginning, and now like Lawson, was trapped into participating in Murphy's scam too. Maybe Greg Little had wanted out, but had been sent a message in the form of Roy Upshaw. Stick to banking, the message had said. It made sense.

I finished my martini and thanked Dr. Stevens for seeing me. Before I left, I said, "If I were you, I would try to recoup as much of my money as I could."

Dr. Stevens nodded his head, but didn't say anything. He guzzled the drink in his hand and poured himself another. I hoped he didn't have any surgeries in the morning. He was going to have a doozy of a hangover. On the way out, I said goodbye to his good looking wife, Cindy, who made fabulous martinis.

CHAPTER FORTY-FOUR

The next morning, I was in my office with my feet propped up on the desk, drinking a cup of coffee and feeling good about what I had discovered about Charles Lawson. There was still a lot I didn't know, but at least I was beginning to make progress. I felt confident I was on the right track to uncovering more dirty little secrets.

Then Lieutenant Matt Davis walked into my office. Without saying anything, he went over to the coffeemaker, poured himself a cup, and added sugar and cream.

"How about a cup of coffee," I said.

"No thanks," Matt Davis said. "I've got one."

He sat in one of the client chairs opposite the desk and stared at me. I waited. I knew he would get around to why he was here in his own time. After a moment, he asked, "Know a woman named Mable Williams?"

I suddenly felt a tightening in my stomach. I took my feet off the desk and swung them around. I looked into Matt's eyes. It was like staring at a brick wall. "Yeah," I said. "She's Charles Lawson's secretary."

"Tell me about her?"

"Like I said, she's Lawson's secretary."

"How do you know her?" Davis asked.

"She's been helping me on the Garrett case," I said.

"Yeah? How?"

Davis stared at me and waited. Something was up. Davis was homicide. He didn't make house calls just to chit-chat. I stared at him a second. The elation I'd felt earlier was gone. I felt the muscles in my stomach tighten a little more.

I said, "She feeds me information."

Matt Davis sipped his coffee, then asked, "What kind of information?"

I sat my cup down on the desk. "Things like Schmitt & Lawson's client list, and Charles Lawson's appointment schedules." I looked him in the eyes again. They were still blank as ever. "What's this all about, Matt?"

"I'm asking the questions," he said. "What did you find out from the information?"

"I think I know what Lawson has been up to," I said. "At least until six months ago."

"What's that?"

"I believe he had been running an investment scam. A Ponzi scheme."

"Got any evidence?"

"Some," I said. "I talked with a guy Lawson scammed."

"And Mable Williams was giving you information about Lawson and his activities."

"Yes," I said.

I looked at him intently. He stared back at me. He was impossible to read.

"What's up, Matt," I said. "Why all the questions about Mable Williams?"

Matt stared at me another second, then said, "She's dead."

For a few seconds I couldn't breathe. The tightness in my stomach twisted into a knot, and suddenly spread up from my midsection into my chest. I felt as if I'd been sucker punched in the gut. It suddenly felt stuffy in the office, and I stood up and opened the window. I sucked in a few deep breaths of the cool autumn air.

Without turning around, I asked, "How'd it happen?"

"Hit-and-run," Matt Davis said.

"When?"

"This morning. Between six-thirty and seven o'clock. She was hit on Mecaslin Street."

Still facing the window, I said, "She was a very careful woman. She wouldn't walk into traffic."

"She was hit on the sidewalk," Davis said. "It looked like they jumped the curb to get her."

Suddenly rage welled up inside me. I clinched my hands into fist and gritted my teeth. They killed her, I thought. They ran her down like an animal and left her lying there in the street.

Davis said, "We think she was hit with an SUV or a truck. The curb is too high for a car without doing damage to it."

I turned back around and looked at him. "Somebody murdered her in the street and left her lying there."

"That's what it looks like," Davis said.

"Any witnesses?"

"No," he said.

I swallowed and cleared my throat. "Who found her?"

"A guy jogging. It was still dark when he called it in. It looks like she was on her way to work. She had one of those zippered, insulated lunch bags with her. We found one of your cards in her purse."

I sat back down at my desk. I felt numb all over.

Davis watched me a second, then said, "Your card had your home number on the back. Why?"

"She called me a few days ago," I said. "She said she was afraid."

"Of what?"

"Lawson had called her into his office and started asking questions about me."

"What about you?"

"He wanted to know how I was digging up so much information on him. He accused her of giving me that information."

"Which she was doing," Davis said. He paused, then asked, "Did Lawson threaten her?"

"Not physically," I said. "But he threatened to fire her. It had rattled her. So I went over and talked with her about it. I gave her my card, wrote my home number on the back, and told her to give me a call if she ever felt threatened."

"She ask you for protection?"

"No," I said. "But Lawson shook her up."

Matt Davis took a sip of his coffee, and then said, "So she leaks information to you and now she's dead."

I nodded, but didn't say anything.

Davis got up and went to the coffeemaker, poured himself more coffee, and then came back and sat down. He said, "You said you know what Lawson's been doing up until six months ago. What's he been up to since?"

I didn't feel like talking anymore. But Davis wasn't going to leave until he got the answers he'd come for.

"I think he's moved on to another scheme," I said.

"You know what kind?"

"Not yet," I said. "But it got Jason Garrett killed. And now Mable Williams."

"So you think Lawson's behind Garrett's murder?"

"I don't think he pulled the trigger himself, but I believe he's involved."

"Got any evidence to back it up?"

"Not right now," I said.

Matt Davis drank more of his coffee, then asked, "And you think Jack Rueben is in this too?"

"You've been doing your homework," I said. I looked at him a second. "Yeah, I think he's the muscle of the operation. He may even be the one that popped Garrett."

"Got any proof?"

"No."

We were silent a moment. I could hear the traffic sounds coming from Broad Street two stories below.

Matt Davis asked, "You think Lawson would run Mable Williams down himself?"

I shook my head. "No. He doesn't have it in him."

"But Jack Rueben does," Davis said. "He has a long rap sheet."

"Rueben would be my number one suspect," I said.

Davis said, "So Lawson went from running a Ponzi scheme to accessory to murder. He must have partners. Know anything about them?"

"No," I lied. Davis gave me the cop stare for a second. I stared back.

Davis said, "So Lawson may have told his business partners Mable Williams had been leaking information to you, and then they send someone, maybe Rueben, to silence her."

"That's what it looks like," I said.

Davis sat his coffee cup on the desk and stood up. He gave me the hard stare some more. "You brought Mable Williams into this mess and now she's dead. That bother you?"

"Yeah," I said. "It bothers me a lot."

CHAPTER FORTY-FIVE

After Matt Davis left, I sat at my desk stunned, staring at a fixed point on the wall across the office. The knot in my stomach had twisted to the point of nausea. I felt like the sole survivor of a train wreck. I sat there for what seemed a long time with a gamut of emotions racing through me: disbelief, sadness, frustration, resentment, and rage. In my mind's eye, I could see Mable Williams the first time I met her in Charles Lawson's office, when for a brief second beneath the ferocious persona she smiled at me. I could still see her sitting in her chair with her feet tucked beneath her, drinking her glass of wine that night she called me. Then a wave of self-doubt washed over me. If I had done more to protect her... if I hadn't dragged her into this mess... if I hadn't taken this case to begin with... she would still be alive.

When someone you know suddenly dies it reminds you how fragile and precious life is, because you never know when it could suddenly end. And murder makes it that much harder to accept.

It suddenly occurred to me that I could use some of Naija's insightfulness, her practicality, and her level-headed common sense.

I snatched the phone and punched her office number. After I identified myself, the receptionist told me Naija was with a patient and asked would I care to leave a message. I said no and told her I would call back later.

I hung up the phone and glanced behind me at the clock on the wall. 11:15. For a brief second I thought about following Julia Garrett's example and tying one on before noon. The office bottle was in the bottom drawer. I could sit here at my desk and get drunk as a monkey. But that wouldn't do me any good. Then I realized the only thing that would make me feel better, bring vindication, would be for me to hunt down the person who killed Mable Williams. Maybe put a bullet between his eyes.

So instead of shaking Jim Beam's hand, I spent the rest of the day going over every detail of the case. I made notes on everything I had discovered, right up until this morning when Lieutenant Matt Davis had walked into my office.

Later Naija called, and I told her about Mable Williams' murder. As always she was empathetic.

"This is getting scary," she said, after I'd finished. "Promise me you'll be careful."

I made an attempt at levity. "If anyone bullies me, I promise to tell the teacher on them."

Sure. Right after I put a bullet between their eyes.

"Do you want me to come over tonight?" Naija asked. "I have my wine tasting group coming over tonight, but I could cancel."

"No," I said. "Keep your plans. I plan to have my own wine tasting soiree when I get home, except it'll be with bourbon."

Naija paused a second, then asked seriously, "Are you sure you're okay?"

"Right as rain," I lied.

Naija said she would call me later, and we hung up.

When I finally left the office, anger still boiled in my veins, but it had been joined by sheer determination. I was certain Richard Murphy had hired Jack Rueben to kill Jason Garrett, and now Mable Williams. I didn't have any proof, but I was determined to find the evidence I needed. How? By going after Charles Lawson. He was the weakest link. I was determined to bring him down with the rest of them, James Barton, Richard Murphy, and especially Jack Rueben.

After I got home, I poured myself a bourbon and went out on the small balcony. It was only about four feet wide, with just enough room for a couple of chairs and a small table. I sat with my feet propped up on the railing. One negative aspect of city living is that you never see the stars at night. The glare from the city lights block them out. Nevertheless, I looked up in the night sky and I made a vow to find her killer.

CHAPTER FORTY-SIX

It was time to poke the beehive and see what flew out at me. The first order of business was Charles Lawson's wife, Amanda. If you want to rattle someone's cage, hassle his wife. Guaranteed to work. It was nine-thirty on a cool Wednesday morning, and I was sitting in my car across the street from Lawson's house on Habersham Road. The house looked like a mansion, probably eight-thousand square feet, no doubt with enough bathrooms that you could use a different one every day for a week. I wondered why the Lawson's needed so much room.

On the way over, I had stopped at a convenience store and bought a coffee and two glazed Krispy Kreme donuts. I took the lid off the coffee, took a sip, and ate a donut. I had two options of what to do next. I could wait until Lawson's wife emerged and then follow her, or I could walk up the long driveway and simply knock on the door. But if I knocked and Amanda Lawson refused to talk to me, then it was ballgame over. So I decided to wait for her to leave the house. Then I would see how things played out from there.

At 10:15, Amanda Lawson pulled out from the driveway in a white Range Rover. She turned left out of the driveway, and I U-turned and fell in behind her. It's easier to tail someone when they don't suspect a tail. I didn't have to be covert. I followed her until she pulled into the parking deck at Phipps Plaza, a high-end shopping mall with stores that catered to Atlanta's affluent clientele. I parked a row behind her and watched as she checked herself in the vanity mirror for what seemed a long time before she finally got out of the car.

She was a good looking woman. She was dressed in black skinny jeans and a long cardigan that covered her derriere. But despite the good looks, my first impression of Amanda Lawson was one of high maintenance. And my first impressions were usually dead-on. I bet she spent a lot of time in front of the mirror. Her blonde hair was perfectly styled. Not a hair out of place. Her makeup deftly applied to perfection. And I could tell by her countenance of arrogance and distain that she thought she was the Queen of Sheba.

This was going to be fun.

I gave her a few moments and then followed her inside the mall.

Then for the next three hours and thirty minutes I watched Amanda Lawson shop. I watched her glide from one ritzy store to another, spending money as if she had just won the lottery. No wonder Lawson had been running an investment scheme. He had to just to keep her happy.

I waited outside a shoe store forty-five minutes while Amanda Lawson tried on shoes. When she emerged, she'd added two additional shopping bags to her growing collection. With shopping bags draped through each arm, she looked like a high-class bag lady. I suddenly realized why they needed such a big house. They needed the space to store all the stuff she bought.

When she came out of the shoe store, I followed her to an Italian restaurant. I gave her about ten minutes, and then I went inside. She was sitting at a table with her shopping bags piled on one of the chairs next to her.

I walked up and sat in the chair opposite her. Her reaction was similar to that of her husband's when I joined him for lunch. Apparently, the Lawson's didn't like unexpected guests dropping in unannounced. She looked up at me from her wine glass first with an expression of surprise, but it quickly changed into a look of disgust and distain. The nerve! A commoner inviting himself to sit at the table with the Queen of Sheba! She glanced around at the empty tables around her, perhaps looking for someone to rescue the queen. There was no one around.

"Hi, Amanda," I said. "My name is Nick Price, and I'm a private detective investigating the murder of Jason Garrett. And now Mable

Williams."

"I don't care who you are," Amanda Lawson said, glaring at me. "I didn't invite you to sit down."

I ignored her remark. "You sure do like to shop. Where does all that money come from?"

"My finances are none of your business," Amanda Lawson said. She reached into her clutch purse and took out her cell phone. It was a pink iPhone. "If you don't leave, I'll call the police."

I said, "And then you'd have to explain to them why I'm here asking questions about two murders. I'll bet they'll be very interested in hearing how much you know."

"I don't know anything about the murders," she said testily. But there was alarm in her voice. She sat her phone down on the table.

"Maybe not," I said. "But you'd probably end up at the precinct for several hours answering questions anyway." I paused a moment to let it sink in, then continued, "Or, you can talk to me now."

"I don't have to talk with you," she said. "You're not a real police officer."

She was beginning to sound like her weasel of a husband.

"You're right," I said. "You don't have to speak to me. But if you don't, I'm going to keep popping up and pestering you until you do."

She picked the phone back up. "I'm calling my husband, and I'm going to tell him you're harassing me."

I reached across the table, plucked it from her hand, and then I dropped it in my jacket pocket.

Amanda Lawson glared at me. The intruding commoner had stolen the Queen of Sheba's cell phone.

"What's he going to do?" I said. "Come and beat me up?"

"You're rude," Amanda Lawson snarled.

"Thanks," I said. "I practice a lot."

She sighed deeply and looked around the room again. No one came to her rescue.

"What do you want?" she said, staring at me.

"What can you tell me about the murder of Mable Williams?"

I knew she probably didn't know anything. But that wasn't why I was pestering her. I wanted to accomplish one thing—push Lawson's buttons. Hearing that I'd hassled his wife would compel him to confront me.

Amanda Lawson shot me a sidelong glance. "I thought Mable Williams' death was an accident."

"The police are now investigating it as a homicide," I said.

So I was going to accomplish two things. Now she could also tell hubby that the police were treating Mable Williams' death as a homicide. More button pushing.

Her eyes suddenly grew wide. "My God," she said. "Why would anyone want to kill Mable Williams?"

"I'd like to know that too," I said. "How well did you know her?"

"Hardly at all," she said. "I only saw her when I went to Charles' office. She never even came to any of the social events Charles invited her to."

A waiter came to the table and tried to give me a menu. I told him I wouldn't be staying. He went away. Amanda didn't call for help. Maybe she had resolved to talk with me so I would leave her alone.

I said, "The police want to know why two homicides happened to people who worked at your husband's law firm."

She took a sip of her wine. "Charles is very upset about both deaths."

"I bet he is," I said. Only because he's up to his rear end in something he has no control over. But I left that out.

I looked at her wedding ring. The diamond looked expensive enough to feed a family of four in Tanzania for five years.

I said, "Your husband's law firm must be doing quite well."

"Charles is one of the best attorneys in the city," she said proudly.

"He has to be," I said, "in order to afford the mansion you live in."

The contemptuous look crept back to Amanda Lawson's face. "How do you know what my house looks like?"

"I followed you from there," I said.

"Oh," she said. She took a sip of wine and looked at me.

"Is the house on Habersham Road the only property you own?"

"No," she said boastfully. "We have another home in West Palm Beach."

I could've guessed the answer to the next question, but I asked anyway. "I bet you have a boat, too?"

"Yes," she said. "At the Palm Beach home. Charles loves to invite friends over and show off his yacht."

This wasn't going anywhere. I needed to wrap it up. But I had learned a couple of things. I knew Lawson was married to a gold digger who shopped like there was no tomorrow. Plus, I had learned about the opulence of their lifestyle. No wonder Lawson had been running a Ponzi scheme. He needed a huge cash flow.

"Thanks for talking with me," I said. I reached inside my coat pocket, retrieved her phone, and handed it to her. "Now you can call your husband and tell on me."

CHAPTER FORTY-SEVEN

It didn't take long before Charles Lawson got his panties in a wad. It was Friday morning, two days after I had accompanied his wife Amanda on her shopping spree. I was sitting in my office with my feet propped up when Charles Lawson barged in without knocking. I love it when a plan comes together. I put my feet down and sat up in my swivel chair. Lawson marched across the office and leaned over my desk.

"You've been harassing my wife," he said.

"I wouldn't call it that. Harassment is such a harsh term."

"I don't care what you call it," he said. He pointed his finger at me. "Stay away from my wife."

"Aren't we grumpy this morning," I said. "Get up on the wrong side of the bed?"

Lawson was wearing a nice navy blue suit with gold pinstripes, a crisp white shirt, gold cufflinks, and a red tie. The suit fit perfectly. It must have cost close to eight grand.

"Nice suit," I said. "Your wife buy it for you?"

"Listen to me," he said, shaking his finger in front of me. "I'm telling you to stay away from my wife."

I ignored him. "Your wife likes to shop. She must have spent a few thousand the other morning. How much does she spend in a week?"

"I told you to lay off my wife," he said.

"No you didn't," I said. "Actually you said to stay away from your wife."

"Don't toy with me," he said.

His finger twitched up and down. His words seemed rehearsed, as if he'd written his lines down and practiced them in front of the mirror. Maybe he practiced the finger pointing too. He probably thought it would intimidate me. It didn't. I wasn't one of his underlings he could frighten by yelling and screaming. He had only been in the office a moment and was already beginning to irritate me.

I said casually, "Amanda and I had a nice conversation over lunch," I said. "Where did you get the money for your houses? And the yacht?"

"Keep your nose out of my business," he said. "Or else."

"Or else, what?" I said.

"Or I'll make you."

He gave me his best courtroom lawyer stare. It didn't work for him. The stare only works if you look intimidating, which Lawson didn't. I wondered if they taught the stare in law school.

"What are you going to do," I said. "Call your friends and have them try to beat me up again?"

"I'll do it myself," he said.

He took a weak swing at me. It wasn't much of a swing. In fact, it might have been the first punch Lawson had ever thrown. I moved my head back and he missed. I was still sitting down, but I hit him with a hard right that landed in his ribcage. It was a good, solid punch. The air whooshed out of him and he backed up. He bent over, panting and gagging like a cat with a hairball stuck in its throat.

I got up and walked around the desk. "Take deep breaths," I said. "It'll pass in a minute."

He tried to talk, and the words came out between gasp for breath. "Why…did…you…hit…me?"

"Because you tried to hit me," I said. I stared at him a second. "Tell me about Mable Williams?"

"It was…an accident."

"Sure," I said. "Do you know they had to run up on the sidewalk to get to her?"

"I had…nothing… to do with that."

"Strange how it happened right after you questioned her about me."

"I don't know...what you're talking about," Charles Lawson said.

His breathing was getting better, but he was still bent over holding his ribcage. He'd have a good bruise in the morning to remember me by.

"Tell me about the Ponzi scheme you were running," I said.

He straightened up and took a couple of deep breaths. He stared at me harshly. He looked like he wanted to throw another punch at me, but then thought better of it.

"I don't know what you're talking about," he said. His breathing was still labored but at least he could talk again.

"Where'd you get the money for your houses?" I said again. "The yacht. The endless shopping trips for your wife. Where's the money coming from?"

"That's none of your business," he said.

I started to say, "Well I'm making it my business," but didn't. Instead, I said, "Why'd you stop the scam? Run out of investors?"

The tizzy he had worked himself up into had dissipated. Nothing like a good punch in the ribs to bring a man back to his senses. He glared at me a second, then said, "You don't know anything."

"I know you were running an investment scam," I said. "And now you've moved on to a different scam with a couple of business partners that play for keeps. Plus, you're involved with two murders."

"I had...." He stopped himself from saying anything else. "I don't know what you're talking about."

"Yes, you do," I said. "You know exactly what I'm talking about."

"Keep your nose out of my business," he warned. He gave me the hard stare again.

"And if I don't?"

"You'll find out," he said.

"What are you going to do?" I asked. "Go tell your new business partners that you need someone else killed."

Lawson didn't say anything.

I looked him in the eye. "You're attracting too much attention," I said. "How long do you think it's going to be before they start thinking of you as a liability rather than an asset?"

"Stay out of my business," he warned again.

I ignored him. He was easy to ignore. "You're in over your head with these guys. The minute they consider you a liability they'll send their hired gun to kill you."

"I'm warning you," he said. "Keep your nose out of my business."

He was still trying to talk tough, but his voice carried a tremble of fear. What I said had shaken him up. I saw the fear in his eyes.

"I'm not going away," I said. "I'm going to keep digging until I find out why two people are dead and who killed them."

"You've been warned," Charles Lawson said. "Stay away from me. And stay away from my wife."

Then he turned around and walked out of the office.

CHAPTER FORTY-EIGHT

Naija's condo was downtown, close to the Georgia Aquarium and across the street from the World of Coca-Cola. It was Sunday evening and we had just finished a shrimp dinner that I had cooked. The shrimp had been fantastic, cooked in the oven under high heat, with garlic, pepper, olive oil, and a sprinkling of my famous homemade seasoning. The famous seasoning was actually garlic and herb dry salad dressing mix, but I wasn't going to tell. To go with the shrimp, I made us a salad with spinach leaves. Of course, mine had bacon chips hidden under the spinach. Naija thought I was Chef Extraordinaire. She was sitting on her couch, her back against the armrest, and her feet on my lap. She was nursing a glass of Pinot Noir. I had a beer.

We sat in silence for several minutes. Then Naija grinned at me and said, "I saw you put the bacon chips on your salad."

I feigned shock. "Shame on you for spying on me. I thought you were relaxing while I cooked dinner."

"I was, but I peeked into the kitchen to see how it was going." She poked my ribs with her toes, then said, "And just in time to see you sprinkle the bacon chips on your salad."

I shot her a sheepish grin. "I can't keep anything from you, can I?"

"No," she said. "So for your punishment, you have to give me a foot massage." She wiggled her toes at me. They had bright red polish on them.

"Well, Ms. Smarty Pants, I was planning on doing that anyway." I put down my bottle on the coffee table and began massaging her left foot, massaging the ball at the base of the toes, and working my way to the arch. She made a small moaning sound and instantly relaxed.

As I worked my magic on her foot, she asked, "Lawson actually tried to punch you?"

I chuckled at her. She made it sound as if Lawson and I had been on the playground at school and he had thrown a punch at me. I said, "It wasn't much of a punch. In fact, I think it was the first punch he's ever thrown."

"What did you do?"

"I moved my head and he missed." Then I added, "Then I punched him in the ribs."

She shot me one of her disapproving looks. Knowing she abhors violence, I realized I should have left out my punch from the narrative. I said in my defense, "He tried to hit me first."

Another strange look came from the other end of the couch. "You know how childish that sounds."

"It's the truth."

I moved my massage therapy to her right foot. She let out a small moan of pleasure. "That feels good," she said. "I could get used to this."

"Nick's massage parlor is open 24-7."

She giggled. "I don't think they're called parlors anymore. But I'll have to remember Nick's *parlor* is open 24-7." Then she sunk further into her pillow. After a few minutes, she said, "It was a terrible thing that happened to Mable Williams. You feel like talking about it?"

I shrugged. "There's not much to say." I reached over and took a drink of my beer. Then continued, "She helped me with my investigation and now she's dead. She was killed because she helped me."

Naija looked at me with an expression of concern. "And now you feel guilty about it."

I nodded. "I dragged her into this mess."

"You had no way of knowing the outcome," Naija said. "And the reason she helped you in the first place was because she wanted to see justice done."

I looked at her. There was genuine concern in her eyes. She knew this was bugging me. Naija had the uncanny ability to see emotions that I kept hidden. Though we'd only been together six months, she could read me like a book, and when I needed her voice of logic and wisdom, she was always there for me.

I said, "I convinced her to help me. I used her for the information she could give me, but I didn't consider the consequences. If I hadn't dragged her into it, she'd be alive today."

"You can't blame yourself," Naija said. "It's not your fault. If you could've prevented it, you would have. But you couldn't. Now you have to make sure justice is done for both Mable Williams and Jason Garrett."

I nodded my head. She was right. I couldn't beat myself up about it. But if I got the chance to shoot the guy that killed her, I would take the shot, and I certainly wouldn't feel any guilt about that.

Naija asked, "And you think Charles Lawson told his business partners about his suspicions about Mable Williams giving you information?"

"I think that's exactly what happened," I said. "And I think Lawson did the same to Jason Garrett. He ratted both of them out, and they killed them."

I reached over and drank most of my beer in a long gulp. Naija took another minuscule sip of her wine. Her glass was still over half full.

I moved my massage therapy back to Naija's left foot. She moaned softly again. After a moment, she said, "So Lawson had been running a Ponzi scheme?"

I nodded. "Until about six or seven months ago," I said. "Then he ran out of investors."

"And that's when he became involved with the other men."

"Yes," I said. "I'm not sure how they came to know one another, but now they're running some other scheme."

Naija thought for a moment, then asked, "And you think the banker...what was his name?"

"Greg Little."

"You think he was involved in Lawson's Ponzi scheme?"

"The payment checks were drawn on First Georgia Savings," I said. "That makes me suspicious."

"And now you believe both Lawson and Little are in business with Richard Murphy and his partner."

"It makes sense," I said. "I think Murphy discovered the Ponzi scheme Lawson and Little were running and then blackmailed them into helping with his own scam."

"What about the documents from Jason Garrett's computer?"

"I think they have a lot of significance," I said. "Though I'm not sure in what way. But I'm going to go over them more thoroughly and see if they lead anywhere. I'm convinced Garrett had discovered something and was killed because of it."

"So you've made progress in the case," Naija said encouragingly.

I shrugged again. "I think the problem with this case is that every time I follow a clue, it only leads to more clues."

"I'm sure you'll uncover more when you look into the documents further."

We were silent for a while. I began to massage her calves. Naija had her eyes closed, and made more of the moaning sounds. After a time, I looked at her and saw her staring at me intently, her dark eyes gleaming.

"Hey, massage boy," she said. "Do you give full body massages?"

"It'll cost you an extra dollar," I said.

"Put it on my tab," she said, and stood up. Then she walked down the hallway toward her bedroom.

And like a good massage boy, I followed her.

CHAPTER FORTY-NINE

I probably had enough on Lawson to have him put away for a long time, perhaps for the rest of his life. Bernie Madoff had gotten a hundred and fifty years for his massive Ponzi scheme after swindling billions. Though Lawson's scam wasn't as big, I was certain he would get twenty to thirty years behind bars. But I wasn't much interested in taking down Lawson for his Ponzi scheme. I was more interested in bringing down Lawson's partners for the murders of Jason Garrett and Mable Williams. The Feds could bring charges against Lawson for his Ponzi scheme later.

There was another reason that kept me from going to the Feds. If I turned Lawson in now, the others he was in business with would run, get off scot-free. Perhaps even set up another scam in another city. Of course there was a chance that Lawson would talk and the cops could snatch the others before they got away, but I wasn't willing to take that chance.

So Monday morning I went to the office early, determined to dig up more evidence. I was convinced the documents from Garrett's laptop labeled DISCOVERY held the key behind Garrett's murder. After all, the documents had linked Lawson, Barton, and Murphy together. So maybe they held other secrets. The answer had to be there somewhere.

But there was a virtual mountain of paperwork. Each document contained around twenty pages, all filled with legalese. Four hours later, I began to get discouraged. I hadn't discovered anything. Besides Lawson's signature, there were a lot of other signatures on the documents of people I didn't know. I realized I could sit here for days and not find anything. The elation I had felt when I discovered Lawson's Ponzi scheme had long since gone.

I needed help.

And I knew just the person to call.

I had a friend who was a documents expert. I turned around and checked the clock on the wall behind my desk. It was 11:15. I gave him a call and he told me to come right over.

I printed out several pages of the documents that contained signatures, copied the files to a flash drive, and headed out.

David Snodgrass had been a forensic document examiner with the FBI for over ten years, before opening his own documents examination business. Since each set of documents had different signatures, and since I didn't have anything to compare them against, I was hoping that David Snodgrass could give me some insight of whether the signatures were forgeries. Again, this was another hunch I had without anything to substantiate it.

David Snodgrass had an office in a small brick office park on North Druid Hills Road, tucked between a debt consolidation company and a pain management clinic. The office had an oak door with brass hardware, and a small black sign with gold lettering that read: SNODGRASS DOCUMENT LABORATORIES. Below the name the words read: Board-Certified Documents Examiner & Handwriting Expert. I opened the door and went inside. A young woman with strawberry blonde hair sat behind a reception desk. She looked to be in her early twenties. A name plate on the desk said her name was Kayla Tindell. She looked bored.

"I'm Nick Price," I said. "I'm here to see David Snodgrass."

She looked at me a second, as if I'd awakened her. "Do you have an appointment?" she asked.

I glanced around the empty office. "Do I need one?"

"Mr. Snodgrass would rather have clients make an appointment first," she said.

She had a slight lisp. Then I saw the reason why. I caught a glimpse of the barbell through her pierced tongue. Ouch. I guessed the piercing was new to her and she was still getting used to talking with it.

"I'm not a client," I said. "I'm a private investigator."

Just then, David Snodgrass came out of his office and immediately recognized me. He strode over and we shook hands, and then I followed him back into his office. "Nick Price," he said, smiling. "It's been a while. How's the private eye business?"

"From the looks of this place, not as good as the document examination business," I said.

Snodgrass sat behind his desk and I sat in one of his plush client chairs.

"There's a lot of funny paper out there that needs examining," Snodgrass said. "I get a lot of documents from divorce cases, mostly from soon-to-be-ex-wives tracking down assets from their husbands. The husbands go to outlandish lengths to hide assets. They fake bank statements, realty documents, titles to personal property, and everything in between. You'd be surprised to see how far they'd go. But if the wife has a good lawyer, and they hire me, I identify the fake documents and track down the real ones. Sometimes, it's the other way around, with the wife hiding property from the husband, but mostly it's the husbands doing it."

"Ever get any threats from the husbands?"

"I had a guy threaten to kill me once because his wife took his two hundred thousand dollar sailboat in a divorce."

"What did you do about it?"

Snodgrass chuckled. "I explained to him that if he made good on his threat, sailboats aren't allowed in prison."

"I bet that shut him up," I said.

"I get threatened all the time by angry husbands," Snodgrass said. He chuckled again. "They think they're slick, but when I find all their hiding places, it kind of makes them mad."

"Let me know if you ever need help with any of them," I said.

Snodgrass shrugged. "They're just angry that they got caught," he said. "So what brings you my way this morning?"

"I need your help with a case I'm working on." I handed him the folder I'd been carrying with me. "I got these documents from the computer of a murder victim."

David Snodgrass nodded, but showed no reaction. To most people, coming into contact with evidence in a murder investigation would raise a few eyebrows, but not a seasoned former FBI agent. Though he had worked in the fraud section of the FBI, David had been involved with his share of murder investigations. People will go to great lengths, including murder, to cover up their fraudulence.

I continued, "Those are just a few of what I found. They all have different signatures on them, and I was hoping you'd take a look and tell me what you think."

"Do you think the signatures are forgeries?"

"I don't know," I said. "I don't have anything to compare them to."

"Let's see what we have," Snodgrass said. He opened the folder and looked at the documents a moment.

After a moment, he looked up and said, "These aren't the originals."

"No," I said. "These were probably scanned from the originals."

"Can you get the originals?"

"No," I said. "I'm not sure where the originals are."

He took the documents from the folder and turned around to a small table to his right. There was a round magnifying lamp with a retractable arm clamped to the edge of the desk. He took one of the documents and studied it under the magnifying lamp. He studied the document at different angles. I didn't know what he was looking for. He did the same procedure with the other seven documents I'd brought. I sat and watched and waited. Then he took out another magnifying glass and studied the documents again. I waited some more.

When he finished, he straightened up and sat back in his swivel chair.

"The signatures on these documents have similar characteristics," David Snodgrass said.

"Meaning they could be forgeries?"

"Exactly," he said. "Here let me show you what I'm talking about."

He took out his huge magnifying glass, grabbed one of the documents, and leaned over his desk. He held the magnifying glass so I could look through it. I leaned forward.

"Look here," he said, pointing with the point of a pen. "See how the E on the signature of Barbara Matthews is slanted to the right. Plus, look at the loop of the E. See how tight it looks."

"Yes," I said.

"Now take a look at this other signature," he said, moving the document a little. Now I was looking at Charles Lawson's signature. "See how the same letters have the same characteristics of the other signature."

I looked at him. "You're right. The letters are the same."

I studied the signatures again. I sat back in my chair. I couldn't suppress a grin. Looks like my boy Charlie was forging signatures. I could add that to my growing list of evidence.

David Snodgrass said, "Judging by your reaction, you found what you were looking for."

"So, you're confident these could be forgeries?" I asked.

Snodgrass nodded. "In addition to the lettering characteristics, the pressure used on the signatures is the same." He explained further. "Every person uses a different pressure when they write. Of course, that alone isn't enough to substantiate forgery, but coupled with the individual lettering characteristics, I would say the signatures were signed by the same person."

"And all the documents I brought in are signed the same way?" I said.

"Yes," he said. "All the documents have the same signature characteristics."

Then I asked the question that had been on my mind even before I walked in. "So you could say with certainty that Charles Lawson forged the other signatures?"

"If Charles Lawson signed his own name to these documents," Snodgrass said.

I stopped breathing for a second. "What do you mean?"

"It's possible that Charles Lawson's signature could be a forgery, too," Snodgrass said. "We don't have any authentic signatures of Charles Lawson to compare to. But if he signed his own name, then he's your forger."

He reached into his desk, pulled out a small white box, handed it to me, and said, "Here you can have this. You can use that to look through the other documents you have."

I opened the box. Inside was a large round magnifying glass. I took it out of the box, held it up, and peered through the glass.

Snodgrass chuckled, and said, "If you get a pipe and carry that around, you'll look like Sherlock Holmes."

"But I'd have to trade my fedora for a deerstalker tweed hat," I said.

Snodgrass smiled. "On second thought, you better stick with the fedora."

We both laughed. I thanked him for his help, and stood up to leave.

Then my curiosity got the best of me, and I asked, "What's the story with your secretary?"

"She's my wife's niece," Snodgrass said. "You noticed the pierced tongue."

"I couldn't help it," I said. "She's sounds like she has a mouthful of marbles."

"She's had it about a week," he said. "She hasn't got used to talking with it yet. Her boyfriend talked her into it."

"Where there is love, there is pain," I said.

"Then she must really be in love," David Snodgrass said. "Just thinking about it makes me squeamish."

In the reception area, Kayla was sitting at her desk still looking bored. She had earplugs in her ears, listening to music on her iPhone.

"Have a nice day," she said, slurring the words again.

As she spoke, I caught another glimpse of the metal barbell through her tongue. It made my tongue hurt to think about it.

CHAPTER FIFTY

I spent the next two days tracking down one of the people whose signatures Snodgrass had labeled as a forgery. Her name was Barbara Matthews, and she tended bar in the Virginia Highlands area. I went over at 3:30 during the lull part of the day, after the lunch crowd had left and before the evening crowd started. Barbara Matthews poured me a draft beer, sat a napkin down on the bar, and placed the mug on top of it.

"Charles Lawson was my lawyer," she said. "He helped me with a problem I had."

"What kind of problem?" I asked.

She shot me one of those it's-none-of-your-business looks. She was good looking, probably in her mid-twenties, with shoulder-length black hair, full lips, and deep-set hazel eyes. She was wearing a sleeveless white shirt and black shorts.

She thought about it another second, and then said, "I had a DUI about a year ago. Charles Lawson helped me with it."

I took a sip of beer, and then asked, "His law firm is pretty expensive, isn't it?"

"All lawyers are expensive," she said.

"If you don't mind my asking," I said. "How much did he charge you?"

"He didn't charge me anything," she said. "I found him through Legal Aid."

"So he helped you pro bono," I said.

She shrugged and smiled. She had a radiant smile. "If that's what they call doing it for free."

"Did he resolve your case for you?" I asked.

"He was great," Barbara said. "I only had to pay a fine and take a DUI driving class. I was lucky. I could have lost my license, and even gone to jail."

"I'm glad it worked out for you," I said. "Has he been in contact with you since he resolved your case?"

"No," she said. She glanced down the bar. The man at the other end was holding up his empty glass. "Excuse me a second."

She went down the bar and mixed another drink for him. He and I were the only two sitting at the bar. When she came back, she poured me another draft and placed it in front of me.

"What's this all about anyway?" she asked. "Why all the questions?"

I knew the reaction I would get, but I said it anyway. "I found your name on some documents on a murder victim's laptop."

Her eyes grew wide. "Murder! Who was murdered?"

"One of the associates at Schmitt & Lawson," I said.

"Why would my name be on documents from a murder victim's computer?" She sounded alarmed and worried.

"That's what I'm trying to find out," I said. "Have you made any large purchases lately? A car? A house?"

She snorted a laugh. "On my salary? I can barely afford rent, much less anything else."

I took a copy of the document with her signature on it, folded it in half so she couldn't see what kind of document it was, and handed it to her.

"Is that your signature?" I asked.

"That's my name," she said, "but not my signature."

She turned around, grabbed an order notepad, tore off a sheet, and signed the back of it. "This is what my signature looks like," she said, handing me the paper.

I compared both signatures, and put both papers in my jacket pocket. There was no question about it. She hadn't signed the document I had retrieved from Garrett's computer.

She asked, "So someone forged my signature?"

"It appears so," I said.

"Who would do such a thing?"

"That's what I'm looking into," I said.

She looked at me with a worried expression, and asked, "What should I do?"

"Check your credit report," I said. "You can do it online. If you see anything that looks abnormal, contact the credit agency."

She nodded, but still had the worried look on her face. Of course, she was going to see discrepancies on her credit report, but I left it alone. I didn't want her running to Charles Lawson and letting the cat out of the bag. I asked her to keep our conversation between us. She agreed. Then I thanked her and left.

Now I knew Charles Lawson had forged Barbara Matthews' signature. She hadn't spoken to him in a year, but the document in my jacket pocket had been dated four months ago.

CHAPTER FIFTY-ONE

It was five-fifteen when I got back to my office. I sat behind my desk and thought about the case some more. I was certain Lawson was forging signatures and that he was getting the identities from people he had helped through pro bono cases. I also suspected Lawson's business partners were stealing those identities to use in the scam they were running. Nothing like extending a helping hand to those less fortunate, especially if you make a ton of money in the process.

Since the files from Garrett's computer were real estate related, security deeds, warranty deeds, deeds of trust, assignment of mortgages, and loan applications, I suspected they were running some type of real estate scam.

To confirm my suspicion, I dove back into the documents from Garrett's computer. First, I printed out several more pages that contained signatures, and spent the next several hours checking them with the magnifying glass David Snodgrass had given me. All the signatures had the same characteristics of the signature of Charles Lawson.

Next, I checked the names against the client list I had received from Mable Williams. She was still helping me. God bless you Mable Williams. Thus far, all the names were from pro bono cases.

I had a hunch about the other names I had checked so far. I called Sergeant Mike Soratelli who was working the night shift this week.

"What do you want?" he asked. It was more of an accusation than a question. Then he said, "No don't tell me. You need a favor."

"You should join a carnival," I said. "You could be the guy that guesses your weight."

"I can guess your weight," he said. "Two-hundred pounds of crap. What do you want?"

I told him what I needed and I emailed him the list of names.

"I'll call you back," Soratelli said, and hung up.

I glanced at the clock behind my desk. It was 9:30. I had been at this for hours and suddenly I felt famished. I hadn't had anything to eat all day. While I waited for Soratelli to call me back, I went into the kitchen alcove to make myself a sandwich. In the back of the fridge, I found some salami and a couple slices of cheese. I couldn't remember how long they had been in the fridge. The expiration date on the salami package was a week old, but the meat didn't smell bad and still looked edible. Nothing was growing on it anyway. I could only imagine Naija's reaction if she could see me standing there contemplating eating expired meat. I shrugged, put everything together with a little mayonnaise on wheat, and ate at my desk, washing everything down with a beer.

Soratelli called back forty-five minutes later.

"All the people you gave me have a record," he said. "They were all arrested for minor offenses: shoplifting, DUIs, public drunkenness, things like that."

"Who's the attorney of record listed?" I said.

There was pause. I could hear him tapping his keyboard, one key at a time. After a moment, he came back on the line.

"It's that Lawson guy," he said, as if he'd just discovered gold. "You gonna tell me what this is about?"

"I don't know what it's about," I lied. "I'm just doing some late night research."

"Stop holding out on me," Soratelli nearly yelled into the phone.

"I wouldn't think of it," I said calmly and hung up.

I knew it was getting late, but I had to continue. With my hunger satisfied, I felt reinvigorated. I knew I was onto something, and I didn't intend to let it go.

For the next hour and a half, I tackled more of the documents. These had the most recent dates on them. I felt I was making progress. Some of the files were assignment of mortgage documents using MERS to transfer the mortgages. I didn't know what MERS stood for. But after a little research, I learned that MERS stood for Mortgage Electronic Registration System, an electronic transfer method that eliminated the need to go to the county courthouse to register property transfers. As I studied the files, I noticed that some of them had mortgages transferred to First Georgia Savings from several other banks. Other had transfers from First Georgia Savings to Tanner Investments under the names from the stolen identities. So far, all the documents I had examined were mortgage transfers from banks and not individual homeowners. That fact could mean nothing, but I found it interesting. There was the possibility that all these properties were foreclosures. When the economy crashed in 2008, there had been a tidal wave of foreclosures in the metro Atlanta area, most of them occurring within three years following the crash. But even now, with the economy still in recovery, there are still more foreclosures than before the housing bubble burst. And all those foreclosures meant a lot of empty homes sitting in legal limbo. They could be easy pickings for a band of criminals who knew their way around the system.

Since I knew Barbara Matthews' signature was a forgery, I examined her documents further. The first document was a loan application for a house in Vinings worth $330,000. According to the application, Barbara Matthews was a registered nurse making $96,000 a year. I grinned to myself. Maybe Barbara Matthews moonlighted as a bartender on her off days.

I sat back in my chair and thought a moment. So I knew they weren't simply forging signatures of pro bono clients. They were also stealing their identities, and creating falsified credit histories, and filing fraudulent loan applications.

So I dove back into the files looking for more clues. Thirty minutes later, another document in particular caught my eye. I hadn't seen it previously, but now it jumped out at me. The name on this loan application was Roy Upshaw. His application was for a house in Decatur worth $220,000, and it had Roy's occupation as a mechanic with an annual salary of $67,000.

I lost it. I burst out laughing. If Roy-boy was pulling down over sixty grand a year, the least he could do was buy some windows to replace the boarded up ones in his trailer home. Maybe even throw down enough for a new front door, since the one he had was about to fall off.

Then the reality of what was in front of me hit home. I sat staring at the documents. These documents were the reason for Garrett's murder. None of the other names on the other documents would have meant anything to Garrett; but Roy Upshaw, initially, had been Garrett's pro bono case and he would have recognized the name immediately. After discovering the document, Garrett had probably confronted Lawson about them. And then shortly after that, Garrett was murdered.

CHAPTER FIFTY-TWO

It was near midnight when I got ready to leave the office. It had been a long day, and I was tired. I had covered a lot of ground and dug-up enough circumstantial evidence to put Charles Lawson, James Barton, and Richard Murphy away for a long time. But I had one problem. The evidence wasn't solid evidence. It really wasn't evidence at all, since I only had copies of fraudulent documents. I didn't know where, or by whom they had originated. For all I knew, Jason Garrett could have created the documents himself. And if I turned everything over to the Feds now, any two-bit lawyer with half a brain could get the evidence thrown out before the trial even started. Another caveat was that I still didn't have any evidence against them for the murders of Jason Garrett and Mable Williams.

I stepped out of the office and locked the door. The building was empty and quiet. The Vietnamese restaurant downstairs had closed at seven. There was an eerie silence in the small hallway.

The wooden stairs creaked loudly as I went down. Every sound was amplified. I sounded like a stampede of elephants coming down the stairs. I came out on the sidewalk and locked the outer door. A light rain was falling. I pulled my hat down low over my eyes and pulled up the collar of my trench coat. I felt like a real private eye as I stood there on the sidewalk in the rain. There was no traffic. The windows on the loft apartments along the street were dark. A bum slept in the doorway of the dry cleaners across the street. The bustling nightlife of Buckhead seemed a million miles away. In this part of town, unless the Hawks are playing at Philips

Arena, or the Falcons have a night game at the Georgia Dome, the businesses close when the sun goes down. Office workers head to the suburbs. City dwellers scurry inside. At night, downtown takes on a sinister atmosphere. And this late at night, it seemed even more sinister.

Suddenly the hairs on the back of my neck stood up. As a cop, I had learned to listen and trust my instincts, and right now, my instincts were screaming. I stood there, thinking. Two people had been murdered. I had annoyed a lot of people. Two goons had assaulted me. Richard Murphy had threatened me. It would be foolish of me not to take the threat seriously.

I walked to my left and paused at the entrance of the alley where I parked my car. My car was at the end of the alleyway. The narrow alleyway emptied into another street that ran behind the Vietnamese restaurant. I listened. After a moment, I heard a noise like a tin can rattling on the pavement. I waited, listening.

There was no other sound.

It might be nothing, a cat in the alleyway scrounging for food, a homeless person moving around between the buildings.

I didn't move. I listened some more.

Nothing.

I saw no movement in the shadows.

If someone were going to come after me, this would be the perfect time. Catch me going to my car in a dark alley, put a bullet in the back of my head, and then walk out to a waiting car on the adjacent street. They could vanish in seconds.

I took my 9mm out of its holster and chambered a round. Then I turned into the alley and took a few steps.

I paused and listened again.

Nothing.

Holding the 9mm at waist level in front of me, I took a few more steps into the alley. My car was parked to the right, close to the adjacent building so other traffic could squeeze by.

I took a few more steps.

Then I heard the shot and saw the muzzle flash simultaneously.

Absolute Justice

It hit the brick wall to my right, close to my face. I felt the sting on the right side of my face as brick particles from the ricochet dug into my skin. Another shot boomed. The bullet hit the brick wall again, this time closer to my head. I felt the sting from the ricochet again.

I saw a silhouette move just beyond my car.

I raised my gun and fired once. I heard a grunt and the sound of a body hitting the ground. I heard his gun clatter to the pavement. Then I heard footsteps running at the other end of the alleyway. I ran toward the sound and I heard a car door slam, and then an engine start. As I reached the end of the alley, I heard the tires squeal. There was a black Ford Explorer pulling away from the curb. I raised my gun and fired four quick rounds into the back of the car. The back glass shattered. A taillight exploded. The SUV swerved right, then left, and raced around a corner.

I stood there a moment, taking a few deep breaths. My heart pounded in my chest. Then I went back to my car and took out a flashlight from the glove box. I looked at the dead man lying face up in front of my car. His gun lay at his side. It was a .38 revolver. The dead man's blank eyes stared up at nothing. The light rain fell on his face. The bullet had caught him just under the left eye and exited the back of his head. There was blood and tissue on the pavement beside the man's head. He looked to be in his late twenties or early thirties. I knew he was dead, but I felt his neck for a pulse anyway. Nothing. I dug in his pockets and pulled out his wallet. Inside were five one-hundred dollar bills and two twenties. His driver's license said his name was Daryl Brock. Someone named Daryl had hired Roy Upshaw to beat up the banker Greg Little. I looked at the birthdate on the license. He was twenty-four-years-old.

I walked back to the entrance of the alley. No one was on the street. The bum asleep in the doorway of the cleaners had not moved. There were no lights on in the loft apartments along the street. I took out my cell and called the police.

CHAPTER FIFTY-THREE

Police cruisers were the first cars to show up. Four cruisers squealed to a halt diagonally in front of both entrances to the alley. I sat my gun on top of my car and put my hands up. One of the patrol officers, who looked fresh out of the academy, told me not to move. He had his gun drawn on me. I didn't move. The other cops had their guns drawn too. I told the rookie pointing his gun at me who I was and what had happened. He watched me closely as I pulled out my wallet to show him my P.I. license. He took the license and told me to wait there. Then he went back to his patrol car.

A few minutes later Sergeant Soratelli drove up in an unmarked car. He parked behind the patrol cars and walked into the alley where I was standing.

"I was on my way home when I heard the radio call," he said.

"Sorry to ruin your evening," I said.

"Tell me what happened," Soratelli said.

I told him what happened.

"This makes three bodies," Soratelli said. "You're attracting a lot of attention."

"It seems that way."

"You hurt?" Soratelli asked.

"No," I said.

"You've got blood on your face," he said.

I touched the right side of my face. There was blood on my hand.

"When he shot at me, he hit the brick wall where I was standing."

"You want to have the EMTs look at you?"

"No," I said. "It's not that bad."

"Who's the perp?" Soratelli asked, motioning toward the body.

"Guy named Daryl Brock." I handed him the wallet I had taken off the body.

"You're not supposed to touch the body," Soratelli said.

"I'll try to remember that next time," I said.

Soratelli walked back to his car and ran Brock's name to see if he had any priors. I stood in the soft drizzle and waited. A few minutes later, Soratelli came back.

"He's been arrested a number of times," he said. "Assault, possession of stolen property, a couple of B & E's. Small time stuff."

"A guy named Daryl hired Roy Upshaw to beat up the banker, Greg Little." I pointed at Brock's body. "Could be the same guy."

"Upshaw have a last name on the guy that hired him?"

"No, just Daryl," I said.

The medical examiner drove up, got out of his van, and came over to look at the body.

"One right through the head," he said. He looked at Soratelli. "You guys through with the body?"

"Yeah," Soratelli said. "You can have him."

The ME motioned and two EMTs took a gurney from the van with a body bag on top. They rolled it over to Brock's body, opened the body bag, and got Brock inside. Then they wheeled the body to the van and slid it inside.

Soratelli asked, "You think he's the one that popped Garrett?"

"I don't think so," I said.

Soratelli gave me a suspicious look. "What makes you say that?"

"This was too amateurish," I said. "The person that hit Garrett was a professional." I motioned toward the coroner's van. "That guy was an amateur. I don't think he knew what he was doing."

"Maybe he was stepping up to the big time," Soratelli said. "And you were supposed to be his first hit."

"Could be," I said. "But he was a bad shot."

"Lucky for you," Soratelli said.

I nodded but didn't say anything.

A crime scene tech came and put Brock's gun in an evidence bag.

Soratelli gave me the hairy eyeball again. "You said there were two of them. Get a look at the other guy?"

"No," I said. "It was too dark. He ran off when I hit Brock. Hopped in his car and drove off."

Soratelli asked, "Get the tag number?"

"No," I said. "He was smart enough not to turn on his lights."

"What kind of car?"

"A black Ford Explorer," I said. "I put a few rounds into the back of it. The back window is shattered. Plus, I shot out one of the tail lights."

Soratelli didn't say anything. He stood staring down the dark alleyway, thinking. After a moment, he asked, "Wasn't the tag number you gave me from a Ford Explorer?"

I looked at him a second. "You figure that out by yourself, or did you have help?"

"Don't be such a wiseass all the time," Soratelli said. "The tag number belonged to Jack Rueben."

"No getting anything over on you," I said.

"We'll put out an APB on the Explorer and Rueben. If he continues to drive it around, someone will notice it. Especially if it's shot up."

"There may be damage to the front end too," I said.

Soratelli stared at me. "You think he was the one who ran down Mable Williams?"

"I think Rueben's the muscle behind whatever is going on," I said.

Then Soratelli asked, "You making any progress on the case?"

"Nothing solid," I said.

I wasn't going to tell him what I had discovered earlier. I didn't know exactly what it all meant, but I wanted to dig into it further before saying anything.

Soratelli said, "You must be getting close. Before they just wanted to scare you away by beating you up. Now they're trying to kill you."

When the crime scene guys finished, Soratelli said he didn't have any other questions for me. It looked like a justifiable kill. I agreed. Soratelli left, and I got in my car and drove home.

I got home at three-thirty in the morning. I went into the kitchen, poured a glass of bourbon, sat at the kitchen counter, and drank it.

I finished my drink, and went into the bathroom and looked at my reflection in the mirror. Now my face looked like five miles of bad road. The right side of my face had several small nicks and cuts from the ricochet. I looked like I'd been in a fight with a thorn bush. The thorn bush must have had a mean left hook. I washed my face to clean the blood and dislodge the brick mortar embedded in my skin. When I checked myself in the mirror again, I didn't look any better. My left eye—still black from my fight with Frick and Frack in the parking garage at Charles Lawson's office—was no longer swollen, but was still a mixture of dark blue and black. Now at least my face was balanced. It was banged up on both sides. I stood there staring at myself in the mirror for a long time. It had been a very long day and it showed all over my face. It had started out early Tuesday morning and it was now early Wednesday morning. In the past twenty-four hours, I had discovered a lot about the case. And I had killed a man. I felt bad about that. But Brock had been intent on killing me. Kill or be killed. It was part of the job.

I took a shower and went to bed.

CHAPTER FIFTY-FOUR

Thursday morning the cavalry showed up at my office in the form of Ray Norris and Tony Veneto. They came in armed to the teeth. Ray wore a black fedora and a black trench coat, and he had his right hand stuffed deep in the coat's pocket. He walked stiffly as if he had a wooden leg. When he opened the coat, he revealed a twelve-gauge shotgun. There was a 9mm strapped to his side. Tony wore a black turtleneck and a black sport coat, and I could see the bulge of his .357 under his left arm. He was carrying a Nordstrom shopping bag. He sat the shopping bag on my desk and pulled out bottles of Maker's Mark, Seagram's 7, and Jack Daniels.

I said, "I didn't know Nordstrom's carried booze."

"They don't," Tony said. "We heard you had a little trouble the other night."

Ray put in his two cents worth. "You know working late is bad for your health." Then he added. "Hey, you look like hell."

Tony joined in. "You get in a fight with a cat?"

I said, "A brick wall took a couple of swings at me." I nodded at their guns. "Where were you guys two nights ago? I could've used the additional fire power."

"I was at home asleep," Ray said.

Tony added, "I was at home, too, but I wasn't asleep." He held his hands out in front of himself as if he were gripping something and motioned with his hips back and forth. "I was showing one of the Falcons cheerleaders a new cheer."

I shook my head in disgust.

Ray asked, "Why didn't you call? We would have come over."

"I was too busy being shot at," I said.

Ray said, "You got nothing to worry about now." Ray was in his late-fifties, with deep-set eyes and black hair streaked with gray that he wore in a sweptback coiffure.

"Yeah," Tony said. "Just tell us who to shoot."

It sounded like a good idea. I could wrap up the case today, and I knew Ray was connected enough to get the job done. But I couldn't do it. Though no longer bound by the stringent rules and regulations as I had been as a cop, I still had to work within the law. But it was a good idea nevertheless.

I pointed at all the liquor bottles on my desk. "Why all the booze?"

Ray took off his coat and sat in one of the client chairs. He said, "We gotta have supplies while we plan our next move."

"I have to resolve this within the law," I said.

"But the other team isn't playing by the same rules," Ray said. "And if they came after you once, they could come after you again. You need to beat them to the punch."

Tony looked at me and raised his eyebrows. "He's right, you know."

Ray said, "Okay, we won't do it our way, but if these guys look like they're getting ready to make another move on you, then we act."

"Okay," I said.

Tony nodded. "So, who was the guy you shot?"

"Guy named Daryl Brock," I said. "He was a small-time hood."

"He'll never make it to the big time," Ray said. "Who hired him?"

"I believe a guy named Jack Rueben," I said.

"That's the guy I tailed," Tony said. "I should've popped him when I had the chance."

He went into the kitchen, got three glasses, and poured each of us some of the Maker's Mark. He sat in the client chair next to Ray.

I explained to Ray, "Rueben is the muscle behind a bigger operation."

Ray asked, "That's the murdered lawyer case you're working, right?"

"Yeah," I said. I explained further. "The ring leader of the group is a guy named Richard Murphy. I think he's running a real estate scam with another guy named James Barton. And they're using the senior partner at the law firm where the murdered lawyer practiced. His name is Charles Lawson."

"Why don't you just turn it all over to the Feds," Ray said. "Let them deal with it. Give 'em something to do."

I shook my head. "I don't have enough evidence. If I turn what I have over to the Feds, they could go after Lawson for fraud and identity theft, but the others will run. Plus, I don't have any evidence on the murders."

Ray said, "So tell me what you've got."

I handed him a few copies of some of the documents, and began telling him what I had so far. I told him about Jason Garrett, how he discovered the documents, and was killed to keep silent. I told him about Charles Lawson, James Barton, and Richard Murphy, about the assault on the banker Greg Little, and about the murder of Mable Williams. Ray listened intently without interruption. He studied the documents as I talked. I finished by telling him about the stolen identities of Charles Lawson's pro bono clients, and how they were using falsified documents on a real estate scam of some sort.

After I finished, Ray was silent a long moment. He drank some of the bourbon while he thought. I sipped the bourbon and waited. I wanted his perspective on the case, his opinion. If you want advice about criminality, ask a criminal. I don't say this out of disrespect for Ray. He was my friend and I had the utmost respect for him. But he was, and forever would be, a member of the underworld. He was his own man, and I admired him for it.

Ray waved the papers, and said, "All these houses were previously bank-owned properties."

"I noticed that too," I said. "The properties are from different counties around the metro area. I figured they picked them up at the monthly foreclosure auctions."

Ray nodded, "I've picked up a few houses at those auctions myself."

I looked at him, surprised. "Is there any racket you're not in?"

"I don't do drugs, or prostitution. Drugs are too risky, and prostitution…well, that's too much trouble." Ray thought for a second, took another drink, then said, "Stealing identities and falsifying documents doesn't justify murder just to pick up houses cheaply."

"You're right," I said. "It's not worth all the trouble. Or the risk."

Ray thought for a second, then said, "But if they were stealing the houses, that would make it worthwhile."

Tony spoke up. "How do you steal a house?"

"It's not as difficult as it seems," Ray said. "In this case, the houses are unoccupied." He shrugged. "Makes it a little easier. You find out what bank owns the property, falsify the necessary paperwork, and then file everything at the county registrar's office."

Tony asked, "Won't the bank find out?"

"Eventually they will," Ray answered, "but by then you would've sold the house to an unsuspecting buyer."

"Take the money and run," Tony said.

I said, "And if you do that on a large scale, you could rake in millions in a short period of time."

"Exactly," Ray said.

I thought for a moment. That could be exactly what Lawson and his partners are doing. They find foreclosed houses, probably ones that have been unoccupied for a while, and then falsify documents to transfer the houses under the names of the stolen identities that Lawson supplies. Then sell the houses to unsuspecting buyers.

Ray said, "But you have to move fast and get out quick." He took a sip of his drink, then added, "And with all the attention they're drawing, I'd say they won't be around much longer."

Tony added, "They'll whack the lawyer before they leave, too. He's a loose end. Same goes for the banker."

Ray looked at me, and said, "It looks like you need to wrap this up in a hurry."

CHAPTER FIFTY-FIVE

It was Saturday morning and Naija and I had decided to take a drive up to Blue Ridge and spend a couple of days in the mountains. Naija wasn't on-call at the hospital, a rarity, so we jumped at the opportunity to spend some quality time together. We rented a cabin for the weekend, packed a couple of overnight bags, and headed north up I-575. It was mid-October and the leaves had started to change. The drive only takes a couple of hours from Atlanta, but we took our time, driving slow and taking in the fall colors.

Blue Ridge is a quaint small town with two-and three-story brick and wood frame buildings built in the 1930s or 40s. We ate lunch at a restaurant with a panoramic view of the mountains. After lunch, we stopped at a local store and bought a few supplies, an assortment of fruits, bread, sandwich meat, eggs, and bacon. They didn't have turkey bacon. Naija was disappointed. I was ecstatic. We also bought a couple bottles of wine. Then we drove further up in the mountains to our cabin.

The cabin was both rustic and elegant. There was a covered front porch and wooden rocking chairs with a scenic mountain view. Inside, were all the amenities you need, a complete kitchen, a huge fireplace, a flat-screen TV, a DVD player, and a bookshelf stocked with a wide variety of books and movies. There was a Jacuzzi on the patio outside the bedroom.

After we unpacked, we spent the rest of Saturday afternoon exploring the area around the cabin. There were walking trails throughout the property, and a stream that ended at a lake about a mile from the cabin. We laughed and shivered at the coldness of the water at the edge of the lake as we splashed each other.

That night the temperature dropped into the thirties, and I built a fire in the fireplace while Naija made us sandwiches for dinner. We ate the sandwiches in front of the fire and watched the flames dance and flicker. Afterwards, we opened a bottle of wine and sat on the couch. I propped my feet up on the coffee table, and Naija sat with her feet tucked beneath her and her head against my shoulder. I put my arm around her. We sat quietly for a time, watching the fire and enjoying the silence.

After a while, Naija asked, "Do you think Charles Lawson hired those men that attacked you?"

"I don't think so," I said. I drank some of my wine, then continued, "I think it was Richard Murphy, trying to make good on the threat he made when I went to his office."

Naija took a sip of her wine, then asked, "So you don't think Lawson was involved?"

I shook my head. "Lawson doesn't have the clout. And he's more of a white-collar criminal."

"But Lawson was the one that told his partners about Jason Garrett."

"That was Lawson's big mistake. He probably thought they would simply scare Garrett the way they did the banker Greg Little. With a beating. But he didn't take into account that Greg Little is a vital part of their operation. Jason Garrett wasn't. So they killed him."

"So why did Lawson tell them about Mable Williams?" Naija asked.

"After they killed Garrett, Lawson probably realized he was in over his head, and he had to be thinking he could be next to die. He got scared. So he pointed the finger at Mable Williams to get the monkey off his own back. Only it doesn't work that way. They killed Mable Williams, and now Lawson is in even deeper than before."

Naija picked up her wine glass and took another sip. Her glass was still over half full. She asked, "So Lawson's business partners could come after him next?"

I nodded. "I think it's only a matter of time. Lawson is becoming too much of a liability."

Naija looked at me. "If you tried to talk with Lawson again, you might save his life."

I knew Naija abhorred violence, and she didn't want to see any more deaths. But to be honest, I didn't care whether Lawson lived or died. He had dealt the cards and now he had to play his hand out. Win, lose, or die. And there was one other reason I felt that way. I didn't like the guy. He was a weasel who had probably swindled millions out of innocent victims. So why should I come to his rescue? I thought about it for a moment longer. Naija looked at me, waiting for my response. She knew I wouldn't sit back and let Lawson get killed. I wasn't that type of guy. If I could save the schmuck's life, I would.

I shrugged. "I'll try to talk with him again," I said. "Maybe he'll listen now."

Naija seemed pleased. She kissed me and held my arm tightly against her body. We sat that way for a long time, silently holding each other, and watching and listening to the fire crackle. There was no other sound. We were comfortable just silently holding each other.

After a while, Naija looked up at me and lightly touched the cuts on the side of my face. "It scared me when you told me you'd been shot at," she said, her voice suddenly somber. "I don't think I've ever been so afraid."

I looked into her eyes. They were rimmed with tears, but she wasn't crying. I think the weight of what had happened suddenly hit home now that she'd had time to unwind and think about it. I kissed her, and said, "I'm sorry I put you through that."

Naija's dark eyes glowed in the firelight. "It would devastate me if something happened to you." She took my hand in hers and held it tightly. "I never want to lose you."

I swallowed the lump in my throat. "You never will," I said.

We were silent a while longer. We drank our wine and watched the fire some more.

Then Naija said, "This place is breathtaking, isn't it?"

I grinned at her. "The view of you here on the couch isn't bad either."

"It would be nice to come up here more often," she said. "It's very relaxing, and it's great for stress relief."

"I know another great stress reliever," I said.

Naija playfully poked me in the ribs. "I bet you do," she said. She stood up and looked at me seductively. "Why don't we go try out the Jacuzzi?"

"I thought you'd never ask," I said.

We went out on the patio and stripped off our clothes. The night air was cold against our naked skin. I held her against me and felt her shiver in the cold. I kissed her and felt her lips part as our tongues locked together. We stood there a moment, kissing passionately. Then we eased into the warm water and held each other until the coldness subsided.

Later, we got out of the hot tub, toweled off, and padded naked into the living room. I put a couple of more logs on the fire. We pulled a blanket from the foyer closet and made love in front of the fire. Then we held each other, drank some more of the wine and watched the flames dance in the crackling fire.

The next morning, we made love again, like newlyweds. Then later we went hiking, and ate sandwiches from a cliff top with a fantastic view of the mountains off in the distance. That evening, as we drove back home, I realized that getting away for the weekend was exactly what we had needed. It had brought us closer together, and for me personally, it had renewed something deep down in my soul.

CHAPTER FIFTY-SIX

It was time to visit Charles Lawson. Again. But if he refused to cooperate this time, then he would have to try to squirm his way out when the Feds came down on him—that is, if his business partners didn't kill him beforehand.

For this visit, I decided to take a different approach. I needed to scare Lawson, convince him his life was in danger, and the only way out was to start talking. There was a pretty blonde woman who looked to be in her late-twenties sitting at Mable Williams' desk. The desk name plate said her name was Stephanie Waters.

"Tell Mr. Lawson, Mr. Rueben is here," I said to Lawson's new secretary.

Since I knew Lawson would refuse to talk with me, I decided using Rueben's name would at least get me into his office. Of course, I was going on the assumption that she didn't know what Jack Rueben looked like.

Stephanie Waters picked up her phone, punched a few numbers, and whispered something to Lawson. I didn't hear what she said.

She hung up, and said, "Mr. Lawson will be with you in a moment."

I didn't bother waiting on him. I walked past her desk to Lawson's office, opened the door, and went inside.

When I swung the door open, Lawson was halfway between his desk and the door. He had the look of a scared rabbit, ready to take off running at the slightest threat. He stopped when he saw me, and his eyes widened with recognition.

"Get out," he said, giving me the hard stare.

"I can't do that Charlie," I said. "We need to talk."

"If you don't leave," he said, "I'll call security and have you thrown out."

"I can't let you do that," I said, "and I'm not leaving until we talk."

He glared at me. "We don't have anything to talk about."

"Sure we do, Charlie," I said, coming up next to him and looking him in the eye. "We've got plenty to talk about."

He looked like he wanted to take a swing at me, but it hadn't done him any good the first time.

We stood there staring at each other for a moment. He had dark circles under his eyes, as if he hadn't slept in days. He looked tired and worn down. Maybe swindling didn't agree with him.

"Come on, Charlie," I said, as if we were old friends. "Let's sit down and talk."

"I have nothing to say to you," he said, but his voice had lost some conviction.

"Well, I've got something to say to you." I walked toward his desk and turned around and looked at him.

He hadn't moved. Then he slowly turned around and moved back toward his desk. That's when I noticed that he walked like a hundred-year-old man, taking short tentative steps. He held his midsection around the ribcage, and I heard him grunt a few times. When he got near his desk, I put my hand on his shoulder to stop him. He didn't look at me.

"What's the matter?" I said. "You're moving like an old lady."

"Nothing's the matter," he said, through clinched teeth.

I knew the telltale signs. I poked him in the ribcage on the left side, and he groaned in pain. "You've been beaten up," I said.

"No I haven't," he said. "I fell off a ladder over the weekend."

He didn't look like the handyman type.

"I don't believe you," I said.

"I don't care what you believe," Lawson said. He moved slowly around his desk and sat down with another groan. I sat in one of the plush leather chairs opposite his desk.

"Who beat you up?" I said.

"It's none of your bus—" but then he caught himself. "I fell."

"Yeah, maybe after someone punched you a few times," I said. "Who did it?"

"None of your business," Lawson said. "Leave me alone." It sounded more like a plea than a demand.

"You need to see a doctor," I said. "You could have a couple of cracked ribs."

"I'll be fine," he said. But he didn't look fine to me.

He took a small bottle of Advil out of his top desk drawer, shook a few in his hand, and drank them down with a glass of water he had sitting on his desk.

"Listen, Charlie—"

"Stop calling me Charlie," he snapped. Then he grimaced in pain.

"Listen, Charlie," I said. "I know how these guys work. They pound your body black and blue, but leave the face alone. That way it doesn't show. Next time, you may not be so lucky."

He didn't say anything. Maybe I had gotten his attention. At least he wasn't telling me to get out of his office. He took a deep breath and grimaced. I've taken my share of body punches before, and I knew he was in a lot of pain. It even hurts to breathe.

To make sure I had his attention, I said, "There's only one way out of this mess, and that's to start talking." To twist the screw a little more, I added, "This time they just gave you a warning. Next time it might be a bullet in the brain like they gave Garrett."

That shook him. His eyes grew wide and the color drained from his face. He looked like a cadaver. He grimaced again and held his ribs with his left hand.

I asked, "When did it happen?"

He looked at me a second, then stared down at his desk. "Saturday night," he said. He paused a moment, still holding his ribs. Then he continued, "My wife and I went out to dinner. When we came out of the restaurant, there were two men waiting beside my car."

"They bother your wife?"

"No," he said. "They pushed her out of the way. One held me and the other did the punching."

"Rueben do the punching?"

Lawson didn't say anything for a second. Then he nodded his head.

Time to make sure I had his attention. I said, "I've got enough evidence on you for the Ponzi scheme you were running to put you away for a long time." To tighten the screw against him, I added, "Plus, I've got evidence on the real estate scam you and your friends are running. If I go to the Feds now, your pals will run and leave you holding the bag. The Feds will pin both murders on you. You'll go to jail for the rest of your life. Meanwhile, your partners will get off scot-free."

He stared at me a moment, his eyes wide. I thought I had his attention now.

"What can you do?" he said, disdainfully. "You're not even a real cop. Just a private eye."

I ignored his comment. Instead, I said, "I've got a lot of connections, and I might be able to help you. But you have to tell me everything."

Lawson looked at me a second, perhaps considering what I'd said.

"If I talk," he said. His voice was desolate. "They'll kill me."

I turned the screw a little more. "They'll probably kill you anyway," I said. "You've become a liability. The only way out is to start talking. If you cooperate, the Feds may work a deal with you."

"But I could still go to jail," he said.

"You're probably looking at doing time anyway," I said. "But how much time will depend on how cooperative you are. If you give up all the information you have, they may go easier on you. But if you don't, I know they'll throw the book at you."

This was total b.s. I didn't know whether the Feds would offer him a deal or not, but it didn't hurt to improvise.

I decided to tighten the screw more. I said, "If you don't make a deal, I'm sure your buddy Greg Little will. He'll squeal like a pig when the Feds barge in on him. That still leaves you responsible for two murders."

Lawson looked around his office, as if he were seeing it for the last time. Outside, clouds had moved in from the west, blocking his cityscape view.

Lawson said, "I need a drink."

He stood up and laboriously walked to a cabinet to the left. He took out two glasses and a bottle of scotch. Then he slowly shuffled back to his swivel chair and sat down with a groan. He then poured about three inches of scotch from the bottle in each glass and handed me one. I took a drink. It was good scotch. Only the best for my swindler buddy, Charlie.

Lawson drank his scotch, poured himself another, and then asked, "Where should I begin?"

"Start at the beginning," I said.

CHAPTER FIFTY-SEVEN

Lawson took another pull of his scotch and looked at me a second. Then he began talking.

"When I first joined the firm, Robert Schmitt operated from a small hole-in-the-wall office on Luckie Street. I was the one that brought in clients. I did all the legwork. In ten years, I built the firm from a one-man operation to one of the most prestigious law firms in the state."

I said, "If the firm was doing well, then how did things get so out of hand?"

"It began when the economy tanked in 2008," Lawson said. "That's when Schmitt decided he'd had enough and retired. I inherited a law firm with serious financial problems. Then our client list started to dwindle, so to keep us in the black I began selling the annuities and settlements the firm held in trust." He paused and took a sip of his drink, then continued, "Selling annuities is legitimate. People who have annuities sell them regularly because they would rather have their money now than later. And you make a nice profit for doing nearly nothing. So I negotiated settlements and offered good returns to investors. It gave us the cash flow we needed."

"And then what happened?" I asked. I took a sip of the scotch. It was good scotch.

"After a while we ran out of annuities to sell," Lawson said.

"And that's when you started your Ponzi scheme," I said.

Lawson nodded his head. "At first I told myself I would quit it when the economy got better. But the allure of easy money was too great. I kept selling the fraudulent documents, and the money kept flowing in. Everything was great."

"So what happened?" I asked.

"When the Bernie Madoff scandal broke, investors got suspicious and started putting their money elsewhere. Then suddenly our pool of investors dried up."

He finished his drink in a gulp and poured another. I took another sip of my scotch, then asked, "Is that when you got involved with Richard Murphy?"

Lawson nodded. "It started when Richard Murphy discovered I was running a Ponzi scheme. He blackmailed me. He threatened to turn me into the FBI if I didn't help him with the scam he was running."

"You could have called in an anonymous tip to the FBI," I said. "Turn the tide on Murphy. Then the Feds may not have listened to him anyway, even if he did squeal."

Lawson sipped his drink. "I was afraid," he said. "Believe me. If I'd known how things would have turned out, I would have turned him in." He looked me in the eye. "Even if it meant my going to jail. But at the time, I didn't think I had a choice."

Out of curiosity, I asked, "How did Murphy discover your scheme in the first place?"

"Murphy's investment company was one of our clients," Lawson said. "I made the mistake of offering Murphy one of our investments, and he recognized the scam right away. And that's when he blackmailed me."

Takes a scoundrel to know a scoundrel.

We were silent a moment. There was one other piece of this puzzle that didn't fit. I asked, "Where does Greg Little fit into this?"

Lawson looked at me a second. "You have been doing your homework, haven't you?"

I didn't say anything.

Lawson took another sip of his scotch. At the rate he was going, he would be plastered in an hour. He said, "The firm has been doing business with First Georgia Savings for years, and when I first started selling the annuities, the legitimate ones, Greg Little helped with the financial end of things. Then when I started selling the falsified documents, I convinced Greg he could make a lot of money, too. So we partnered up."

I said, "And having an attorney and a banker involved in a Ponzi scheme only adds to its perceived legitimacy."

Lawson nodded. "We had investors throwing their money at us."

"How did Greg Little get involved with Murphy's scam?"

Lawson sipped his drink, then said, "When I got involved with Murphy, Greg didn't want any part of it. He wanted out. But Murphy saw an advantage in having a bank manager, and an attorney, as a part of his scam. It would give the scam legitimacy. So Murphy blackmailed Greg the same as he did me. So Greg went along with it for a while, but after a few months he wanted out again."

I said, "And that's when Murphy sent him a message in the form of a beating."

"Yes," Lawson said. He sipped his drink some more, then continued, "Greg was lucky a cop just happened by at the time, or he would have ended up like me, or worse."

Lawson grew silent and looked around his office again. Then he looked out the window at the low passing clouds. With the clouds pressing against the windows, Lawson must have thought the world was closing in on him. In a sense, it was.

He finished his drink and poured another. After a moment, he said, "I've really made a mess of things, haven't I?"

It was a rhetorical question, so I didn't say anything.

Lawson continued, "I've ruined my life." He looked at me, and said, "I'm sure Amanda will leave me."

"Sometimes couples find a way to work things out," I said. But I didn't think this was one of those times. Not Lawson's wife. She was a gold digger and the minute the money stopped, she would look for someone else to bankroll her shopping sprees.

As if Lawson had read my mind, he said, "Not with Amanda. She's too self-centered. The marriage oath 'for better or for worse' doesn't mean anything to her."

I suppressed a grin by taking a sip of my scotch.

Lawson looked at me, and asked, "So do you think you can help me?"

"I'll talk with the Feds, and the DA, and see what kind of deal they'll offer," I said. "But we'll need a mountain of evidence against Murphy and Barton."

"I'll do whatever you need me to do," Lawson said.

"Good," I said. "Now tell me about Jason Garrett."

CHAPTER FIFTY-EIGHT

It was nearly six o'clock by the time I left Lawson's office. The clouds had finished moving in and it had started to drizzle. I pulled from the parking lot where the two goons had assaulted me and headed down Peachtree Street toward downtown.

Lawson had come clean and told me everything, and by the time he had finished, I knew all about the swindle Murphy was running.

Richard Murphy had a nearly perfect setup for his real estate scam. James Barton was the middleman who found the vacant houses and handled the necessary paperwork for the property deed transfers. Charles Lawson handled the legal aspect of things. Lawson also supplied Murphy with the information needed to steal the identities of his pro bono clients. Murphy used the information and created fraudulent documents that supported the stolen identities. Greg Little helped by falsifying credit reports under the stolen identities. Little also handled the banking aspect of the transactions. Murphy had all the bases covered. And since the paperwork looked authentic, no one questioned anything. If Murphy had not had Jason Garrett murdered, he may have swindled millions and gotten away with it.

But Murphy did have Jason Garrett killed, and then Mable Williams. He even sicced the dogs on me, and now a twenty-four year old kid will never see twenty-five. Not to mention the countless lives he had ruined with his scheme.

I had no reason to think Lawson had been lying about any of it. He was a broken man who was looking at years behind bars, even if he did get a deal from the Feds.

When Lawson told me about Jason Garrett, I saw a part of him he probably kept hidden from everyone, even his gold-digger wife Amanda. He nearly cried with grief. Of course, some of Lawson's grief could have been the booze talking, but I thought he was genuinely broken up about Garrett's murder.

Lawson told me that Jason Garrett had discovered the documents, and had noticed the name of his new pro bono case, Roy Upshaw. In an instant, Garrett had known the documents were fraudulent, and he had confronted Lawson about it. Not knowing what to do, Lawson told Richard Murphy. Lawson swore he didn't know Murphy would have Garrett killed. He thought he would have him beaten up the way he'd done with Greg Little. But he hadn't taken into account that Greg Little was a vital part of their scam and Jason Garrett wasn't. So Murphy had Jason Garrett killed to keep him silent. Lawson said he didn't know who killed Garrett, but he was positive it was Jack Rueben. Rueben was the muscle of the operation. Rueben was the enforcer and kept everyone in line.

Lawson told me that when they discovered Garrett's body, he realized what he'd done. He told me he felt terrible about Garrett's murder. That's when Lawson nearly broke down and cried. He said he never thought that anyone would be killed because of the scam they were running. Again, I had no reason not to believe him.

Then I had asked him about Mable Williams. He said he didn't have anything to do with her death. He said that he suspected that whoever had been following me probably had seen Mable Williams talking with me. Then Lawson added that Murphy probably had Mable Williams followed as well. He said he didn't know of her death until the police told him. Lawson said he suspected Rueben again for Mable's death too.

After his narrative, I told Lawson not to say anything to anyone about our conversation. Not his wife. And not Greg Little. I told him that Little would have to work his own deal when the Feds swooped down on him. Maybe if he agreed to testify against Murphy and Barton, they might offer him a deal too.

Absolute Justice

As I drove, the drizzle changed into a steady rain. The traffic going down Peachtree crawled at a snail's pace. The rain made the normal heavy traffic even worse.

I had two problems to work out. I needed hard evidence against Murphy and Barton on the real estate scam. The copies of the documents I had weren't enough. I needed irrefutable evidence. I also needed evidence against them for the murders of Jason Garrett and Mable Williams. Okay, three problems. I wanted to bring down Jack Rueben for both murders, not to mention the attempted murder on *moi*.

The traffic wasn't moving, but my mind was racing. What I needed was a plan. I needed some way to get the evidence. Then suddenly an idea bloomed, as if someone had turned on a light in my brain. The way to get the evidence was to beat them at their own game. What I needed was a real estate swindle, something to entice Murphy into a trap, something big enough to make him want a piece of the action. Men like Murphy are driven by only one thing—greed. If I waved easy money if front of him, he might take the bait.

And I knew just the person to help me with a plan. *If you want to know about criminality, ask a criminal.* I knew I could depend on my friend Ray Norris for help. If anyone knew how to develop a good racket, it was Ray.

I thought some more as I listened to the rain drum on top of the car. I could use Lawson as the inside man to put the plan in place. He could present the plan to Murphy and help setup everything. Then when the deal went down, the Feds could swoop down on them like vultures. Of course, Lawson would get caught up in the sweep, but I could talk with the DA and the Feds beforehand. Maybe they would offer him a deal. Plus, if Lawson wore a listening device, he may get Murphy to incriminate himself on the two murders. It would be a double play, a pitcher's best way to get out of a tight spot. I would entrap Murphy on the real estate scam, and get evidence on the murders. I liked the idea. It was vague and didn't have any substance, but at least I had the beginnings of a plan. I felt it could work. As the traffic inched further along on Peachtree, I listened as the wipers swished back and forth and thought some more.

CHAPTER FIFTY-NINE

It was 5:45 in the morning and I was at a diner on Luckie Street with FBI Special Agent Luther Higgins. We sat in one of the vinyl booths next to the window.

After we ordered, Higgins took a sip of his coffee, then asked, "What do you need?"

"What makes you think I need something?" I said.

Higgins shot me a sidelong glance. "You wouldn't invite me to breakfast if you didn't need something."

"Maybe I just want to spend time with a friend," I said.

"Right," Higgins said. He sipped his coffee again, then said, "I heard you were in a shootout the other night."

"Good news travels fast," I said.

"What happened?"

"A couple of guys were waiting for me when I came out of my office," I said.

"And you shot one of them," Higgins said. "What happened to the other guy?"

"He got away."

"Too bad," Higgins said. "Now, are you going to tell me why we're here or not?"

Luther had played football at the University of Georgia as a running back, but in his sophomore year he suffered a catastrophic knee injury that ended any aspirations of a professional football career. Luther and I sometimes worked out together.

I said, "What can you tell me about mortgage fraud?"

"What's the matter?" Higgins said. "The gumshoe gig not paying enough?"

"I'm a curious guy," I said.

Higgins gave me a suspicious look. "What's the real reason?"

"I'm working on a case that may interest you," I said.

"Alright, you've got my attention," he said.

I took a sip of coffee. "Tell me about mortgage fraud. Is it a popular crime nowadays?"

The waitress brought our food and refilled our coffee cups. She was a large black woman who smiled brightly and was full of energy.

When the waitress left, Higgins said, "Mortgage fraud has always been a popular crime among scam artists. It's grown considerably since the housing bubble burst."

"How does it work?" I asked.

Higgins ate some of his eggs, and then said, "There are several variations of mortgage fraud, but there are a couple of methods that we investigate the most. One is property flipping. Although flipping property is a legitimate business, there is a shadier side of it too. That's when a con artist inflates the value of a property with false appraisals. He then has associates purchase the property repeatedly at the inflated prices. Then when the payments aren't made, the bank forecloses on the property and ends up taking a huge lost, while the scam artist walks away with the money."

Higgins stopped to eat more of his breakfast. He was passionate about his job and enjoyed talking about it. He drank some of his coffee, and then explained further, "But the most common type of mortgage fraud comes from insider knowledge. This happens when scam artists use corporate shell companies, stolen identities, and fraudulent documentation to scam buyers and lenders." After taking a few more bites, Higgins continued, "There's different ways to do it. One way is to find a house you want to steal. It doesn't matter whether it's occupied or not. Then you research who the true owner is, steal their identity, and then fake documentation to transfer ownership of the house to you."

"And then I can sell the property to an unsuspecting buyer," I said.

"Exactly," Higgins said. "You run off with the money and leave the bank and the original homeowner holding the bag. Not to mention the poor guy you sold the property to. He loses his down payment, but the biggest loser is the bank that financed the house under the fraudulent papers."

I ate some of my breakfast, then said, "Meanwhile, I have a load of money and I'm living the good life."

Higgins nodded. "And some guys even pull the same scam over and over in a short period of time and walk off with millions."

"Nothing like maximizing your profits," I said. "What happens to the original owner of the house?"

Higgins answered, "He'll end up maintaining ownership, but it turns into a big legal mess that'll cost him thousands to straighten out."

We ate in silence a moment. I put a dab of strawberry jam on my toast and took a bite. Higgins slurped up some of his grits.

After a while, Higgins asked, "Now are you gonna tell me the real reason you invited me to breakfast? And why the sudden interest in mortgage fraud?"

For my plan to work I needed Higgins' help, so I told him everything I had so far. I left nothing out. I finished by telling him about Lawson, about how Murphy had him beaten up, and how Lawson now wanted a deal for his testimony against his partners.

When I finished, Higgins asked, "You got any of the documents from the dead guy's computer with you now?"

I reached inside my suit jacket, pulled out a few copies of the documents, and handed them to him.

When he finished looking them over, he asked, "And all these signatures are forgeries?"

"Yeah," I said. "Lawson admitted everything to me. He stole the identities of his pro bono clients."

"Nothing like helping out the less fortunate," Higgins said, still looking at the documents. When he finished looking at them, he said, "These are copies. Got the originals?"

"No," I said.

Higgins glanced up at me. "Lawson doesn't have them either?"

I shook my head. "Lawson said Murphy keeps all the originals."

Higgins nodded. "Smart move on Murphy's part. Without the originals, you don't have much to go on. Got any other evidence?"

"Only what Lawson told me," I said.

"Lawson could be lying," Higgins said. "He could have cooked it up to take the heat off the Ponzi scheme he was running."

"I don't think Lawson is lying, though," I said. "I talked with him. He's scared of Murphy. And he says he'll help with the investigation any way he can."

"What does Lawson want in return?" Higgins asked.

"He wants a deal," I said.

We were silent a moment as we finished our food. Then our waitress came by, cleared the table, and sat the check face down.

After she left, I asked, "So what do you think? Think Lawson will be able to cut a deal?"

Higgins shrugged. "If Lawson didn't have anything to do with the murders, and if he cooperates fully and testifies against his partners, the U.S. Prosecutor may cut him a deal. That's a decision the prosecutor will make. But first, if we're going after these guys, we'll need a lot more evidence. As it stands now, you don't have enough for a warrant, much less a conviction."

"That's the reason I invited you to breakfast," I said. "I've got an idea how to get the evidence, but I need your help."

"Okay," Higgins said. "I'm listening."

CHAPTER SIXTY

After I left the diner, I walked the few blocks back to my office. It was almost seven and there wasn't much traffic on the streets. Downtown wouldn't get hopping for another hour. The sun was starting to rise, and I could see faint light off to the east. Back at my office, I sat behind my desk and began working out the final details of my plan. I had given Higgins the gist of the plan, but I still had a couple more details to work out. Putting a plan together requires a lot of legwork, a lot of details to work out, and in this particular case, a lot of negotiations. I had to make sure all parties involved were on the same page. So I sat in my swivel chair and went over the details of what I needed. When I finished, I sat back in my chair and propped my feet up. I thought I had a good plan, nothing complex, just a good old-fashioned sting operation. I could almost hear Scott Joplin's *The Entertainer*—the theme song from one of my favorite movies, *The Sting*—playing in the background.

At ten o'clock, I grabbed my suit jacket and fedora and headed out. Time to get the last piece of my plan in place. I had my car parked in the same alley where I had shot Daryl Brock. The rain from two days before had washed away any indication a death had occurred there. Now it was just another dingy, stinking alleyway.

I drove to Ray Norris' liquor store on Peters Street. The store had just opened, and Tony Veneto was behind the counter. Today he was wearing a black T-shirt that clung to his muscles like a second skin. Depicted on the T-shirt in white was a snarling wolf gnashing its teeth, and below was the legend: DON'T PISS ME OFF. If that wasn't enough warning, Tony had his .357 strapped under his left arm. The only customer in the store was an ancient wino with a network of deep lines chiseled on his face. He wore a tattered brown coat, and he reeked of cheap wine. Without saying a word, the wino splashed a handful of change on the counter, and Tony counted out the amount he needed. Then Tony handed him a pint of Mogen David 20/20, also known as Mad Dog 20/20, the preferred wine for winos everywhere. I was certain Naija and her highbrow friends had never featured it at one of their wine tasting soirees.

After Tony handed him the wine bottle, Tony said, "See you tomorrow, Clyde."

Clyde grabbed the wine bottle, dropped it in his coat pocket, and then left without looking at me.

I walked over by the counter. Tony nodded at the door, and said, "He waits out front every morning until we open. Then he buys his wine with whatever money he's panhandled the day before. If he doesn't have enough, I give him the wine anyway." He glanced at the clock behind the counter. "So, what brings you here so early?"

I nodded toward the back. "Ray in his office? I've got a favor to ask him."

"Sure," Tony said.

I went around behind the counter and we walked toward the storage area at the back of the store. In the back, cases of every kind of liquor imaginable were stacked shoulder-high. Off to the left, was another storage area in a locked cage of chain-link fence. Inside was an array of flat-screen TVs, computers, laptops, and printers, all new and in the original boxes. On a shelf to the left, I saw a neat row of ladies handbags, all lined up as if they were on display at Macy's.

Ray's office was in a walled up area next to the locked storage area. The office was no bigger than a walk-in closet, with just enough room for a desk, a metal file cabinet, and a couple of chairs. Tony and I crowded into the tiny office space.

I motioned toward the caged storage area. "Don't you worry about the cops raiding you?" I asked Ray.

Ray grinned at me. "They raid the place about every six months," he said. "But they can never pin anything on me." He patted a stack of papers on his desk. "I'm just as legit as those big-box stores."

Tony spoke up. "Except we have lower overhead."

"Right," Ray said. "We eliminate the middle man. Sell direct from the manufacturer."

Not to mention the merchandise Ray sold was hot as a blowtorch, but I didn't say that. Instead, I asked, "What's with the ladies' purses?"

Ray sat back in his swivel chair. "I just got those in a couple of days ago," he said, smiling. "Louis Vuitton. Retail, those things go for a couple of grand. I took one home to the wife. She loved it." He thought a second. "You should take one to Naija."

Though Naija had a variety of purses, I bet she wouldn't appreciate it if I gave her one that was so hot it could burn her hand.

As if reading my mind, Ray said, "She doesn't have to know where it came from."

"She would ask," I said. "It's not like me to go out and buy her a handbag that's worth a couple thousand bucks."

"Give it to her for Christmas," Ray said, shrugging his shoulders. "She'll never know the difference." Then Ray asked the same question Tony had asked. "So what brings you here so early in the morning?"

"I need some help from you with something I'm planning," I said.

"Whatever you need," Ray said.

He didn't ask what kind of help I needed. To him, it didn't matter. That's the true meaning of friendship. Being there for your friends no matter what.

Then I told them both what I had in mind. I mentioned that I had spoken with an FBI friend of mine about helping, too.

That raised a couple of eyebrows around the cramped office.

Ray interrupted. "We'll be just concerned citizens helping law enforcement, right?"

"Exactly," I said. "I haven't mentioned your name yet. I wanted to make sure you're onboard with the plan first." I explained further, "This is going to be an old-fashioned sting operation. We get the evidence needed, and then we get out of the way and let the Feds take over."

Ray nodded. "Okay, I'm in," he said. "I'll have someone draw up the papers we'll need."

Tony looked over at me. "I'm in, too," he said. "Whatever you need, Kemosabe."

CHAPTER SIXTY-ONE

Next, I went to see Lieutenant Matt Davis at his office at police headquarters. His office was on the fourth floor with a window to the right that overlooked a parking lot. Not much of a view, but at least he had a window to look out of. Matt's metal desk looked like it had been new around 1975, but Davis kept the desk immaculately neat. The only items on the desk were a laptop, a pen set, and a cube with pictures of his family in it. I walked in and sat in one of the chairs opposite the desk.

"I need your help," I said.

"I didn't think you came in just to join my fan club," Davis said. "What do you want?"

"I know who killed Jason Garrett," I said.

That got his attention. Davis put down the pen he was holding and looked at me a second. "I'm listening."

"The shooter was Jack Rueben," I said. "He was hired by a guy named Richard Murphy."

Davis looked me in the eye. "And you know this how?"

"For right now, call it a gut feeling."

"I can't arrest someone on a gut feeling," Davis said. "Got any evidence?"

"No," I said. "That's why I need your help."

He motioned to the coffeemaker on the counter next to his desk. "Pour us a cup of coffee and tell me what you have on your mind."

I got up, poured both of us a cup, handed Davis one, and then sat back down. I took a sip. The coffee was hot and strong. Cops love their coffee strong enough to kick you in the teeth.

Davis took a sip of his coffee, then said, "So you know who killed Garrett, and who ordered the murder?"

"Yeah," I said. Then again, I told my tale. I finished by saying, "And I suspect Rueben was the one who ran down Mable Williams."

Davis leaned back in his swivel chair. "We've got an APB on Rueben already," he said. "When we find him, maybe he'll talk."

I shook my head. "You've seen his rap sheet. He's not going to talk. As soon as you bust him, he'll lawyer up. Meanwhile, Murphy will be on the next plane to the Caribbean."

Davis looked at me and rubbed his chin. "Okay. Let's say you're right. What do you have in mind?"

"We need two things," I said, counting them off. "First, we need more evidence on the real estate scam Murphy is running. I've got a plan for that. Second, we need evidence on the two murders. And since Murphy and Rueben are hardened criminals, the only way we can pin the murders on them is for them to admit to the killings."

"How are we gonna do that?" Davis asked skeptically. "Go over and ask them to confess?"

"Close," I said. "But not exactly."

Davis gave me a strange look. "What are you talking about?"

"We need to record them talking about the murders," I said. I shot him a devious smile. "And like I just said; I've got a plan."

"Okay," Davis said. "You've got my attention. Tell me about it."

So I told him what I was thinking and how I proposed to pull it off with Lawson as the inside man. Davis listened without interruption.

When I finished, Davis said, "Lawson has been uncooperative since the beginning. What makes you think he'll cooperate now?"

"He'll cooperate," I said. Then I told him how Murphy had Lawson beaten up, and that Rueben had been the one doing the beating. I added, "Lawson's scared. He's afraid he'll be the next one murdered. And he very well could be next. Plus, he's worried about having the two murder charges pinned on only him, not to mention a slew of felony charges. Believe me, he's ready to cooperate."

"And Lawson has agreed to help you with this plan, as well as testify against his partners?"

"Yeah," I said. "He knows he's in a lot of trouble for the scam, but he claims he had nothing to do with the murders."

Davis looked at me. "You believe him?"

"I don't think he was personally involved," I said.

Davis said, "But if Lawson had kept his mouth shut Jason Garrett and Mable Williams would be alive today."

I nodded. "I didn't say Lawson was a saint. But I believe he didn't know Murphy would have Garrett murdered."

Davis drained his coffee cup, got up, poured us some more, and sat back down.

"What does Lawson want in return?" he asked.

"He wants a deal," I said.

Davis passed me a suspicious look. "What kind of deal?"

"He's terrified of going to jail."

"He's not coming out of this unscathed," Davis said. "Even if he didn't have anything to do with the murders. He's swindled a lot of money out of people in his own Ponzi scheme. He could be looking at several years behind bars for that alone. Then you add the other scam he's been running with Murphy. That could add up to a lot of time, even if he is cleared of the murder charges."

I took a sip of my coffee. We both were silent a moment. Then I said, "What if you talk with the DA, see what kind of deal Lawson can get."

Davis sat back in his chair again, propped his elbow on the armrest, and rested his chin in the palm of his left hand. He was thinking about something. Then he said, "Under the Felony Murder Rule, Lawson could still be charged with murder even if he wasn't directly involved." Davis explained further, "If a murder is committed in the commission of a felony, all participants can be charged with murder. For example, if you drive the getaway car in a bank robbery and your partner kills someone in the bank, you can also be charged with murder." Davis paused a moment, thinking some more. "But that's up to the DA. If Lawson assists us in gathering evidence against his partners, the DA may—and I mean may—

Absolute Justice

cut him a deal. As far as the Ponzi scheme charges and the real estate scam charges, they are federal offenses. That's an entirely different ball game."

"I talked with an FBI friend of mine about the federal charges," I said. "He said he could talk with the U.S. Prosecutor about the federal charges."

"Who's the FBI guy?"

"Higgins," I said. "Luther Higgins."

"I know him," Davis said. "He used to play for Georgia. Got hurt, ended his career. He's a good guy."

I nodded, took a sip of coffee.

Davis said, "If Lawson's going to get a deal, he has to help us gather evidence. And you say he's willing to do that?"

"Yeah," I said.

"And you got a plan?" Davis asked.

"Yeah," I said again. Then I told him how we could use Lawson as the inside man, and how Ray Norris was willing to help.

When I finished, Davis said, "Ray Norris." Davis paused and thought a second. "He's the guy that sells stolen property out of his liquor store on Peters Street, right?"

I didn't say anything.

Davis wouldn't let it go. He said, "Norris is slick. We can never pin anything on him."

"I don't know anything about that," I lied.

"Sure you don't," Davis said, giving me the suspicious look again.

I decided to change the subject. I said, "If we send Lawson in wearing a listening device, we may be able to get evidence for the murders."

"If they discover he's wired," Davis said. "They'll probably kill him."

I nodded. Davis was right, though. If Lawson went in wired and they discovered it, he would be the next one on the hit parade.

I said, "It's the only way we can get what we need. And Lawson did say he would help any way he could. I'll talk to him again, make sure he's willing to do it before we go any further."

"OK," Davis said. "You talk with Lawson. I'll talk with the DA's office and see what kind of deal they can offer him."

I said, "Plus, I'll give Higgins a call. Let him know we're moving ahead. Maybe he can talk with someone at the U.S. Attorney's Office."

"After you talk with Higgins, I'll set up a meeting with everyone involved and we'll go over the plan."

I stood up. "Thanks for the coffee."

Davis nodded. "If we pull this off," he said, "everybody will get what they want. You'll solve your case, and get a nice fat check. I'll clear two murders off my books. And the U.S Prosecutor will uncover a huge real estate scam. Hell, Lawson may even get his wish."

CHAPTER SIXTY-TWO

The District Attorney's office was in the Fulton County courthouse building on Pryor Street. It was a little after eleven in the morning, and I was waiting for Matt Davis at the top of the steps at the entrance to the courthouse. Davis had put together a meeting with the DA, scheduled for 11:30. I was early. I was dressed in a black suit with gold pin-stripes, black shirt, a solid red tie, and a gray fedora. I carried a brown leather shoulder bag stuffed with documents. Ten minutes later, Davis showed up, and we rode up together in the elevator to the DA's office on the third floor. The DA's name was Tony West. When we got to his office, West came around his desk and we all shook hands. Tony West was a light-skinned black man with an angular face, a strong jaw line, and a touch of gray at the temples. West had held the DA position for the last eight years and was known as a hardnosed but fair prosecutor.

"Detective Davis has brought me up to speed," West said. "We'll be meeting in the conference room."

He led us out of his office and down the hallway. As we walked, he said, "Deborah Northcutt from the U.S. Attorney's Office got here a couple of minutes ago, and I was just getting ready to brief her, but now that everyone is here, we'll move ahead."

We walked down the hallway to a huge conference room big enough to accommodate a baseball team meeting. But the large cherry wood table looked too uptown for ballplayers.

Inside the conference room, on a counter up against the far wall, a coffee urn had been set up, and everybody was standing around drinking coffee, waiting to get things rolling.

The only person in the room I didn't know was the woman from the U.S. Attorney's Office, Deborah Northcutt. Tony West introduced us and we shook hands.

Deborah Northcutt looked to be in her mid-thirties, and though I had never met her, I knew of her reputation. As a federal prosecutor, she was a barracuda in the courtroom. Defense attorneys both respected and feared her. And rightly so. In court, she'd tear her adversaries apart. I wouldn't want to be a defense attorney and face her in court.

Also in the conference room was FBI Special Agent Luther Higgins. We shook hands as everyone took seats at one end of the large conference table. Tony West thanked everyone for coming and then began bringing everyone up to speed. He finished by saying, "Nick Price here," with a nod in my direction, "has been working alongside the APD on two murder investigations."

The barracuda interrupted. "Murder isn't a federal offense unless it was committed in the commission of a felony. So why am I here?"

"If you will allow me to finish," Tony West said, shooting her an impatient hard look. There were a lot of big egos in the room, and Tony West and Deborah Northcutt had two of the biggest. Though they played for the same team, they regarded each other as adversaries. Go figure. But my money was on Deborah Northcutt.

Tony West started again. "As I was saying, during Mr. Price's investigation into the two murders, which could turn out to be felony murders," again another hard look at Deborah Northcutt, "Mr. Price uncovered a real estate scam that the prime suspects have been running in the Atlanta area."

"How big of a real estate scam?" Deborah Northcutt asked.

I spoke up. "Several million. They've been running the scam for over six months."

Deborah Northcutt looked over at me, nodded. "OK. You've got my attention. Tell me what you've got."

"It's a four-man operation," I said. "But two of the four are unwilling participants. I'll get to them in a moment. The two primary participants are Richard Murphy, the ring leader of the group, who operates out of a company called Tanner Investments. The other person is the workhorse of the outfit, James Barton. He operates out of South Realty Group. The third is Greg Little, a bank manager at Georgia Savings and Loan. He's one of the unwilling participants. Murphy is blackmailing him into going along with the scam. And the fourth guy is Charles Lawson, the senior partner with the law firm of Schmitt & Lawson."

I took a sip of coffee, then continued. "Here's what they're doing." Then I told everyone what Lawson had told me. I went through every detail. No one interrupted to ask questions. Deborah Northcutt took notes on her legal pad. Tony West also took notes.

After I finished Deborah Northcutt said, "That's a unique way to steal houses."

"Gutsy, too," Luther Higgins said. "Most scam artists jump in, scam a few houses, make a bundle of quick money, and then move on the something else. But these guys have been doing this a while now."

"And they know what they're doing," I added. "They only steal unoccupied bank-owned properties."

"And I assume they're selling the stolen houses to unsuspecting buyers," Deborah Northcutt said.

"At cut rate prices," I said. "Say, they steal a house worth three-hundred thousand, but they sell the house at two-hundred thousand. They still make a good profit, and the buyer thinks he's getting the deal of a lifetime."

Deborah Northcutt took some more notes. Then she asked, "Got any evidence?"

I reached in my shoulder bag, pulled out a thick manila folder, and plopped it down on the conference table. "These are copies of some of the properties they've stolen. I'm sure this isn't all of them. There's more."

"Where did you get the documents?" Northcutt asked.

"Off the computer of one of the murder victims," I said. "Jason Garrett. He was the first victim."

Deborah Northcutt took the folder, and glanced through some of the documents. When she finished, she asked, "How do you know these aren't legitimate transactions?"

"The signatures on the documents are forgeries," I said. "Charles Lawson, one of the unwilling participants in the scam, was forced to steal identities from his pro bono clients."

Then I explained how Charles Lawson and Greg Little ended up involved with Murphy.

When I finished, Deborah Northcutt summarized just to make sure she had it straight. "So this Charles Lawson and Greg Little were committing a felony and this other felon, Richard Murphy, blackmails them into participating in his scam. Is that right?"

"Exactly," I said. "No honor among thieves."

Deborah Northcutt handed me the stack of documents back, and said, "These aren't the originals. Do you have the originals?"

Then I went through the same song and dance routine I had with Higgins and Davis. I told her how Murphy kept the originals.

When I finished, she said, "This Richard Murphy is slick. This isn't his first rodeo, is it?"

Then Luther Higgins joined the conversation. "I've done some background checks on both Richard Murphy and James Barton. Barton's done four years of a ten-year stretch for embezzlement in Colorado. Murphy has an even longer rap sheet. He did two years out of an eight-year sentence also for embezzlement, and another four years for racketeering. These guys are professionals."

Matt Davis spoke up. "And the muscle of the group is a guy named Jack Rueben. We like him for the two murders."

We were all silent a moment as Deborah Northcutt finished her notes. Then she put down her pen and sat silently a moment biting her lower lip. Her eyes knitted together as she thought. Something didn't sit right with her. After a moment, the barracuda in her surfaced again. "If we have evidence against Charles Lawson and Greg Little for the Ponzi scheme, why haven't they been arrested?"

Luther Higgins answered. "If we arrested them for the Ponzi scheme, Murphy and his cohorts will run, right after they destroy any evidence that implicates them in the scam they are running. They'd get off scot-free with the scam they've been running, not to mention two murders."

The barracuda shot him an incredulous look. "Why not just sweep in and raid everybody at once? Get the evidence before they get a chance to destroy it."

Luther Higgins said, "Because all we have is Lawson's statement against them. And that's not enough for a warrant."

Deborah Northcutt nodded. I was certain she had thought of the same thing, but just wanted to hear it from someone else. She thought another second, then said, "And Charles Lawson is willing to testify against the others."

"Yes," I said.

"What does he what in return?" Deborah Northcutt asked.

"He wants a deal," I said.

Deborah Northcutt looked over at me, and said, "That will depend on what he can give us."

Tony West asked, "Was Charles Lawson involved with the murders?"

I answered. "I don't think he was," I said. "Granted, he's a white collar criminal, but I don't think he's a murderer."

Tony West pointed at Davis and me. "And you guys think Jack Rueben is the person who killed Jason Garrett and Mable Williams? Right?"

Matt Davis spoke up before I could answer. "Right. We believe he was the triggerman for the Garrett murder, and we think he was the one driving in the hit-and-run on Mable Williams."

Tony West asked, "Does Lawson have specific knowledge of the murders?"

I answered. Davis and I made a great tag team. "Not directly," I said. "But that brings me to my next point. Lawson has agreed to help gather evidence for us."

Deborah Northcutt gave me a skeptical look. "And how do you suppose we get the evidence?"

I smiled at the barracuda. "I have a plan," I said.

She still looked skeptical, but said, "Tell me about it."

Then I told her my plan. As I began to lay it out, I still saw skepticism in her face, but as I continued, the skepticism dissipated. At one point, I caught a glimpse of a faint smile as she bit her lower lip. She listened without interruption.

After I finished, Deborah Northcutt asked, "And you set all this up?"

"Yes," I said. "And I'm the person that got Charles Lawson to talk."

She nodded but didn't say anything. After a moment, she asked, "And one of your associates is going to help with this plan you've developed?"

"Yes," I said. "His name is Ray Norris, a local business owner."

Matt Davis smirked and harrumphed. But he didn't say anything.

Tony West spoke up first, playing devil's advocate. "Your plan sounds like entrapment. It could get us into hot water."

"Neither the police, or the Feds are entrapping anyone," I said. "I am. You're going to get an anonymous tip from a concerned citizen about illegal activity."

Everyone was silent a moment as they thought about it. Then Tony West said, "If everyone else is onboard, then I'm good with the plan."

Deborah Northcutt said, "How do you want to handle your guy on the inside?"

"I want to make sure his safety is secure," I said.

Luther Higgins spoke up. "We can separate him from the others after we make the bust."

Deborah Northcutt looked at Luther Higgins, and said, "One final question. Why use a civilian for this? Why not use FBI undercover operatives?"

"We're under a tight time constraint," Higgins began. "It could take weeks for us to set up a sting, and James Barton and Richard Murphy are already antsy." He motioned over at me. "And besides, Mr. Price already has a good plan."

I put in my two cents. "Time is a major factor. Murphy and Barton could run any day now."

Higgins added, "I'll have a strike team ready to move in when the time comes."

"And I'll have a team ready as well," Matt Davis said.

Everyone was silent a moment.

Then I glanced at Deborah Northcutt and Tony West, and asked, "Do you think you can offer Lawson a deal?"

Deborah Northcutt asked me, "Why is Charles Lawson entrusting you to negotiate a deal for him? Why doesn't he do like most other criminals and hire an attorney?"

I answered, "I asked Lawson the same question, and he told me he'd take his chances dealing with you guys without an attorney."

Tony West said, "If Charles Lawson didn't have anything to do with the murders, we may give him a deal for his testimony in the murder trials. Ms. Northcutt will have to address the federal charges against him."

"I can't make any promises," Deborah Northcutt said. "It's going to depend on how much evidence Lawson provides us. But if he provides good evidence, and he testifies, and we get a conviction of the others, we may offer him a reduced sentence. Maybe a minimum security facility."

I nodded. "I'll pass the information along to Lawson."

Deborah Northcutt thought another minute. Then twisting her lips into a devious grin, she looked over at me, and said, "I like your plan. It's a good old-fashioned sting operation." Then she said something that nearly knocked me out of my chair. She said, "I can almost hear Scott Joplin playing."

CHAPTER SIXTY-THREE

I was sitting at my desk and had the windows open with a light autumn breeze blowing in when two unlikely characters strode into the office. It was Charles Lawson and Ray Norris. I had put them in touch with each other to work out the paperwork for the sting, but seeing them together struck me as strange. The original odd couple, a prominent attorney who had bilked millions, and a gangster who sold stolen merchandise from his liquor store. They both wore business suits as if they were on their way to a board meeting. They came into the office and sat in the client chairs. Ray had a huge accordion folder stuffed with documents.

Lawson still moved gingerly and occasionally grimaced and held his left side as he walked. I had already spoken with him regarding a deal, and he knew he wasn't getting off unscathed. But he was sticking up to his end of the bargain in hopes for a reduced sentence, maybe in a minimum security prison.

I took three glasses from my desk drawer and poured each of us a shot from the office bottle. It wasn't the high-priced stuff Lawson had in his office, but it was good bourbon, nonetheless.

Ray took a belt and began. "Take a look at this paperwork." He passed the folder over to me. "These papers look like the real thing. I bet pros couldn't tell them from legitimate documents."

"What about the signatures?" I asked. "You know Murphy will check them first."

"Take a look," Ray said. "I've got different signatures for each set of papers."

Lawson spoke up. "No forgeries this time. Those signatures are the real thing."

I took a moment and glanced through the documents. They looked legitimate. Then I saw why. He did have legitimate signatures on them.

"Is this Clyde the wino's signature?" I asked holding up a document.

"Yeah," Ray said. "I had to get a couple of drinks into him to steady his shakes, but he managed to sign it. Great, huh?"

I couldn't resist a grin. According to the documents in my hand, Clyde the wino was now the proud owner of a home in the Vinings area worth four-hundred thousand dollars. Well…there goes the neighborhood.

I asked Lawson, "How'd it go with Murphy?"

Since Richard Murphy and James Barton knew who I was, I couldn't be directly involved in setting up the meeting with Murphy, so I was depending on Lawson to handle it.

Lawson said, "When I first told Murphy I had a client that has some vacant houses he needs to unload, he said he wasn't interested." Lawson motioned over to Ray. "Then I told Murphy my client was connected and that the mob knew of our illegal activities."

"I'm listening," I said.

"Then I told him my client had acquired the houses by the same means that we'd acquired ours, and that he has clean titles that can't be traced." Lawson paused, took a drink, made a face as if he'd taken bad medicine, then continued, "Then I told Murphy—how do you say in mob-speak—my client 'would consider it a personal favor' if he would take the houses off his hands."

"What did Murphy say to that?" I prompted.

"He told me he didn't care who my client was, and for me to tell him to take a hike."

I looked over at Ray. "So much for making new friends," I said. "He probably doesn't know what a nice guy you are." Then I turned my attention back to Lawson. "What happened next?"

"Then I told Murphy that he may not want to piss off the mob. I told him they could make trouble. Plus, I said it was a one-time deal and my client wanted to unload the houses and retire to Florida." Lawson took another drink, made the face again, and continued, "Then I told him the houses are worth over three mil, and he could make a bundle on the deal." Suddenly Lawson was sounding like a wiseguy. Maybe Ray was starting to rub off on him.

"Never underestimate someone's greed," I said. "How did it go when you showed Murphy the paperwork?"

"Great," Lawson said, still playing his wiseguy role. "Murphy was still cautious about the deal. Kept asking how Ray Norris got wind of our operation." Lawson took another belt, but this time didn't make the face. Then he continued, "I told him the same thing as before. I said that Norris was connected and that one of his associates told him about our scam."

Ray spoke up. "To give Murphy a little push. I gave him a call myself. I reiterated what Lawson had told him. Told him everything was on the up-and-up."

"Murphy believe you?"

"Yeah," Lawson answered. "But he still seemed leery. Then I gave him copies of the documents to check out. He looked them over for a long time, but then said he was in. He said that he'll have Barton draw up the paperwork needed on his end." Lawson paused for effect and shot us a conspiratorial grin as if he'd just pulled the biggest scam of his life. Then he said, "Murphy bought it. Hook, line, and sinker."

I asked, "You set a time for the meeting?"

"Yeah," Lawson said. "Day after tomorrow. Two o'clock in Murphy's office."

"Think Jack Rueben will be at the meeting?"

"I'm sure he will be," Lawson said. "Murphy doesn't trust people. He'll want to make sure he has his goon there."

"What about James Barton?"

"He'll be there, too" he said. "He'll have the new paperwork made out that transfers the properties. That's when they'll hand over the money to Ray."

"And that's when the Feds will barge in and arrest everyone," I said.

"Speaking of such," Lawson said. "What's the plan for me? Am I going

Absolute Justice

to be arrested too on Thursday?"

"They'll have to take you in," I said. "But I told them to keep you separated from the others. But they can set bail for you quickly, and since you're helping they'll probably let you stay out on bail until your sentencing."

Lawson finished his drink. "Looks like we have a plan," he said.

CHAPTER SIXTY-FOUR

After Ray Norris and Charles Lawson left, I called Julia Garrett.

Without preamble, she asked, "Have you found my husband's murderer?"

"Yes," I said.

"Who killed him?"

"I can't say right now," I said. "But I've got something in the works that should tell us everything."

"When can you tell me?" she said.

"In a couple of days," I said. "We'll have all the answers then. I just wanted to let you know that we're close."

"That's good," Julia Garrett said. There was a pause on the line for several seconds. "Tell me one thing," she said. "Why was my husband killed?"

No matter the subject, Julia Garrett's voice still held that soft, seductive quality to it.

"Your husband uncovered a real estate scam," I said. "They killed him before he could go to the authorities."

Julia Garrett's voice cracked, and she said through tears, "Since all this has happened, I've been trying to make sense of it. But I can't. Why did they have to kill him? It doesn't make sense."

I wanted to say something to give her comfort. But what could you say to the grieving widow of a murder victim? When someone you love suddenly dies, it leaves a void in your heart. But when the loved one is murdered, coupled with the senselessness of the act, you're left with nothing but grief, loneliness, and the unanswerable question of why. Why did they have to die? I didn't have an answer. So what could I say? A few seconds of silence passed, and then I said the only thing I could say. "It never makes sense."

CHAPTER SIXTY-FIVE

It was Wednesday afternoon, the day before our big meeting with Richard Murphy, and I was in my office with my feet propped up. I had just gotten back from the Vietnamese restaurant downstairs where I devoured a plate of lemon grass chicken. A healthy choice, grilled chicken over rice with a salad. Naija would be proud. But she would frown upon the ten chocolate chip cookies I picked up for dessert at the bakery around the corner. Or she would eat one herself. Fresh baked chocolate chip cookies could make the staunchest health nut fall off the wagon.

I was just finishing my first cookie when there was a light knock on the office door. I knew who it was immediately. He was the only guy I knew who knocked on my office door. Everybody else just waltzed in as if I were giving out free chocolate chip cookies. I yelled to come in, and Billy Hobbs strode in carrying a laptop bag and a small attaché case.

Billy Hobbs fancied himself a covert operative for the CIA, and he dreamed of exposing international spy rings using his expertise in counterintelligence and espionage. He had all the latest gadgetry for surveillance: audio and video devices, bugging devices, and network sniffers that could track email and Internet traffic. Hobbs was a genius. He wasn't in the CIA, however, because he couldn't meet their stringent physical requirements. Standing 4'9" and frail as a twig, Hobbs looked as if a strong gust of wind could topple him over. But he never allowed his physical limitations to stop him. He had a master's degree from M.I.T., and he ran a little shop called Atlanta Spy Equipment Company.

Hobbs has always known he would be at the butt end of short jokes, but he deftly turned the jokes around. I've always teased Hobbs about him being at the CIA recruiting office (if there is such a thing), and him glaring up at a life-sized display of a spy with a red line drawn through it with a sign that read: You must be this tall to be in the CIA. But Hobbs always threw it back at me, telling me I couldn't meet the intelligence requirement. Touché. But Ouch!

Hobbs and I were the best of friends, and I had called him and asked about some of his surveillance gadgets to use on my sting operation. Hobbs was ecstatic and agreed to help.

I stood up when he walked in. Hobbs looked at me, and said, "Sit back down, Jolly Green Giant, so I don't have to talk into your navel."

"So, Grumpy where's the rest of your clan?" I asked.

"Is that all you've got?" Hobbs said, grinning at me. He had a high-pitched voice that always reminded me of screeching tires. "We haven't seen each other in weeks and that's the best you can come up with."

I sat back down at my desk. "I'm a little rusty with my short jokes."

"If that's the best you've got, you're a lot rusty." Hobbs put the attaché case on my desk. "Give me a cookie," he said in that screechy voice.

When he finished the cookie, Hobbs reached into his attaché case and held up what looked like at tie-tack with a black onyx stud in the middle. "This is a new gadget I just got," he said. "The latest in audio surveillance. It has a tiny microphone installed in the middle. Very sensitive."

He took out a magnifying glass from the case, hobbled around behind the desk, and showed me the tiny microphone. Without the magnifying glass, you couldn't tell it wasn't a real onyx stud.

I handed the tie-tack back to him. "I'm impressed."

"Check this out," Hobbs said, and reached into his case and took out a lapel pin of the American flag. "This one has tiny microphones in the stars." Again he showed me the microphone with the aid of the magnifying glass.

"What's the range of something so small?" I asked.

"It can pick up voices from twenty-feet away," Hobbs said. He sounded proud of the fact. "Plus I have something else for you."

Hobbs thrust out his small chest as if he were a rooster patrolling the henhouse, strutted back around the desk, dove into his bag of tricks, and produced a tiny tan device smaller than the tip of my pinky finger.

"Check this out," he said. "This is a listening device that fits into the ear canal. It's virtually unnoticeable. This little baby enables you to give your guys instructions. And you can track the signal up to five-hundred yards away. Perfect for this type of operation." He beamed at me, proud of what he'd come up with for this operation.

Just then, Ray Norris and Charles Lawson walked into the office. They didn't knock. They probably smelled the chocolate chip cookies.

When they walked in, Billy Hobbs immediately noticed Charles Lawson's elongated neck. He glanced at me with an evil smirk, and then turned his attention back to them. "It looks like this circus is complete," he said. "Now we have the dancing bear, and he's brought along the sword swallower."

"Bite me, pipsqueak," Ray Norris said, grinning at Hobbs.

Ray Norris and Billy Hobbs had known each other for a number of years. In fact, Hobbs had installed the security equipment at Ray's liquor store, complete with HD cameras, motion detectors, and a silent alarm system that instead of notifying the cops, it notifies Ray Norris and Tony Veneto. If I were a burglar, I'd rather the cops catch me than Ray and Tony. The survival rate would be higher.

Ray made the introductions, and Hobbs and Lawson shook hands. Hobbs explained what he and I had been discussing. He finished by showing them the tie-tack and lapel pen.

Hobbs said, "Each of you will wear one of these, and we'll be able to hear everything that's happening inside." Then he displayed the two ear pieces. "Plus, you'll have one of these in your ear. This allows us to give you instructions."

"Let's test everything out," I said.

"I'll wear the lapel pin," Ray Norris said.

Hobbs pinned the microphones to Lawson and Norris. He had each man bend down and Hobbs inserted the ear piece into each man's right ear using a tiny pair of tweezers. Then he opened his laptop and punched a few keys, and took out a headset with a wraparound microphone and put it on. The headset looked too big for his small head.

Then both men left the office heading in opposite directions. Hobbs said to me, "I can adjust the ear devices where each man hears everything, or we can give each man individual instructions."

Hobbs tapped a few more keys. Then he whispered into his mouthpiece, and a few seconds later Lawson repeated what Hobbs had said. We could hear it coming through the small speakers on Hobbs' laptop. Next, he did the same with Norris. The devices checked out great.

When they came back into the office, I said, "I'll let the Feds know we're ready to go."

CHAPTER SIXTY-SIX

Thursday morning I awoke before dawn. The digital clock beside the bed said it was 5:10. I got up, drank some orange juice, and ate a blueberry muffin. Then I put on my sweats and my Nike running shoes and headed out for a run. I didn't bring a gun with me. I didn't think anyone would try to kill me this early in the morning. I ran down Marietta Street and then turned right on Spring Street, heading north. I reached my athletic club on Peachtree a few minutes before six. I worked out on the Nautilus equipment, starting with lateral raises and then worked on my biceps and triceps. I finished with several sets on the bench press. When I finished my muscles were good and tight. Back in my apartment, I hit the shower and then got dressed. I sat at my kitchen counter and ate two more muffins and a bowl of cereal. While I ate, I thought about the case.

What had started out as a missing person case had ended up as a double murder case involving a real estate swindle worth millions. Buddha once said: There is no fire like greed. And I believed it. Look at what greed had caused in this case. Two people murdered, one other dead, and by the time it's finished a lot of lives will lay in ruins. All because of greed. One of the seven deadly sins.

If it all went according to plan, by this evening Jack Rueben and Richard Murphy would be in jail for murder, and James Barton would be behind bars for his part in the real estate swindle. I had a good plan. The only aspect of it that bothered me was the fact that Ray Norris was going into the lion's den unprotected. But Ray was a seasoned businessman-slash-criminal. He could take care of himself.

After I finished eating, I left my apartment and went to my office.

At eleven o'clock Ray Norris and Charles Lawson arrived. A few minutes later, Billy Hobbs arrived and rigged up Lawson and Norris with their microphones and earpieces. Then we tested the equipment again.

Ray Norris and Charles Lawson went downstairs. Lawson stayed on this side of the street, while Ray walked across to the other side.

Hobbs put on his headset and punched a few keys on his laptop. Then he said to Ray in his screechy voice, "Hey, goombah, while you're out why don't you pick up us a pizza?"

Ray Norris' voice boomed through Hobbs laptop. "Go buy your own damn pizza, pipsqueak."

So the equipment checked out great.

Thirty minutes later, the three musketeers showed up. Luther Higgins, Matt Davis, and Mike Soratelli. Luther Higgins carried a bag of sandwiches and a six pack of soda. He put the bag on my desk, pulled a sandwich out, and said, "Compliments of the Federal Bureau of Investigation."

"Glad you thought of lunch," I said. I smirked at Ray. "I ordered a pizza but it never arrived."

Each of us took a sandwich from the bag and opened a drink. All the sandwiches were the same. Cuban with provolone.

We were all silent as we ate.

Higgins finished his sandwich first. He drained his can of soda, and then looked over at Lawson. He asked, "Have you spoken to any of your partners lately?"

"No," Lawson said. "Not since setting up the meeting."

Higgins gave him the hard stare a second. "You wouldn't tip them off, would you?"

I noticed Lawson hadn't eaten much of his sandwich. Probably too nervous. I understood why. His life was already in shambles and after today, he would probably end up in jail. Even if he made a minimum security prison, it was still incarceration.

Everyone looked at Lawson, waiting for the answer to Higgins' question. If Lawson had tipped his partners off then we couldn't go ahead with the operation. All of this preparation would have been for nothing.

Of course, it would nullify his deal. But that wasn't what was on my mind. I was thinking about Murphy and Rueben getting away with murder. A few tense seconds ticked by.

Lawson took a sip of his drink, and said, "Absolutely not. They killed one of my associates and my secretary. They've beaten me up. They've ruined my career, my marriage, and my life. And it was probably only a matter of time before they killed me too." He paused and looked at each one of us. "So to answer the question unequivocally...no, I haven't tipped anyone off."

Higgins nodded at him. The tension cleared a little. But the tension wasn't going away completely, not until we were finished.

After a moment, Higgins asked Lawson and Ray Norris, "And both of you know exactly what to do, right?"

Lawson answered. "Yes." Then he motioned toward Norris. "We'll record them as we make the transaction. Plus, if I get a chance, I'll see if I can get them to talk about Garrett's murder."

"Don't be obvious about it," Higgins said. "If you start asking questions about the murders, they might get suspicious."

I stepped in. "We've been over it a thousand times," I said to Higgins. "They know what to do."

Higgins nodded. "I've got an FBI surveillance van for our operation, along with another agent named Hinson. Officially, we're not part of the operation. I told the higher-ups I had a tip from a snitch that something big may go down today. Hinson volunteered to help."

Matt Davis said, "Acting on the same tip from the FBI, the APD is keeping an eye on the situation. But officially we're not part of the operation either."

We all knew Higgins and Davis had to say they weren't part of the sting operation to avoid entrapment allegations later if it came up in court.

I looked at my watch. "It's show time," I said.

Higgins pointed at me. "You and Hobbs can ride with me," he said. "Lawson and Norris will go there alone."

We left the office in single file, heading down the narrow stairs to the street. Billy Hobbs brought up the rear, carrying his attaché case and laptop bag.

CHAPTER SIXTY-SEVEN

Forty-five minutes later, Luther Higgins, Matt Davis, Mike Soratelli, Billy Hobbs, and I were crowded in the FBI surveillance van down the street from Tanner Investments. We had strapped on our Kevlar vests over our shirts. Though he wasn't part of the attack team, Hobbs wore a vest too. It hung on his thin shoulders like a lead shield. The van looked like a telephone repair van. We parked it next to a switch box on Piedmont Avenue. FBI agent Hinson, dressed as a telephone repairman, was outside the van at the switch box. He had it open and looked as if he were working.

After a few minutes, Lawson's Range Rover passed the van and then turned right into Tanner Investments' parking lot. We tested our equipment again before Lawson and Norris went inside. Everything checked out.

Using binoculars I watched as Ray and Lawson got out of the car and walked to the office door.

I said, "I wish we had eyes in there with them."

Hobbs said, "There are glasses that have optic capabilities, but they're bulky and have a limited view range. You only see what the wearer is looking at."

"That would have been better than running blind," I said.

Higgins said, "Nothing we can do about it now."

We were silent a moment. Then we heard Lawson's voice again.

"Mr. Murphy," Lawson said, "this is the man I was speaking to you about, Ray Norris."

"Mr. Norris," Murphy's recognizable voice said through Hobbs' computer. "Do you mind waiting here in the reception area for a moment while Mr. Lawson and I talk?"

"Of course not," Ray Norris said. "Take your time."

Higgins and I exchanged a look. Higgins shrugged. This wasn't part of the plan. But if things got out of hand this early, we could tell both of them to abort and get out. For now, the only thing we could do was wait and see what happened next.

We heard a door close and then shuffling footsteps.

We all listened as the conversation in the office unfolded.

Murphy's voice again. "I don't like you bringing outsiders into our operation. How'd he find out about it?"

"I don't know," Lawson said. I picked up a quiver in his voice. I suspected there was someone else in the office.

Murphy: "Maybe you told him?"

Lawson: "No. Norris came to me."

Another voice spoke up. I recognized it as that of James Barton.

Barton: "How he'd find out then?"

Lawson: "Like I told you guys before. He's connected. He must have found out somehow through his business dealings."

Murphy: "You said he was a client of yours. What do you do for him?"

Lawson: "I'm one of his attorneys. I look out for some of his business interests."

Murphy: "Maybe you added to his business interests by running your mouth about us."

Lawson: "I would never do that. I've never said anything to anyone about our operation."

The nervousness in Lawson's voice had intensified. I didn't think Lawson would be so jumpy if he were alone with Murphy and Barton. Rueben was probably in there too.

I heard Barton say, "And now here we are with you bringing an outsider in."

Another voice spoke up I didn't recognize.

"Maybe I should beat the crap out of him again," the voice said.

Absolute Justice

Jack Rueben.

Lawson: "I'm not afraid of you, Rueben." Lawson's voice didn't sound convincing. It trembled as he spoke. But at least he confirmed who else was in the office.

Rueben: "What happened? You grow a pair since I beat the crap out of you last time?"

Then I heard a very familiar sound, a sound I knew all too well. An old friend. I had been on both the receiving and the giving end of that sound before. It was the slap, smack of a punch. It sounded like a body punch. It was immediately followed by a groan. I heard Lawson struggling to catch his breath.

I grabbed the headset from Hobbs and asked Ray Norris, "Can you see what's going on in that office?"

His voice came back as a whisper, "No, they have the blinds closed. But it sounds like someone's getting knocked around in there. Want me to go inside?"

"Not right now. Let's see where this goes. Lawson can take care of himself."

I didn't believe that, but at this point, we just had to wait and see what happened next. Then as an afterthought, I added, "If it gets bad, I'll let you know and I want you to get up and walk out. Don't go in and try to save Lawson, just get out. Got it?"

"Got it," Ray whispered.

Back in Lawson's office, I heard Rueben say, "Why don't I beat the crap out of him again, just for fun."

Murphy: "We're not here for that."

Rueben: "Lucky for you."

Lawson: His breathing labored. "I'm not scared of you."

Rueben: "You guys should have seen him the other night. He was crying like a little girl. Right in front of his wife. 'Don't hurt me. Don't hurt me.'"

Lawson: "Shut up. You don't scare me."

Rueben: "I can put the fear back into you."

Then I heard the smack of more punches. One, two, three times. Each punch followed by argh! aargh! aaargh! Then Lawson wheezing to catch his breath.

Murphy: "That's enough."

Everyone was silent a moment. The only sound was Lawson trying to breathe. Inside the van, Higgins said, "This Lawson guy has guts. Gotta give that to him."

I said, "I just hope it doesn't get him killed."

When Lawson got his breathing under control, he said, "What are you going to do? Kill me like you did Jason Garrett?"

"Maybe I will," Rueben said. "I'll make you piss in your pants just like Garrett did. Right before I put a bullet in his head."

CHAPTER SIXTY-EIGHT

Inside the van, everyone looked at each other astonished. In the span of a few minutes Lawson had accomplished what none of us had after weeks of investigations. Now we knew for certain who pulled the trigger that killed Jason Garrett.

"That sounds like a confession to me," I said.

"Now all we need is for Murphy to admit to hiring him to make the hit," Matt Davis said.

Soratelli said, "That Lawson is one smart cookie. He's only been in there a few minutes and already got a confession."

Hobbs had plugged in a couple of small speakers he'd brought. We listened more to what was going on in the office.

Lawson said, "You're not all that tough without a gun to stand behind. Or a car."

"What are you talking about?" Rueben said.

"You know what I'm talking about," Lawson said. "My secretary."

"That old broad," Rueben said.

"Her name was Mable Williams," Lawson said. His voice was no longer trembling. Now it was laced with a tinge of anger. "She was just a secretary. She didn't have anything to do with this."

Murphy spoke up. "We had been watching her for a while, and she had been talking with that detective. We saw her talking with him several times."

"You didn't have to kill her," Lawson said.

Rueben said, "Accidents happen. She shouldn't have been walking so early in the morning." Then Rueben laughed. "You should have seen the look in her eyes right before she disappeared beneath my bumper. Looked like a deer in headlights. Eyes wide like saucers." He laughed again. "I could hear bones crunching under the car."

Inside the van, a wave of rage washed over me. I clenched my teeth and both hands tightened into fist. I felt my pulse throbbing in my neck. My blood began to boil. Rueben was in there bragging, whooping it up about killing Mable Williams. I felt like barging in and putting a bullet between his eyes.

Soratelli must have noticed something in my expression. He put his hand on my shoulder, and said, "We'll get 'em. Just take it easy."

I glanced around the van. Everyone else was giving me the hairy eyeball, wondering what was going on. Or perhaps they knew. I think everyone has felt that urge at one point in his life, to serve as judge and jury—especially when you hear of a horrible crime against a vulnerable person, a child, an elderly person, or simply an innocent secretary walking to work early in the morning—and you secretly wish someone would shoot the guy. That's exactly how I felt at that moment.

To ease the tension, Soratelli said, "Lawson's two for two." He glanced at Matt Davis, then at Luther Higgins. "We got a confession for the murders. Think we should go in now?"

"We only have Rueben," Higgins said. "We want them all. Let's wait and see what happens next."

Back in the office, Lawson said, "Do you want to do the deal or not?"

Murphy said, "Yeah, we're still going to do the deal, but this better be the last time you bring anyone else in. Understand?"

"Understood," Lawson said. Then he added sardonically. "It'll definitely be the last time."

CHAPTER SIXTY-NINE

Inside the van, Luther Higgins spoke into a PTT microphone on his wrist, alerting the FBI strike team down the street to get ready to move. Matt Davis notified the APD team to move closer in from their position a block away. Outside the van, Special Agent Hinson replaced the panel on the telephone box where he'd been stationed, climbed into the driver's seat, and we slowly inched closer to the parking lot of Tanner Investments. Everyone checked their weapons. I checked the clip of my 9mm, pumped a round into the chamber, and clicked the safety off.

Earlier when Ray Norris and Charles Lawson had first entered the office, I had asked Ray to look around and give us feedback on how many office workers he saw. A crowded office could present a problem if we encountered resistance. But we didn't have to worry about employee interference. There weren't any. The reception desk where Cheryl Swanson had sat was vacant. Plus, there were no other workers in the cubicles leading to Richard Murphy's office as there had been before. Ray reported the place was a deserted office, only the desk and chairs remained. We had set up the sting at the right time. What with two murders and the unwanted attention Lawson was stirring up, Murphy had decided it was time to close up shop. And I'm certain that they wouldn't have left a couple of liabilities behind either, namely Charles Lawson and the banker Greg Little. They would have been murder victims' number three and four.

Now from inside the van I said into Ray Norris' earpiece, "You're on, Ray." Then as an afterthought, I added, "Let's bring these guys down."

"My thoughts exactly," Ray whispered. We had left his earpiece open during the conversation inside the office so he heard everything that went on.

After a couple of beats, I heard Murphy's voice. "Sorry to keep you waiting, Mr. Norris. We had to iron out a few details."

Then there were footsteps as Ray walked into the office. Then Ray said, "Everything okay, Lawson?"

Rueben blurted. "What's it to you?"

"Call off your gorilla," Ray said, presumably to Murphy. "I came here in good faith, and don't want any rough stuff."

Murphy said, "Like I said. We had to work out a few details."

Lawson said, "Everything's fine. Let's do the deal and get out of here."

Murphy spoke up. "Before we go any further," he said, his voice full of suspicion, "how did you find out what we were doing?"

We had covered this in our preparation. I had suspected Murphy would ask how Norris found out about them.

Staying on script, Ray Norris said, "I have a lot of friends."

Murphy replied. "I have lots of friends too. But you still didn't answer the question."

Norris said, "I found out about your operation by accident."

"What kind of accident?" Murphy asked.

"One of my associates bought a man's identity that you had previously stolen," Norris said. "When I checked him out, I found out that he had already purchased a house a few days before."

"Who was that?" Murphy asked.

"Guy named Roy Upshaw," Norris said.

Rueben spoke up. "That screw up. I should have taken him out when he screwed up beating up the banker."

Inside the van, Soratelli said, "This keeps getting better. Every time that guy opens his mouth he confesses."

Billy Hobbs snickered. He was enjoying playing FBI agent on a stakeout.

Inside the office, picking up where Murphy left off, Barton asked, "How'd you know it was us that stole his identity?"

Norris was following the script exactly. We had anticipated this question also.

Norris answered. "I had friends check into it, and they paid Roy Upshaw a visit. From what they reported, Upshaw isn't in the position to purchase such an expensive house. So I suspected a scam of some sort and had friends dig a little deeper. They discovered, after Upshaw's arrest, an associate had represented him from Schmitt & Lawson. A law firm I use from time to time."

"So Lawson did tell you about us," Murphy said. Anger rising in his voice.

"No," Norris said, keeping his cool. "Nothing like that. Since I suspected a scam, I had a friend of mine at police headquarters check the records of other indigent people arrested represented by the same firm. Then I checked those names out too. And here we are."

Lawson said, "I told you he was connected."

For the first time Ray got off script. "And my ties run deep. Police, federal agents, and even a few judges."

Which may be true, I thought.

Norris asked, "Are we going to do this deal or not?"

Barton spoke up. "You got the paperwork?"

"Yeah," Norris said. "You got the money?"

"It's ready to be transferred into your account," Murphy said.

Barton said, "Let me see the documents."

Ray handed the manila folder over that contained the fake documents. We heard papers shuffling. A minute passed. No one said anything. Another minute passed. The tension inside the van increased. Barton was Murphy's expert and knew what to look for to make sure the papers were legit. But we had had the FBI's documents team go over every line of the papers to make sure they looked authentic. Nevertheless, everyone was on pins and needles.

The tension built and everyone in the van appeared to have stopped breathing. The tension felt thick enough to slice through. A bead of sweat swept over my forehead. More seconds ticked away.

After another minute, Barton said, "These look good."

A cumulative sigh of relief raced through the van. I raked my shirt sleeve across my forehead.

Inside the office, Ray Norris said, "So we have a deal?"

"Yeah," Murphy said. "Give Barton your account information."

Ray gave them the account number. We had set up a bank account just for the transfer. But certainly not at First Georgia Savings. After the bust, the Feds would seize the bank account and the money as evidence.

Inside the van, everyone was silent a moment. Again, we collectively held our breath. More silence passed. We waited. Our entire operation hinged on this moment. We had to wait for the money transfer to make the bust.

At the same instance, two other FBI strike teams were waiting on our signal to go. One stationed outside James Barton's office, with an Evidence Response Team with them to gather evidence, and the other team outside First Georgia Savings waiting to arrest Greg Little.

Everyone waited for the signal to move in.

After another moment of silence, Barton said, "It's complete."

Ray Norris said, "I should get a text message stating that the transaction is complete."

Five seconds later, Ray's phone bonged announcing a text message. The text was from the team of FBI agents monitoring the bank account. Ray checked his phone, and said the funds were there. That was the signal to move.

Higgins yelled into his PTT microphone, "Go! Go! Go!"

CHAPTER SEVENTY

Now it was time for the *coup de grâce*.

Agent Hinson gunned the van across the parking lot and screeched to a halt. An FBI attack van pulled in directly behind us. An APD swat team pulled in behind it. Agent Hinson bolted from the van carrying a police battering ram. He pounded the lock on the door and on the second strike the wood splintered with a loud crack and the door flew open.

I led the charge inside, all the running and strenuous exercise paying off. Matt Davis was on my heels. Luther Higgins with his bad knee came third, and Mike Soratelli brought up the rear. Murphy's office was in the back of the building, about forty-feet from the front entrance. They would have heard the crash of the door splintering.

We had to move fast.

If we didn't reach Murphy's office quickly, Rueben would kill both Ray Norris and Charles Lawson before we could save them.

I raced forward knowing that my friend's life depended on what would happen in the next few seconds.

I had known we would have some ground to cover to reach Murphy's office, but there was no other way into the building. I had discussed this with both Ray Norris and Charles Lawson beforehand. Both knew the risk and accepted it. Charles Lawson really hadn't had much of a choice. But Ray had agreed to help because of our friendship. And a person who would put his life in danger for a friend is rare. I had to save my friend.

I raced forward, my gun clutched in my hand.

It all happened in a blink of an eye.

I banged through the office door with my gun raised and yelled, "Nobody move."

As planned, Ray Norris was standing by the office doorway.

When I burst into the office, Murphy stood up behind his desk, and yelled, "It's a set up."

I grabbed Ray's arm and shoved him out of the office, out of harm's way.

Out of the corner of my eye, I saw Jack Rueben reach into his jacket, and produce a Glock.

"You sonovabitch," Rueben said and shot Lawson in the right shoulder. Lawson screamed, banged against the wall, and slumped to the floor.

I raised my gun and shot Rueben high in the forehead.

The bullet tore a hole about the size of a nickel on his forehead. But when the round exited, it blew the majority of the back of his head out. Blood and brains splattered the wall behind him. For a split second, Rueben just stood there with a stunned, dazed expression on his face, and then he crumbled to the floor dead.

James Barton turned to stone and raised his hands. Luther Higgins shoved him out the office door to the other waiting FBI agents who had come in after us.

With my attention focused on Rueben, I hadn't noticed Murphy's open right hand desk drawer.

When I turned my attention back to Murphy, I saw his right hand disappear and when it came back into view, it held a Sig Sauer .380.

I yelled, "Gun!"

But I was too late.

Murphy raised the pistol and shot me.

CHAPTER SEVENTY-ONE

Though it all happened in a split second, it seemed to have moved in super slow motion, as they used in old movies to slow down the action.

After I shot Rueben, in the corner of my eye, I saw Murphy's hand disappear below the desk.

Then I saw him come up with the pistol.

I yelled, "Gun!"

But it had come out sounding like, GUUUUUNNNNN! As if I were yelling in a cave.

I instinctively raised my 9mm.

Then Murphy and I both fired simultaneously.

Murphy's shot slammed into my chest.

Fierce pain exploded through my upper body, the impact knocking me off my feet. I went sprawling backwards. It felt like I'd been hit by a '57 Buick.

In the same instance, on either side of me, two other shots rang out. They came from Matt Davis and Mike Soratelli.

My shot hit Murphy high in the chest. The two shots from Davis and Soratelli tore through Murphy's body, one hitting him in the head, just below his left eye, the other in the middle of his chest, right in the heart. Murphy crashed into the wall behind him from the three impacts and dropped like a sack of potatoes.

Both Soratelli and Davis kneeled down to check on me. I was sprawled out on the floor, the pain still surging through my chest.

Soratelli said to me, "Where are you hit?"

"In the chest," I croaked, grimacing from the pain. "It hit the vest."

The Kevlar vest had saved my life. Soratelli unstrapped the vest and unbuttoned my shirt to reveal a huge bruise the size of a softball on the left side of my chest. The round had hit just above the ribcage to the left of my breast bone. If I hadn't had on the Kevlar, the shot would have probably killed me.

Grimacing again, I sat up and looked around.

Richard Murphy lay face down in a heap next to his desk. A river of blood ran from beneath his body. Next to the wall, Jack Rueben's body leaned against the wall. His eyes were still open, staring at nothing.

Luther Higgins rushed up to check on his star witness, Charles Lawson. Lawson was propped against the wall, whimpering like a little girl. Higgins ripped open Lawson's shirt sleeve to get a look at the wound. The shot had just grazed him, what they called in the old western movies as "just a flesh wound." Lawson saw the blood spurting from his shoulder and moaned some more. From the sounds he was making, you would have thought he had lost a limb.

Higgins said to Charles Lawson, "You'll live. It doesn't look too bad."

"He tried to kill me," Lawson said with astonishment in his voice. His voice had a high pitched tone as if he was ready to sing soprano. "He really tried to kill me."

"You'll be fine," Higgins said. "By the way, you handled it great."

An EMT came in and gave Lawson a bandage to hold on the wound to stop the bleeding. Lawson grimaced as he held the bandage in place.

Then Lawson looked at Higgins through red-rimmed eyes, and asked, "What happens now?"

Good question. Since the two biggest culprits lay dead, the only two left for Lawson to testify against was James Barton, and Lawson's partner-in-crime Greg Little. But I was certain the Feds would still hold up their end of the bargain and honor the deal with Lawson.

Higgins said, "First we'll get the EMTs to take you to Grady Memorial and get you patched up. Then you'll be booked as we outlined earlier. But you'll make bail quickly and be home in time for dinner."

Lawson didn't say anything, but nodded his head.

A couple of EMTs came in and helped Lawson stand up. He was a little woozy, maybe from the loss of blood, but more likely from the shock of being shot. I saw tears in his eyes. I couldn't tell whether the tears were from the pain in his shoulder or of the reality of what just had taken place. Maybe a little of both. He had faced death and he came out alive. Lawson was now a certified tough guy. He would have something to brag about to his prison buddies.

CHAPTER SEVENTY-TWO

After the EMTs escorted Lawson out, Matt Davis kneeled beside me, and said, "Looks like you took one for the team. Want me to poke it to see how tender it is?"

"It hurts plenty," I said. "Take my word for it."

Soratelli and Davis helped me to my feet and we walked outside.

There were eight APD cruisers parked at different angles in the parking lot. Plus, an assortment of unmarked detective vehicles.

An FBI Evidence Response Team truck was parked close to the door. As we passed the truck, a team of agents bailed out to begin gathering evidence. They would confiscate the computers and any documents they found, and label them in boxes and evidence bags. They worked like a choreographed team of movers.

Ray Norris, who had calmly walked out of Murphy's office like he was out for an afternoon stroll, emerged from our surveillance van. Billy Hobbs came out next, still wearing his Kevlar vest like a badge of honor.

An EMT came over, took me by the arm to guide me to a waiting ambulance. I'd go and get some x-rays to make sure I didn't have any broken ribs. But I knew they weren't broken. Bruised maybe, but not broken. I'd been banged up enough to know what broken ribs felt like, and this wasn't it.

At the ambulance, I stopped a moment. Ray Norris, Mike Soratelli, Matt Davis, Luther Higgins, and Billy Hobbs were standing there looking at me.

I couldn't resist. I said to Soratelli, "For a fat guy, you move pretty fast."

Soratelli said, "You guys think you're hot snot with your six pack abs, but you're nothing but a bunch of rookies." Then he rubbed his amble belly. "This is what you get when you work hard enough. Twelve pack abs."

We all burst out laughing.

I climbed into the ambulance. Looking out, I gave my group of friends an appreciative nod. They all nodded back. Suddenly, I felt a lump in my throat. These guys were my friends and they had gone to bat for me when the chips were down. The true meaning of friendship is having someone you can depend on when you need them the most. Without true friends, you're nothing.

An EMT climbed in the ambulance with me, slammed the door shut, and we sped away.

CHAPTER SEVENTY-THREE

"**So they were stealing houses using** stolen identities?" Naija asked.

I nodded. "Charles Lawson stole the identities from his pro bono clients," I said. "Then James Barton, along with the help of Greg Little, falsified documents under those names, giving the person fake work records, income, and credit histories. What they did next was pretty clever—"

"But not clever enough," Naija interjected.

"Not with *moi* on the case," I said, tooting my own horn. "But they knew how to pull off a good scam."

"What did they do, exactly?" Naija asked. Her dark eyes gleamed at me from across the table.

It was a Friday night, a week after the bust, and we were at The Sun Dial restaurant atop the Westin Peachtree Plaza Hotel. The cylindrical glass building stood seventy-three stories tall, and the elegant restaurant at the top slowly revolved completely around every thirty minutes, giving a panoramic view of the city. On a clear night, you could see for miles. I had never been there before, but Naija had with her highbrow friends. We were sharing a bottle of William Hill Cabernet Sauvignon.

I explained, "First they would go to the monthly auctions on foreclosed homes in the area counties. Then they would keep an eye on the houses that didn't sell."

"Why would they do that?" Naija asked.

Absolute Justice

"They wanted to make sure the houses stayed empty," I said. "In order for them to pull off their scheme, the houses had to be empty and bank owned. So if the houses remained unsold for a time, they would steal them under the stolen identities. Then they would sell the houses to unsuspecting buyers."

"That's very daring," Naija said. She was always genuinely interested in my cases. She thought for a second, then asked, "Why steal the identities of only pro bono clients?"

I answered, "People in financial straits are less likely to check their credit, or make big purchases that require a credit check. So the identity theft sometimes goes unnoticed."

Our waiter came up and took our orders. I ordered a ribeye steak with roasted red potatoes. Naija ordered the faro risotto with a vegetarian chickpea tomato ragout.

After the waiter left, Naija said, "So tell me exactly how they did it, stole the houses, I mean?"

I explained, "They researched to find which bank owned the house they planned to steal. Then using the stolen identities and falsified credit histories, they transferred ownership under those names. And having two inside men, Charles Lawson and Greg Little, helped them to pull it off."

"So it was that simple," Naija said. "They just went to the courthouse and transferred the titles under the stolen identities?"

I took a sip of my wine. It was good. Maybe this wine tasting stuff was beginning to rub off on me. I answered, "In some cases, they did just that, took everything to the courthouse. The fraudulent paperwork was that good. It didn't raise any red flags. In other cases, since they had an inside man, Greg Little, they used MERS—"

"What's MERS?" Naija interrupted.

"It's an electronic method to transfer ownership of real property." I explained further. "Instead of having to go down to the courthouse to transfer property, lienholders can use MERS to transfer property. Again, Greg Little made it easier for them."

Naija took a tiny sip of her wine, then said, "So after they transferred the property, the people whose identity had been stolen were then homeowners."

"Yes," I said. "On paper. Homeowners that didn't know it."

"But wouldn't the banks eventually find out about the stolen properties?"

"Yes," I said. "The key word being eventually. A risk Richard Murphy and James Barton were willing to take. They figured they could swoop in, steal as many homes as possible, dump them off to unsuspecting buyers, make a pile of money, and move on to another city before the banks made the discovery."

"But they didn't do that," Naija said. "They hung around longer than they planned to."

"Right," I said. "They let their greed take over. And that was their downfall. Had they made their money quickly and moved on, and not committed two murders, they might have gotten away with it."

"But they didn't," Naija said. "And you solved the case, and here we are in a nice restaurant in an elegant hotel."

"Exactly," I said. "With a lot of help from my friends."

The waiter brought our appetizers, an order of fried yellow corn grits. Naija had urged me to try them. I was a little apprehensive about trying any food Naija recommended, since I could end up eating something healthy. But since it was grits, I decided to give them a try. But I wondered why such an expensive, elegant restaurant would sell fried grits. Maybe highbrow dining took on a different flare in the South.

I took a bite of the fried grits. Naija was right. They were good.

Naija asked, "What's going to happen to the other man who was in on the scam?"

"James Barton," I said. "After the bust, Barton confessed to everything. He has a slew of federal indictments against him. Not to mention accessory to murder. He'll probably spend the rest of his life in prison."

Naija watched as I finished one of the cakes of fried grits. She shot me a knowing look of satisfaction. "What do you think of the grits?"

"Good," I said. "Despite my apprehension at trying some of the foods you like, I'm glad you're nudging me along."

"Sometimes it's more like a shove." Naija smiled at me and took a sip of her wine. Then asked, "And what's going to happen to the banker, Greg Little?"

"He confessed, too," I said. "Since he didn't have anything to do with the murders, he'll only face the felony charges against him. I spoke with the federal prosecutor, Deborah Northcutt, and she said they'll probably put him in a minimum security prison. But he will probably get ten to fifteen years."

The waiter brought our entrées and we ate in silence. Naija's faro risotto didn't have any meat in it, so it wasn't appealing to me. Plus, it didn't look like enough to eat. If I had that for dinner, I would have to stop on the way home and get a burger.

After a while, Naija asked, "What's going to happen to Charles Lawson?"

"Since Lawson helped with the sting, they'll go easier on him," I said. "Plus, with Barton's and Little's confessions, Lawson won't have to testify against them."

Naija asked, "So they'll send him to a minimum security prison, too?"

I nodded, taking a bite of my steak. Then I said, "When I spoke with Deborah Northcutt, she told me she requested Lawson be sent to Butner Federal Prison in North Carolina. It's a minimum security prison."

Naija paused a moment, looking at me. "Butner," she said.

From her expression, I could tell she was thinking about something, formulating her next question.

Then she asked, "Isn't that where Bernie Madoff is?"

"Yes," I said. "Maybe Lawson and Madoff can compare notes on running a Ponzi scheme. How not to get caught." I took a sip of my wine, then continued, "Anyway, I've heard that if you've got to go to prison, Butner's the place to go."

"So Lawson didn't have anything to do with the murders?"

"No," I said. "He didn't know that Murphy would have Jason Garrett killed. And he didn't have anything to do with Mable Williams' murder either."

We finished the rest of our meal in silence, enjoying the view of the city lights in the distance. When we finished eating, the waiter cleared the table, and brought coffee for me and tea for Naija.

We sipped our drinks, and after a while, Naija asked, "Is your client—what did she call herself, 'The Goddess of Love'—was she satisfied with your results?" She was looking at me and smiling again.

I smiled at her. "Are you picking on me?"

"You're the seasoned investigator," she said. "You figure it out."

"Yes," I said, giving her a playful look. "She was very satisfied with my performance. I found her husband's killer and uncovered the reason why. She paid me a good deal of money and gave me a nice bonus."

"And that's why we're here at this nice hotel," Naija said.

Exactly," I said. "And at this nice restaurant. The fruit of *moi's* labors."

Naija took my hand from across the table and held it. She had a playful twinkle in her eyes. "She didn't proposition you again, did she?"

"Do I detect a hint of jealousy," I said, playfully.

"No," Naija said. "I'm just curious."

"No," I said. "She didn't proposition me again."

I moved my chair around closer to hers. And we held hands for a time and watched the city lights twinkle in the distance.

Then it occurred to me that now was a good time to say what had been on my mind for a long time. Really ever since meeting Naija. For me, the moment I first saw Naija, it was love at first sight.

I was having a mental debate with myself. *Just say it*, I told myself. *Take a swing and see what happens. What have you got to lose? Everything*, I answered back.

Naija tilted her head to one side, one eyebrow raised, and looked at me. She could tell I was thinking about something.

"What?" she said.

I looked into her eyes, and then said those three words that had been bouncing around in my mind since meeting her. I said, "I love you."

At first Naija didn't say anything. She just looked at me with her eyes gleaming in the dim light of the restaurant.

A few seconds ticked by that seemed like hours.

I was on pins and needles. I held my breath.

Sometimes I can tell what Naija was thinking by her expression. But not tonight. Tonight she wore her poker face and she was impossible to read.

But she hadn't snatched her hand away from mine, which I took as a good sign.

After a few more antagonizing seconds, she said, "I love you, too."

I wiped away a tear that had appeared at the corner of my left eye. Then I leaned over and kissed her. Naija wasn't one to display affection in public, but this time she let her inhibitions fly out the window. She kissed me as if we were the only two people in the restaurant.

Then I said, "I've wanted to say that for a long time."

"And I've wanted you to say it for a long time," she answered.

We sat there a while longer, holding hands again and watching the city lights below.

After a time, I said, "We don't have anything to do in the morning."

Naija glanced over at me, giving me a playful look. "Are you propositioning me?"

"You're the one with the M.D." I said smiling. "You tell me."

She rubbed my forearm lightly back and forth. It was arousing. "What did you have in mind?" she asked.

"Since I've got a pocket full of money, and since we're here in this fancy-schmancy hotel, I was thinking we could get a room."

Naija gave me a playful smile. "I thought if I dropped enough clues, you would catch on," she said.

I laughed. "After all, I am a seasoned investigator."

THE END

Larry W. Pitts

ACKNOWLEDGMENTS

I have a small pocket dictionary on my writing desk that was given to me years ago, and the inscription reads, *This will help you become a great writer.* I keep that small dictionary as a reminder to write at the best of my ability. A man I both admire and respect, Robert (Bob) Harkins, gave it to me. He has been my friend for most of my adult life. Bob and his wife Olivia Rossi, along with their two sons Bobby and Billy Harkins, made me an honorary member of their family, and for that, I am eternally grateful.

I would like to thank everyone at Yawn's Publishing, especially Nadine and Farris Yawn who made the book possible. Their suggestions have made the book what it is, a good read.

I would also like to thank my first readers, Hugh Gardiner, Diane Ludington, and Don O'Briant (a great friend and a wonderful writer). Their insight and suggestions have made the book better.

I also would like to thank the following friends who have always supported my writing: Jacqueline LaScala, Poorva Pandya, Kay Roberts, Lisa Axelberg, and the previously mentioned Don O'Briant, who also gave me my first writing gig.

Last but certainly not least, I owe a big sense of gratitude to my wife Ethel Rafferty for without a happy, stable home front writing the novel would not have been possible.

I want to mention a good friend of mine, Tracy Downer, who was killed in a tragic car accident in 2012, and who gave me encouragement to write the novel when I first started the project. There is a section in the novel where I mention, *"When someone you know suddenly dies it reminds you how fragile and precious life is, because you never know when it could suddenly end."* When I wrote that passage, I was thinking of Tracy.

I also want to mention my good friend Charles Porter, who left this world too early in life. He was always happy and full of life, and always supported my writing.

I owe a big thanks to my friend Earl Heinz, a body-builder whose muscles have muscles, who gave me a fabulous mahogany writing desk.

Thanks to David Fulmer, a fantastic novelist, who gave me suggestions and insight into the business-end of writing. There is a lot more to being a writer than simply putting thoughts down on paper.

I also would like to thank New York Times bestselling author John Lescroart who answered my goofy questions about writing and publishing in general.

It takes a lot to write a novel, and without the help of the aforementioned friends and acquaintances, this book may not have been possible.

CPSIA information can be obtained at www.ICGtesting.com
Printed in the USA
LVOW05*0045281014

410783LV00001B/2/P